MW01680219

JOSIAH RUSH

JOSIAH RUSH
DELANEY BAKER

Josiah Rush

By Delaney Baker

Cover Art and Illustrations by Jordan Brill

Map by Debbie J Scott

Author photograph by David Bergman

delaneybaker.com

Paperback ISBN: 979-8-9850628-0-9

eBook ISBN: 979-8-9850628-1-6

Printed in the United States of America.

FOR THE KINGDOM

AUTHOR'S NOTE

I love art. It took a pandemic for me to realize just how much.

Some works of art are meant to reflect the world in which we live or the people within it. Some art instructs, challenges, or questions deeply held personal and cultural ideas about ethics and values. Some art provides a balm for our pain and sadness, or it may satisfy our thirst for vengeance and control.

I think, however, better art leads us to pursue inner renewal, healing, and an appreciation for whatever it is we cherish. It leads us to harness our passion as fuel for our life's work and challenges us to live virtuously. Better art reminds us that there is comfort for (and acceptance despite) our shame, as well as forgiveness to exchange. The best art admonishes us to never succumb to sensualized alternatives to true and lasting joy.

Despite my opinions on what constitutes great art, I did not start writing this book with an understanding of what I loved about it. I did not necessarily endeavor to capture or create it because during that season I was still sorting out my own heart, elements of which you will likely observe throughout Josiah Rush. I wrote this book in autumn of 2020 simply to develop the discipline needed to do so.

I have no expectations about how this may stack up against my favorite works of art and literature, I just wanted to tell a story. It is my first, and I am growing as an author. Consider this an invitation to grow with me.

I have always loved the atmosphere of the wild west, so I created a fictional world where cowboys can still inspire men to honor and pursue the freedom which, for me, they represent.

I feel compelled to state up front, regarding certain events described within, that this is no field manual. I encourage you to educate yourself on proper first aid and survival methods. The characters here are flawed and make mistakes; to expect perfection from them limits their human-likeness. Nothing that follows should be considered an endorsement of skills, tactics, or practices undertaken by the characters.

As a final note, this is not a children's book. While the situations contained herein do not glorify the licentious or perverse, I do not shy from their reality. Thank you for exercising appropriate discretion.

Someone once told me that writing a book is an audacious task because the author assumes their words are worthy of the reader's time. Thank you for spending your precious time reading my story. I appreciate the responsibility and do not take your investment lightly.

Enjoy,

Delaney

ACKNOWLEDGMENTS

This book would not have been possible without the grace of God, my wife and daughter, and a wealth of others. Thank you Grant for your encouragement, David for your example, and Jonesy for your generosity. I owe a debt of gratitude to Curt for your motivation, Monty for your wisdom, and Toby for your friendship. Your collective influence in my life makes me a better man. Thank you to the McBride family for letting me play cowboy for a time. Thank you Mom, Gwen, and Aunt Sharon, my early readers, for your honest and constructive feedback. Thank you Jenny Rone King, Jana Aplin, Steve Sutton, Rhonda Robirds, and Marcie O'Neal for your help making this into something tangible. Jordan Brill, thank you for crushing the cover and illustrations.

JOSIAH RUSH

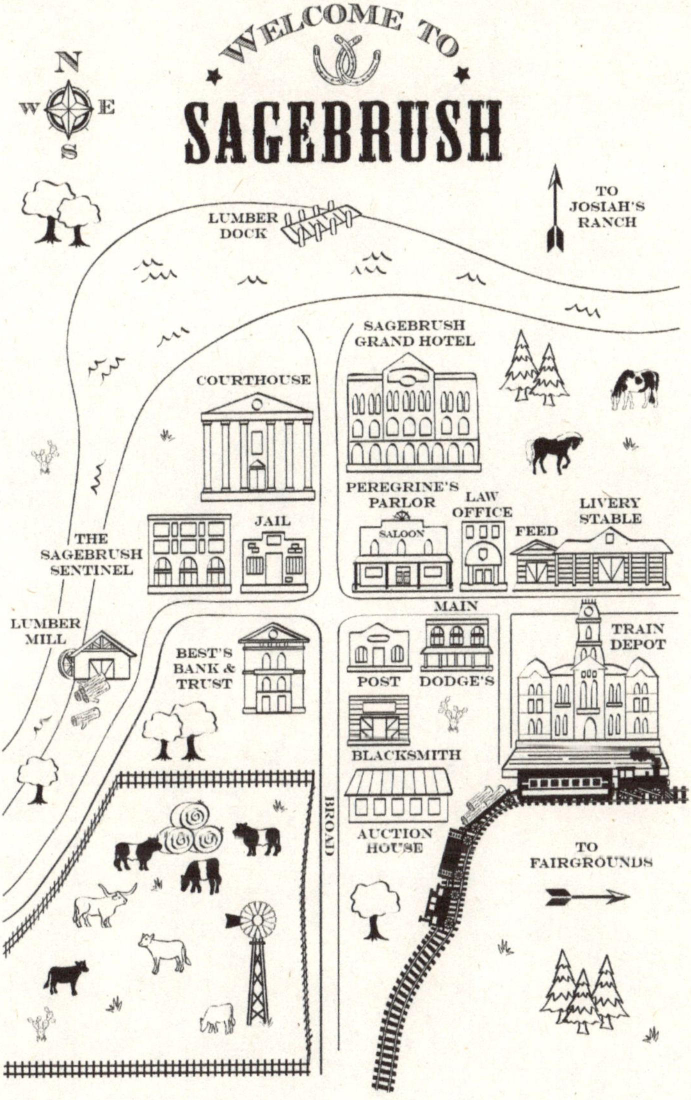
WELCOME TO
SAGEBRUSH
N
W
E
S
LUMBER DOCK
TO JOSIAH'S RANCH
SAGEBRUSH GRAND HOTEL
COURTHOUSE
PEREGRINE'S PARLOR
SALOON
LAW OFFICE
LIVERY STABLE
FEED
JAIL
THE SAGEBRUSH SENTINEL
MAIN
LUMBER MILL
BEST'S BANK & TRUST
POST
DODGE'S
TRAIN DEPOT
BLACKSMITH
BROAD
AUCTION HOUSE
TO FAIRGROUNDS

PROLOGUE

10 years earlier

The sound of gunfire usually results in ringing ears. That was not the case this time for Josiah Rush as smoke poured from his barrel. He would have preferred the ringing to hearing the cries of the young boy.

"PA!? Pa! Wake up, Pa!"

"Good shot," a voice reassured. "There was a weapon. That was a good shot," Marshal Oglesby repeated. "Take a seat. That's it. Someone get that kid outta here! Josiah, relax."

The room seemed to spin as shock set in. It felt to Josiah like someone else was in control of his body when he released the cylinder of his revolver and emptied the chambers. Cartridges clattered to the floor. Marshal Oglesby picked up the lone, spent casing and handed it to Josiah.

"You'll have to reckon with this one someday. Part of the job."

Josiah stared into the distance, removed the badge from his lapel and walked out of the shack without saying a word.

1

Somewhere outside the sun was shining, but it was certainly somewhere other than the town of Sagebrush. Main Street was so deep with muck that the horses stumbled as much as the whiskey-fueled cowboys struggling to lead them to the livery. The gray skies and drizzle offered a welcomed relief, however, from the biblical onslaught of thunderstorms the town had received the night before. As a result, any man attempting to grow a crop this year had forgotten his midnight prayers negotiating for safety and was celebrating the rain at Peregrine's Parlor by noon. The saloon was full of folks racking up their tabs, one drink after another.

"Them doors keep swingin' as folks see this weather ain't lettin' up 'fore afternoon chores," Lawrence Hoak said. The bartender capered at the expectation of a busy day.

Josiah Rush offered a subdued smile, tipped his hat, then grabbed his whiskey. Turning around, he rested his elbows on the bar and took inventory of the place. A piano clamored to life with a novel stride as the talented Philippe La Brune, a transplant from the bayou, finessed the out-of-tune upright. The piano lived against the far wall near a stage where a red velvet curtain was drawn closed. The air was thick with tobacco, but the smoke was pierced every so often by the scent of expensive perfumes. Men shuffled cards at the crowded wooden tables; the ladies laughed, and the drinks flowed. It was not holy, but it was not hell. The gamblers wagered real coin, gold and silver pulled from the very hills that skirt the territory; and the ingenious of industry in the form of a timepiece dangled from every silken vest pocket that graced their chests. Most were known to be decent men, not usually given to the debasement of high moral conduct. Civility, not savagery, was the social veneer. Reason, not violence, the first language. Josiah reckoned that such pretense was merely the ends toward which men strive, but not the means in which they truly deal. *After all*, he thought, *every man wants his own way for the world.*

At a card table to Josiah's right convened a couple men notorious in these parts. Jacoby Sutton sat there desperately trying to understand the nuances that governed the art of poker. Across from Jacoby was Will Richardson who had become quite frustrated with, and frankly astonished by, the sheer dumb luck Jacoby found by having simply shown up and received fortune's favor. Jacoby's pot was the current inspiration of envy among the other gentlemen at the table.

Peregrine's Parlor was the finest saloon in the west. Black paneling lined the bottom half of the walls and above the chair rail was an exotic paisley papering. It matched the carefully chosen oil lamp sconces. A French chandelier swung from the checkered tin ceiling, and glass windows lined the two walls facing Broad Street and Main. Outside, old men would often rock in the chairs along the boardwalk, keeping company with the dogs at their feet and the horses at the hitching posts. The weather, however, had driven a few of them inside where they sat bunched together at a corner table chewing tobacco and tapping their toes on the pinewood floor along with the beat of ole La Brune. The bar propping up Josiah ran the length of the far wall and found its terminus at a discreet staircase leading up to the second-floor rooms of the contiguous and estimable Sagebrush Grand Hotel.

The Parlor's proprietor, Peregrine "Perry" Page, was savvy to have acquired the lease on the great room of the Sagebrush Grand, only the most recent home to his saloon. When Perry first came to town, his establishment was across the way in a lowly false-front pole building. Then the promise of gold attracted the prospectors, and the early settlers and homesteaders of Sagebrush prospered. They spent a great deal of their earnings with Perry; and that was before the growth that occurred once the railroad came through. The saloon now occupied prime real estate with one entrance on the corner of the town's central intersection and the other inside the hotel to lure weary travelers with a hot meal and a strong drink. No one in Sagebrush knew the truth of how Perry managed to negotiate such a feat of commerce with George Best, the wealthy hotel owner and big city banker not known to be a generous benefactor. Josiah had heard rumors concerning untoward dealings between the two men but remained skeptical.

Josiah sipped his whiskey and let it roll over his tongue a while, savoring the medium-bodied offering, salty on the palate with a smoky finish. His beaver pelt hat bore a kind of cattleman's pitch across the crown not by design, but from improper handling. Its flat brim sat slightly canted atop his head and was faded black after having endured years of abuse from midday rays of sunshine. His vibrant eyes illuminated his otherwise deeply shadowed face which was beginning to show signs of weathering and age. He sported the stubble of a recently greying beard. A triangular bandana adorned his neck and behind it one might catch a glimpse of an eagle claw on a braid of gold. Josiah sat the empty glass down on the bar and took an interest in the happenings at a table by the window overlooking Broad Street.

"Lawrence," he said, "I'll take another. And bring over a round on me for that table right there." Josiah pointed out the distant patrons for the bartender before meandering through a maze of revelers. He gave Will Richardson a clap on the shoulder as he passed by, then pulled up a chair at an adjacent game next to the merchant from Dodge's Emporium.

"Hello Mr. Kelly! Plenty of traffic in town today. Surprised to see you here," he said.

"Oh? Will ye be takin' yer dry goods home in this rain, then?" the Irishman asked.

"Fair enough," Josiah said, "I meant no disrespect."

"Aye, none taken. T'was but a gag. How d'ye do Mr. Rush?" Martin Kelly removed his hat revealing a mess of red hair and stood to shake hands.

"Quite well, thank you. That is, despite havin' failed to learn *not* to presume another man's business." Josiah nodded to the other players at the table as he sat.

"Oh, not at all! Yer right, in fact. Had it not been fer the carpenter replacin' a rafter in the upper level, ye'd find me hard at work, no doubt."

"Well, it's no waste to invest in your diggins, I suppose."

"Invest, aye, with Mr. Best's quid to boot; interest is cheap."

"Martin, tsk tsk," Josiah said. "You do well. Why not plank your own profit?"

"Yer concern is appreciated, but I'll gladly pay tomorrow to keep well enough on hand today." Martin placed a bet.

"As I said, I'll make no presumptions about your business, my friend."

"Shall we deal ye in, then?" Martin inquired just as an unknown woman entered through the swinging doors and caught Josiah's interest.

"Hmm, not today."

"Does the same principle that keeps ye from a loan also keep ye from a game of poker, Mr. Rush?"

Josiah watched the woman navigate the crowd. She held her head high and moved with grace, gliding across the floor.

"Ah, no, I've been known to play a friendly game," Josiah said. "Just . . . not every day." His eyes followed the stranger.

"Is this not a *friendly* game, sir?" Martin teased, graciously choosing to address the manner of sport rather than the aimless commentary on the frequency of his participation in it.

"Oh, sure," said Josiah. He made no eye contact. Intending to take his leave of the purveyor and approach the woman that captured his attention, his speech slowed, "but it's just *not* every day that . . . uh . . . ah, well, if you'll excuse me." With that, Josiah tipped his hat and stood, accidentally pushing his chair backward into Lawrence Hoak. The drinks Josiah had ordered crashed to the ground, spilling beer all over Will Richardson who was still at the next table losing to Jacoby Sutton. The sound of breaking glass caused an immediate hush to fall across the room. Even La Brune interrupted his tune and turned from the piano to look on. Will stood up slowly. All eyes were on the three men as Will used the back of his hand to brush the liquid from his leathers. Coupled with the storm clouds outside the window, his burly figure cast a menacing presence. Lightning cracked, thunder pealed, and Will's top lip quivered, animating the ends of his wide, curly mustache. Lawrence Hoak instinctively took a step backward toward Josiah who, despite his guilt, chuckled at the fear the large man evoked in the bartender. Josiah gave Will a quick wink then nodded in Lawrence Hoak's direction. Playing along, it was a still, tense moment before Will let out an audible sigh. He collected his wager from the table, then in one swift motion grabbed his duster off the back of the chair and pushed his arms through. After a few paces he stopped shoulder to shoulder uncomfortably close to a paralyzed

Lawrence Hoak. Will deposited a coin into the bartender's vest pocket with a gentle pat.

"Well, I weren't stayin' dry today, anyhow," he said. Will brushed past Lawrence out the saloon doors into the rain as Josiah struggled to contain his laughter. Lawrence wiped his brow then made a start for the broom.

Philippe La Brune returned to his ivories and the murmur of activity began to fill the air again. With Lawrence placated and the glass swept, Josiah offered his apologies and scanned the room, in vain, for the woman he had seen a few minutes earlier.

MARSHAL

2

The wagon trail that led into Sagebrush descended from the heights of the eastern mountains. It had been washed out in places where the springtime run-off chiseled its way to and fro across the fraternal scars that straightened into a plain and split the landscape. On either side of the deep ruts were disparate portraits. The trail followed a river along the northern parallel which provided sustenance for lush grasslands and roaming bison. A ridgeline on the trail's southern panorama, however, was lifeless and arid. Like estranged lovers, both halves of the frontier were inextricably bonded yet irreparably cloven.

Upon reaching the base of the range, it was but a half-day's ride into Sagebrush. The clop of hooves and the creak of shifting saddles were as naturalized to the environment as birdsong or the rustling of an armadillo. Manure and wildflowers were the burden and blessing of the wind. This stretch of dirt was frequently met with empty bellies and full hearts as travelers might experience exhausted rations yet remarkable joy at the promise of nearing their journey's end.

There was a point on the trail where the ridges crowning the hidden gables of the town's facades became visible over the mirage on the horizon. Here the rhythmic banter and brass whistles of distant steam engines could be heard on the other side of a slow rise to the north. Track, paid per mile with government funds, wound its way through redundant twists and turns until it eased southward, spanned the river, and intersected with Main Street. From there it joined tracks funded by private capital which headed southwest straight out of town all the way to the coast.

On the second day after the storm rolled through, a rider from the trail galloped into Sagebrush just before noon. He passed over the tracks but did not stop at the livery. The Livery Stables, operating within the first structure to the north after crossing into town, boarded horses for visitors, but the grounds also included a pasture behind the building which extended toward the river. The adjoining feed store kept the troughs along the shared fence row full of fresh hay, and this five-acre plot proved successful in reducing the instances of colic among local equine populations. It allowed the tenants to more frequently attend to their grazing so the stable boys could more frequently attend to their stalls so the cowboys could more frequently attend to their spirits. The livery's owner, Dillon Turk, managed the place with the help of his bride Rebecca, a talented and industrious seamstress, along with their two sons, Jasper and Cassidy.

The rider arrived on a hot day, so everyone and everything else was moving slowly. The road had dried out and his appaloosa kicked up a mess of dust, causing the women out front of the Emporium to hold kerchiefs over their faces and fan themselves. Certain women would gather there for gossip and business, enticing new arrivals and convincing them to replenish dwindling provisions at Dodge's Emporium and Dry Goods, courtesy of Martin Kelly. The Emporium benefited from its location as The Depot's nearest neighbor. When travelers arriving by rail disembarked, the train station's platform intuitively ushered them through an alley next to the store out to Main Street. The Depot stood proud as Sagebrush's newest evidence of the progress of man. It had been constructed with what the owners referred to as resplendent archways, but the prevailing opinion of the townsfolk was that it looked obnoxious. The Depot replaced several aging buildings, including the former home of Peregrine's Parlor, after a fire broke out that had mysteriously coincided with the ingress of surveyors from the railroad.

The rider came to a halt at the Post Office, situated next to the Emporium, and dismounted his winded stallion. The local postmaster, Charles Crandall, had grown up as an orphan and once served a pivotal year riding for the Express. He knew this land—its tempests and dangers—better than just about anyone. Consequently, he was a frequent consultant for any sojourner with business beyond the well-trodden paths of the wagon trails. These days, though, he rarely strayed from the road between town and his cabin. It was never difficult for anyone to recognize the fondness he carried for both his roving brethren and the time he spent reared by the wild.

The rider shimmered with sweat in the late morning sun and noticed white foam forming around his horse's bit. After pulling something from a saddlebag, the jockey tossed the reins quickly over a banister. He burst through the doors of the Post Office with profuse apologies.

"I got caught up in a terrible storm and the pass was flooded. I persevered, sir, but the route I managed set me behind nearly two days," the youthful rider recounted.

"Alright now, son . . . just-just take her easy." Charles Crandall smiled paternally. "Here, have some water. I'll see to it that your horse is cared for."

The official correspondence the rider carried was marked "URGENT" and addressed to the marshal. Crandall left the young man to recover on a bench and went across the street to recruit some help. On his way, he passed an old spinster that he surmised had been critical of the courier, for she was now being castigated by a mysterious woman. The unfamiliar young lady clearly understood the gravity of news carried in such a hurried fashion.

The door hinges squeaked as Crandall stepped into the law office of Nicholas Scoville, Esq. When Scoville, a man of small stature, first came to town he perplexed the locals by leasing an uptown front but securing the land deed to an unattractive property further south on Broad. That property became home to the commercial docks when the railroad finally did come through and soon boasted an Auction House adjacent to the stockyards. In keeping with appearances, Scoville maintained the lease for the office on Main Street where he has continued to not only provide legal counsel, but also serve as Public Treasurer. Scoville readily agreed to take the rider's appaloosa to the livery and then drop by the Emporium for some dried apples and jerky for the famished youngster. Crandall left to seek out the mail's intended recipient.

"Marshal! Marshal!"

"Over here, Crandall." A ray of sunlight flickered off a bronze star pinned to the lapel of Marshal Felix Oglesby. Oglesby's spurs clinked as he stepped toward the center of the intersection to meet Crandall. Some old men stopped rocking to lean in and listen. A couple young boys let the dirt clods they were throwing at each other fall to the ground.

"This just arrived special by messenger, not rail, so I reckon you need to see it straight away."

"Obliged." The marshal took and unrolled a warrant issued by a judge from back east. He began to read it as he turned and casually strolled away. Anxiously, Crandall watched. The marshal suddenly stopped and lowered his head for a split second before glancing back over his shoulder. He nodded slightly then proceeded to the courthouse.

Charles Crandall whistled for the boys at play. "Jasper, run along and tell your Pa to saddle up my horse." The younger Turk's widened eyes conveyed his understanding of the situation's gravity. "Cassidy Turk," Crandall lowered his head and raised his eyebrows, "you go fetch me Josiah Rush."

3

An unbridled gelding circled the round pen at a trot. Its eyes darted left to right, skeptical and panicky; it seemed reluctant to acknowledge confinement. A flaxen mane cascaded down a chestnut coat. It fell onto muscular shoulders toned by the fortuitous circumstance of a formidable lineage and the restless vigor of youth. Josiah stood in the center of the pen, intensely focused, and squared up to the four-year-old Morgan horse. A bead of sweat formed on his brow. It remained undisturbed as he held the long lines and let Nero tire himself, pass after pass, as though a lone brute on a platform carousel.

As Nero grew fatigued, Josiah began to gently toss the reins across the horse's loins and let it run out from underneath them. He was conditioning Nero to the feel of leather. Josiah kept a keen eye on the horse's movements watching for signs to make an approach.

When Nero began to drop his head, and the laps he made grew more constricted, Josiah initiated the dance. He confidently approached the horse who ran from him until it grew weary, then Josiah approached again. Over and over and over this occurred; all the while Josiah gently encouraged Nero, trying to calmly alleviate any anxiety.

"Shh, ole boy. That's right, just settle down now," he said. "I know. That's a good boy."

Then, finally, as if Nero had an epiphany, he stood still and let Josiah reach out and caress his symmetrical white blaze from crown to nose. The horse bowed its head working with, not against, Josiah who was able to place the bit and slip on a bridle.

Two onlookers were perched atop the fence passing a flask. Levi Holdegel and Cooper Emmons exchanged glances, each impressed with Nero's improvements. Cooper, the local blacksmith and farrier, was there on a house call to shoe the gelding. He had stayed for the education. Nero belonged to Levi, who hired Josiah to train the horse before it went to auction.

After more than an hour in the oppressive heat, Josiah remained hesitant to mount up. The bronco had had a fit upon the initial cinch of the saddle and took to kicking and bucking. Josiah was in no hurry to find out how Nero would react to the weight of a full-grown man on his back.

The horse was smart. Although Josiah remained on the ground, Nero almost intuitively understood the rein commands. In that pen, man and beast beheld one another with a reciprocal reverence demonstrated by seemingly unprecedented cooperation.

"He's relaxed now boys, and he's thinkin'." Josiah spoke half to himself, unconcerned with whether Levi or Cooper heard a word he said. Although Josiah was there for the benefit of the two men, they did not, in fact, hear him and were instead preoccupied with a longhorn in the south pasture. It was nearly two hours on when they missed Josiah triumphantly kick a leg over and finally take Nero on the horse's first ride.

Staring out over a stamping and snorting bull, Cooper Emmons asked, "You reckon I could break *him*?" Cooper showed no interest in the reaction he had garnered, causing Levi to think the wiry metal worker just might have been serious.

"Do what?" Levi inquired.

"You know, throw a saddle on him, ride him through town. Break him like Josiah done yer pony here."

"Ah Cooper, this ain't breakin'," Josiah said riding up on Nero. "Nah, his spirit's still there." He patted the horse's crest.

"Well, I'd break that bull," Cooper said. He was half-drunk and oblivious to the magic that had just transpired in the pen before him. "I wouldn't want no spirit left in that sum' bitch if I's to take him fer a trot."

Josiah and Levi were still shaking their heads when Cassidy Turk came sprinting up the hill.

"Mr. Josiah!" the boy shouted. He closed the distance in a hurry.

"Cassidy? Boy, what brings you up this way? And why are you soakin' wet? Levi, help me out here." Josiah dismounted and handed the reins to the one-armed breeder, then strolled curiously over to the sopping young man.

"I had to cross the river, sir; just upstream of the lumber routes."

"You did what!?"

"It was the most direct way, sir, and Mr. Crandall made it sound mighty urgent."

"Cassidy Turk, you know better than that! You coulda been killed! That river is too wide and the current too strong north of the mill, what if you'd have drifted into them loggin' channels? You coulda been crushed. Ain't nothin' so urgent as to risk your life like that, you hear?"

"Yes sir."

"Now, about Mr. Crandall?"

"He just said to come fetch you is all."

Josiah huffed a bit. He scanned the western pasture where his cattle grazed on sparse patches of grass. He then looked over to his branding iron next to a crush pen and thought about all the work he'd planned to do that afternoon.

"He say why?" Josiah asked.

"No, sir," Cassidy said.

Levi spoke up. "Ain't like Crandall to send a summons if it weren't important."

"Yeah," Josiah said, "I reckon so. Well, I suppose we'd better see what all this is about then."

Levi and Cooper moved to untie their horses. "What do you have planned for Nero?" Levi asked.

"He's had quite the day already," Josiah said. "We ought to get him to the barn and let him rest."

Just then Nero snorted.

"I don't think he cares too much for that idea."

"Well, I don't want to overwhelm him." Josiah turned toward the barn.

Nero whinnied and threw his head back one time.

"Ain't that somethin'?"

"Look, I know what you're thinkin' and there's no way that horse is ready. I ain't ridin' him into town for you right now, he still needs a week's worth of work or more."

"Might be good for him to see these other horses in action."

"Yer drunk and that ain't gonna happen." Josiah laughed. He took the reins and led Nero to a stall in the barn. He saddled up an old mare as Levi watered his horse then watered himself. Cassidy Turk climbed up with Cooper Emmons, and the four of them headed for town.

Meanwhile, Charles Crandall had been tasked with hanging wanted posters around Sagebrush. The posters announced a reward for a man by the name of Colton Waddell and enumerated a censored list of his alleged abuses including rustling and murder. The last known whereabouts of Waddell were a two-days' ride from Sagebrush in an old mining settlement known as Buffalo Junction where he was believed to be hiding out with one of his brothers.

Marshal Oglesby was of a mind to pursue the outlaw Waddell and see him brought to trial to answer for his crimes. In the interest of justice, he and his deputy, Butch Eaton, planned to muster a posse. Among the recruits were Will Richardson and Jacoby Sutton, pulled fresh from the Parlor gaming tables. They were all out front of the Emporium stocking up on a week's worth of supplies.

". . . and you're sure I can't convince you to come join us? I'd greatly appreciate the help," Marshal Oglesby implored the merchant, Martin Kelly.

"Oh, and who would keep these lasses comp'ny whilst I was away?" Martin joked. Spreading his hands before him, he motioned to a few ladies by a bench on the store's boardwalk.

"Come now, Martin, this is serious business."

"Aye, Marshal," Martin said. His face lacked its usual jovial smile, "I am serious. Dis is business." Martin dared the insinuation at the risk of displeasing the marshal who looked away but nodded his head.

"Alright Mr. Kelly, well, I trust that a man capable of protecting his . . . friends, is also capable of keepin' the peace in Sagebrush in my absence?" The marshal made the charge with his most adroit charm and manners, bowing to the ladies.

"Have ye no worries, sir. I shall look after her as one of me own." Martin tipped his hat as though a gentlemen's agreement had just been struck.

"Very well. At some point this week stop by Scoville's regardin' payment for the . . . uh . . . provender." Marshal Oglesby motioned toward Will and Jacoby who struggled to attach one side of a bedroll to a saddle as Deputy Butch Eaton untethered the other.

Charles Crandall had finished hanging posters and rode over from the livery with another man at his side.

"Felix, err, uh, Marshal," he stuttered, remembering his manners. "This here's Henry Olt. He comes with the favorable recommendation of Dillon Turk." Crandall dismounted and began to load up a mule.

"Pleased to meet your acquaintance, Mr. Olt. I appreciate your willingness to proffer aid to our modest company, I do fear we need it. However, and forgive my forwardness, I do not know you. Have you no other business than to be ridin' out with our lot after a man presumed to be as dangerous as our suspect, the outlaw Colton Waddell?" As the marshal posed his question, Josiah and Levi appeared on horseback from around the corner.

"It is mighty fine to meet you, sir. Yours is a fair inquiry, and my abbreviated answer is no. Mr. Turk is brother to my late wife and I'm just arrived here in Sagebrush. Havin' not yet secured work, I figure my assistance will be the opportunity to prove my salt and get to know some of the men."

"Just fine, Mr. Olt. My condolences, and you're welcome to join us." At that, Marshal Oglesby noticed Josiah and greeted him with a tip of the hat.

Due to the excitement, a crowd of curious townsfolk gathered about, including a certain woman who peered at the posse from the window of the Emporium.

"Howdy gentlemen," Josiah said. "Pray tell, Crandall, what's the meanin' of all this? Have anything to do with your beckonin', I presume?"

Crandall nodded.

Josiah's eyes caught the spying woman give him a contemptuous look before hastily drawing the curtain closed. He recognized her from the Parlor two days prior and was unsettled by her expression, but more pressing matters demanded his attention.

Marshal Oglesby spoke. "Josiah, I'm glad you're here."

Crandall handed Josiah a copy of the wanted poster. He perused it carelessly as Cooper Emmons rode over, having dropped off Cassidy Turk with his mother, Rebecca, at the livery. Josiah passed the poster on to him and Levi.

"Alright, so you're goin' after him," Josiah said.

"I'd rather hoped to hear you say, '*we're* goin' after him,'" Crandall interrupted. Josiah looked down from his horse at the postmaster with respect and regret, but simply shook his head.

"Marshal, you've got men," Josiah said. "You don't need me." He glanced around at the five others and observed that the curtain in the window of the Emporium had been drawn open once more.

"These are good men, yes. I am confident in their abilities, but I am certain of yours." He paused. Josiah knew better than to think Marshal Felix Oglesby was flattering him with an appeal to hubris merely to garner his consent, and the marshal confirmed it when he walked closer and quieted his voice. "Look, I need a man who, if it comes to it, is proven able to pull that trigger."

"I just . . ." Josiah took a deep breath. "I don't really wanna do that anymore," he said.

"Then why even carry that barkin' iron?" Will accused, regarding Josiah's pistol. His mustache twitched.

Cooper chirped up in Josiah's defense. "If he never drew that gun again, he'd still be deadlier with it than you are with yours."

"Are you dense or have I done somethin' that makes you think you can get away with talkin' to me like that?" Will took a threatening step toward Cooper.

"E-he-he-easy ladies! If Josiah decides to break peace, I doubt it'll be to keep you two mules from anointin' one another right here in the dust of Main." Levi spat, and the two men dropped their bickering.

"C'mon, Rush," Charles Crandall insisted again. He squinted and there was excitement in his invitation. "*Ride* with us."

"You don't know what you're askin', partner." Josiah winced and continued, "It's been a decade or more since I last drew on a man, and I mean not to do it again. An' if'n I do, it's gonna be on my terms, not for anyone else, and certainly not because I went lookin' for trouble, you hear."

"I *do* know what I'm askin' of you, but—"

"Reuben Ward wasn't lookin' for trouble either," the marshal interrupted.

Josiah took off his hat by its crown. He rubbed his head deliberately from front to back before returning the hat crooked to his head. "And who's that?" he asked as though he knew better.

"Reuben Ward. He was runnin' cattle just like you when he hired on this son of a bitch, Waddell, as a ranch hand. They drove a herd north together for two weeks, breakin' bread and sharin' a fire every night. After the stockyards, Waddell shot him and left him for dead, the profit from three hundred head of cattle ripped right out of his dyin' hands. Only he didn't die, he was nursed back from the brink by some medicine woman. After finally makin' his way home, well, there wasn't any home left. It had been razed to the ground, his wife and boy locked inside."

Suddenly everyone seemed to take an interest in their boots. Everyone except the woman inside the Emporium, who was transfixed on Josiah with tears forming in the corners of her eyes. Not even Cooper Emmons had anything to say.

4

The trail from Sagebrush to Buffalo Junction followed the river westward out of town. It was a well-trodden trade route that eventually intersected with the southern fork. There, the pines gradually gave way to desert brush. Josiah rode behind the marshal with the rest of the men trailing single file. It was still early in the journey, and everyone relaxed in their saddles.

Distant crows joined an opus of burbling water bounding over river rocks. The occasional scampering of a skink accompanied the steady breathing of horses. Josiah knew that at this point in the expedition, being well provisioned and fresh to saddle, there was a certain peace that befell most men. Josiah envied that peace.

"Somethin' is just eatin' away at you, I can tell." It was Levi who disrupted his thoughts.

"Nah," Josiah lied, avoiding eye contact. "And if there was?"

Levi knew better. "You keep on broodin' like a beat pup and folks is gonna start to assume you been licked."

"Watch your mouth." The kindly admonition was met with laughter from Josiah's friend.

"Oh, come on," Levi said, "ain't no shame in it, but how can you be so glum out here in all this beauty?"

"Don't get too comfortable, Levi. Behind all this beauty is just a different set of dangers."

"Don't I know it? Ain't even the terrain that'll getchya." Levi looked long past the horizon. "Almost like it's...alive ...ain't it?" He broke off a plug of chewing tobacco. "Like it's remindin' us that one day we won't be?"

Josiah watched a hawk dive out of sight behind the dwindling trees across the river. When it reappeared, the bird was clutching prey in its talons. "She offers more than a reminder of death. I think we get the chance to settle with it, overcome the fear of it. That's when men start to live."

"Thing is, I never give it any thought 'cept when I get away for a little while," Levi confessed.

"Good for the soul to have the freedom to get away now and then. Suppose that's why some men'll bleed for it." Josiah motioned to Levi's old wound.

A silence persisted between them for a while until Levi resolved to try his inquiry again. "Surprised to see you out here, Josiah," he said.

"To tell the truth, part of me is, too."

"And the other part?"

Josiah shook his head, "Tryin' to tame it. Don't wanna live for the thrill that comes from the prospect of a fight no more."

"Even if you're fightin' the good fight?"

"Even so. Good fight ain't always cut an' dried. Men have a way of spoilin' just causes."

"That don't mean you can turn a blind eye to evil, Josiah."

"No, it does not, which is why we're here havin' this conversation, not back at the Parlor havin' a different one."

Josiah rode on, certain in the moment only of the inescapable err of his ways as he considered the absurd extremes of his competing convictions. On one hand he knew the undeniable horrors of partaking in violence. On the other was the truth that non-violence results in the perpetuation, by others, of the very horrors such a creed seeks to preclude. Josiah supposed he was not culpable for the violence of others but could not bring himself to ignore the victim's cause. He rationalized his continued involvement by concluding, "Peaceful don't mean harmless."

"Remember the war, Levi," Josiah said after a moment of reflection. "I held the lines then, damned though I may be, and you got no cause to doubt me now. You hear?"

"I hear you. Anyway, I ain't here to agitate you. Just checkin' in 'cause you don't look so good."

"Well, sometimes a man has got to face the truth about the worst in himself 'fore he reckons with the worst in others. Since we're about to reckon with the worst in Waddell, I guess it'd be cause for concern if I was lookin' my best."

"Should I be worried?"

"Only if you've given yourself an honest assessment." Josiah glanced at Levi for the first time with a smirk. It was the sign that Levi had hoped for, that little bit of life that restored his confidence.

"Josiah, you'd give a man hell on his deathbed, but then pour your heart into his eulogy. Hope you don't come to regret that someday." Levi mocked the smirk.

"Can I ask you somethin'?" Josiah stared forward again. "Are you uncomfortable with silence?"

Levi shook his head to himself. Not one to forfeit the last word, he fondly replied, "I don't understand how you can be mean enough to eat from the same plate as a rattler, but dumb enough to allow it the first strike." With that, Levi wheeled his horse around, announced to the men that Josiah Rush was back, and fell in with Cooper toward the rear of the party. Josiah pocketed the jab, in part because he knew Levi was right.

That night the group camped under the canopy of the heavens. They had made good time and reached the southern ridge by dark. After scouting a location, they set up at the base of a mesa in a flat spot where a sheer wall was cleft from the hills in a semicircle. A crackling fire animated the shadows it cast on the sandstone and sent smoke plumes upward into a cloudless, star-filled sky. A chill settled on the air as Josiah laid on his bed roll and stared up into the swirling expanse. In the distance, a coyote howled while the rest of the men supped on beans and pemmican.

The marshal and his deputy sat around a campfire with Charles Crandall entertaining the newcomer, Henry Olt, with stories of the townsfolk. Cooper Emmons walked up to the fire and took a seat between Will Richardson and Jacoby Sutton. Will, recalling the previous day's squabble, stole a sideways glance at Cooper whose hand disappeared inside his vest for a beat. Retrieving a flask, Cooper took a swig and offered it to the big man. Will paused a spell before nodding and accepting the drink. After another nip, Cooper returned the flask to his pocket oblivious to an eager Jacoby's outstretched hand.

Henry Olt finished his rations and stood up, wiping his hands on his ill-fitting pants. He took leave of the men and walked over to Josiah who had turned to the wall.

"Excuse me, Mr. Rush. I was hopin' for a word before you turned in."

There was a time when Josiah would have sat around the campfire with the rest of the men. He would have been all laughs, the center of attention, but also the most hospitable and welcoming of all the men upon meeting someone new. There used to be an ease with which he spoke and an authenticity to his warmth and curiosity. Josiah used to love people effortlessly and naturally. These days though, he did well just to acknowledge that he ought to love people at all.

These days, it took a great deal of effort to even feign a smile in the attempt to communicate that he was not outright hostile. Josiah's abbreviated patience for interruptions had little to do with the interruption itself, and more to do with the fact that he required greater time to revive his own energy; such time was sacred and increasingly difficult to come by. He fought a heap of guilt for, and indeed grieved, the loss of his ability to react graciously to requests for his attention. He held conflicting desires to obviously regard others with favor but also settle the persistent contradictions of his principles that relentlessly plagued him with a crippling sense of immediacy. Mustering the last bit of available energy, he propped himself up on one elbow and turned, trying not to seem perturbed.

"What's on your mind, Mr. Olt?"

"I just wanted to say what an honor it is to be ridin' with you, sir."

Josiah's eyes found the fire. He pursed his lips sideways and chewed at the inside of his cheek. After inhaling sharply, he said, "It's a lot of work tryin' to live up to another man's expectations. Perhaps you'd ought to find somethin' inside yourself that makes you honored to be ridin' in your own saddle."

"Don't mind that angry bastard, Mr. Olt," Levi hollered. He had been eavesdropping. "It's when he's *not* givin' you hell you ought to be worried."

Mr. Olt tipped his hat coldly before returning to the fire. Josiah watched him go and felt disappointed with the way he handled the man's appreciation. He wanted to apologize, but for his manner not the content of his words. That would require a bit more delicacy than he was up for, however, so he rolled over and drifted off to sleep.

The next morning Josiah was the first to wake. In the peaceful pre-dawn, he stoked what remained of the previous night's fire, releasing cinders that ascended to the sky like aspiring stars and burned themselves out just the same. He added more kindling then threw on another log. As the flame died down to a good bed of embers, he boiled enough water for everyone in the party to have a cup of coffee or two once they awoke.

The constellations began to fade as his eyes followed the western horizon up and around to the east where the faintest gradient of the softening morning blue was cresting a barren silhouette. The effect of the golden firelight dancing from the walls of the camp waned as the sun's rays began to assert their governance over the morning. Josiah rubbed sleep from his eyes and poured his first cup of coffee. He inhaled the steam deeply and, filtering grounds through his teeth as he sipped, he savored a moment to himself.

"Just in time," a voice from behind him whispered. Josiah turned to see Charles Crandall yawn. He was still wrapped in wool when he took a seat next to the fire. Crandall produced a tin cup from under his blanket and Josiah poured him coffee. The two men sat in silence; each ultimately concerned more with wrestling into submission their internal afflictions in order to face the day rather than hazard conversation about even the most trivial matters. Crandall eased the pressure in his chest by contemplating the phenomenon that everything he beheld was alight due to the power of something else set destructively ablaze. Josiah fought against his urge to dwell on the fiery fate of the Wards as he prayed deliberately through each line of an ancient prayer.

Before long, he finished his recitations as the camp brimmed with life; bedrolls were packed, horses were watered, and breakfast tins were splashed clean. The deputized posse meant to get an early start so as to scout Buffalo Junction by mid-afternoon.

They were not long on the road when Jacoby Sutton began to have issues handling his proud cut appaloosa. He had been trailing Josiah's immediate rear for a few miles when the horse grew increasingly disobedient, jumpy, and desirous to run up alongside Josiah's mare.

"You need some assistance, cowboy?" Deputy Butch Eaton asked from behind Jacoby.

No sooner did an embarrassed Jacoby shake his head "no" than that horse of his reared up on its hind legs and lunged forward in a failed attempt to mount the mare. Fortunately, she spooked and whipped sideways, bringing Josiah with her out of harm's way. She faltered, however, and when she regained her footing, blood poured from a gash on her front left fetlock. Josiah and Jacoby both shared a long wide-eyed look. Plenty of communication was exchanged in that look; there was an apology from Jacoby for endangering Josiah, shame from Josiah for the trouble of bringing along a mare, and more than a little relief that no one was injured. Levi and Crandall laughed, Butch cursed them under his breath, and Cooper could not stop remarking on how terrified Henry Olt seemed. He kept saying it was as though it had just dawned on the rawheel how far they were from a doctor and how dangerous their adventure could become. They were "on a manhunt, after all." Josiah addressed the horse's injury then made good use of his bandana to avoid eating the dust of the others as he rode last in line the rest of the way.

After a long day on the trail, they paused upon finally cresting a hill overlooking Buffalo Junction. The shadowy cavalry, saddled atop their steeds, spread out to take in the lay of the land. The village was once a waypoint for a spur track off the mainline that the railroad abandoned once the local mines proved unprofitable. It had since become a ghost town of sorts, falling to disrepair. Along with a few hardscrabble homesteaders, it was reputed to have collected its fair share of outlaws. It was fertile ground for fugitives due to its proximity to a maze of old navigable mineshafts well-suited for hiding loot, as well as evading or ambushing bounty hunters.

The men carefully made their way down to the town square where they rode in formation to a centrally located stone well to refill their water supply. Cold stares from hardened bandoleros welcomed the party. Marshal Oglesby glared right back at a small gang near the entrance to a tavern. He squinted, cocked his head slightly, and made his silent announcement. Slowly, he adjusted the duster's lapels revealing his badge, and by dropping his hands to his hips he brought their attention to a pair of pistols in black studded leather holsters that matched his chaps. For the marshal, honorable work required honorable attire. Deputy Butch Eaton dismounted and retrieved a lever action repeater from his saddle. The stocky deputy joined the marshal at his right shoulder and noticed a sombrero disappear from the back of the group around a corner. Josiah was still at the well filling his canteen when he heard a gunshot.

5

Back in Sagebrush things had been business as usual since the marshal left. That was until late one afternoon when Martin Kelly came hurtling out of the Sagebrush Grand Hotel into the road, shrieking like a barn cat, and tripping over everything in his way. The uproar from the whiskey bent merchant caused the old men out front of Peregrine's Parlor to wager whether he had collided with a water basin or pissed himself.

"Lorraine! Lorraine! Fer da love o' Pete, where are ye, Lorraine!" he shouted.

Hearing the commotion, Lawrence Hoak temporarily abandoned his post behind the bar of the Parlor and attempted to restrain his friend in hopes of salvaging a shred of dignity. He was not the only one rushing toward the Celtic cries, though, and his eyes found a pretty woman in blue when they should have found a step off the boardwalk. Alas they did not, so down went Lawrence Hoak, sprawled out onto the hardpack ground. Having fallen face first into the dirt he then rolled over, wailing and cussing, into a pile of fresh horse manure. He grabbed hold of his wrist, and spit blood from a busted nose all over Martin Kelly who had stumbled over to offer help.

Peregrine Page had been upstairs overlooking the chaos. He made his way down as the woman in blue rushed past the bluster into the hotel. A departing train whistle sounded in the distance. Upon reaching the boardwalk, Perry peered down at the two men, one drunk, one bloody, both putrid. Just then a handful of new arrivals found their way from the Depot's platform through the alley out to Main Street. Perry's exasperation turned to horror as he noticed a small trickle of dignified ladies and refined gentlemen gawk disapprovingly from the scene on the ground up to the Parlor's namesake then back to the scene on the ground. Perry's scathing eyes darted to Lawrence, then to Martin. The merchant was too busy vomiting to notice or care. Perry then turned his attention back to the alley as the last of the passengers to disembark took their initial assessment of the blossoming town. Perry felt a sense of relief, but it was short-lived. From around the corner emerged a man in a top hat and bowtie spinning a walking cane. The black suit belonged to none other than Perry's financier, the banker George Best, owner of the Sagebrush Grand Hotel.

Perry ushered Mr. Best into the saloon offering assurances that business was well in hand. A few patrons with empty glasses stood up and left while another helped herself to a top-shelf selection. Perry's guarantees to Mr. Best had to compete with the intensifying sound of a woman's screams coming from the stairwell leading to the second floor of the hotel.

Upstairs, Lorraine was a rush of blue fabric that swished down the hall and burst through the door of room 213. She got straight to work washing her hands in a basin while comforting Martin Kelly's pregnant courtesan. Rebecca Turk, the seamstress from the livery, sat in the corner offering further reassurances to the blubbering beauty.

"Have you ever served as a midwife before, Mrs. Turk?" Lorraine asked.

"My husband runs the stables, ma'am. We've brought in a couple of foals over the years, and I have two sons of my own. That's the extent of it." Rebecca replied.

"I'm sure that'll do," Lorraine said. She offered an encouraging smile to hide her diminishing faith. "Now, a train just arrived and I'm expecting Dr. Hoyle. I wrote for him when I discovered Ms. Pearl here was carrying breech. Until he shows, we'll just have to be responsible for making sure our friend is comfortable and we're prepared for delivery. Can you seek out some more clean linens and towels?"

"Of course, ma'am."

"Oh! And inquire about another feather pillow or two, please." Rebecca exited the room and Lorraine sat down on the bed with Pearl. "How's the pain, darling?"

"Currently fine enough, though a heartbeat ago I'd sworn to join a convent 'fore I'd find myself in a family way again," Pearl said as she relaxed on the bed in a familiar fashion.

"Come now," Lorraine frowned, "it's still early and I'm going to need you to be tougher than that."

Rebecca Turk had made her way downstairs. Seeking the necessities for Lorraine and a respite from the crassness of the laborious Ms. Pearl, she passed by Lawrence Hoak without notice. The valiant klutz was headed back to the Parlor from the hotel where he had stopped his nose from hemorrhaging and procured a makeshift sling. Upon his return he found Philippe La Brune clanging away on the piano in the saloon. The barroom was completely empty save for a comatose

Martin Kelly curled up on the stage using the red velvet curtain as a blanket.

Despite the pulsing of his temples, Lawrence managed to yell, "Philippe! Please, sir, my head. Just take five . . . you know what?" He softened, "Enjoy the rest of your day, sir. Thank you." The freeman stood up from the piano and pulled a corn shuck from his sleeve garter. He rolled a cigarette with expert dexterity and precision, lit it, then pushed through the swinging doors without saying a word. Lawrence closed the saloon and retired to a room to sleep off his headache.

Meanwhile, Perry was failing in his attempts to appease an unhappy George Best. On top of the colorful display of sport which, earlier, ran off customers, Best's preferences for whiskey and accommodations were nuanced and he grumbled that his own establishments were short of both. Best's penchant for imports would go unsatisfied until next week's rail delivery, and his personal suite was presently inhospitable as it was apparently below the "Sagebrush Grand's Maternity Ward," as he put it. Once settled in another room on the far side of the hallway, Mr. Best bid Perry good evening and the two retired without broaching much in the way of financials.

The ladies in 213 awaited Dr. Andrew Hoyle, who had in fact been on the train that afternoon but had yet to find his way to the hotel. Upon his arrival earlier in the day, unaware of the premature urgency of Ms. Pearl's predicament, he had seen a familiar name on the building sidelong from the Depot. Ignoring the tumult of the two men also in need of his talents out front of the Parlor, Dr. Hoyle had stopped in to see an old acquaintance from his university years, one Nicholas Scoville, Esq. The two spent time catching up and reminiscing well into the evening over a few highballs.

"This sure is a treat, Nicholas. I expected to find nothing but rotgut available this far out."

"While the tint of tobacco does color the local wells, Andrew, this is a railroad town. The enterprising fellow at the

Emporium has extensive networks that provide us with the finest Aqua Vitae," Scoville said.

"Of course, a market the Eastern Distillers are quite happy to oblige, I'm sure."

"And a market that you, yourself, are now able to service from what I understand. How is your venture blooming?"

"Surprisingly well, and I am enjoying the travel. Speaking of . . ." Dr. Hoyle retrieved a pouch from his duffle and laid it on the mahogany desk between them. Nicholas Scoville leaned forward from his brass-buttoned leather chair and drew a long breath savoring the scent of the spicy vanilla tobacco. The two men each lit a pipe.

"So, tell me more about your operation," Scoville pressed. "Last I heard you were completing a residency in a state asylum studying phrenology, is that correct?"

"The broader field of neuropsychiatry, but yes." Dr. Hoyle said.

"How is it that you've found yourself a nomadic general practitioner?" Scoville asked.

"Oh, well, let's just say I now offer my services in order to finance my heart's true desire: to be a wayfarer across these magnificent lands. It's not difficult to trade the sterility of an institution for the vibrance of the frontier. I now have several towns much like your own across the west with talented nurses in my employ. They are all equipped to provide emergency assistance because of wartime experience, and they keep me apprised of patient conditions as I make my rounds." Dr. Hoyle stood as he spoke and began to admire the library of works available at Scoville's disposal, including the Platonic Dialogues and multiple volumes on Colonial Common Law. "Caring for pioneers, prospectors, and cowboys is fascinating because I'm not only helping these poor people, but I'm continuing my work in the service of civilization by gathering a great body of evidence about the cranial maladies of our lesser compatriots."

Scoville balked. "Why, I'm not sure I know what you mean. I've found these modest people quite admirable. In fact, in my experience, if your interests are in the correlation between character degradation and the skull, then your time would be better spent massaging scalps in the halls of our statesmen."

Dr. Hoyle just laughed, cheerfully esteeming his old friend's fondness for his quaint neighbors. "Of course, of course these are good people, to be sure. But enough of them, tell me about *your* adventures. Surely the 'Bane of the Bench' has an interesting tale of abandoning the bulwarks of society for this dusty junction." Dr. Hoyle waved his fingers playfully as Scoville rolled his eyes.

"Ugh, please don't *ever* call me that again! Truth be told, I've got an entrepreneurial streak that cannot be satisfied by the legislatively erected bureaucracies of the capital. I, too, like to help people, not spend half my time justifying my work to an appointee who only holds a position of oversight because he's the second cousin of some politician or other who was probably ousted during the last election cycle."

Scoville stood and began deliberately perusing his collection as well. "So, upon resigning my post-collegiate debut into public service, I truly entered the realm and set about to see the expiry of the most vexatious assault on free men. I used my influence to help persuade our politicians to extinguish the wartime income tax. I then grew weary of political power brokers syphoning from the social productivity of free trade between mankind, so I set out to support the pioneers at the vanguard of our nation's untapped resources. I have been proudly overseeing land deed transfers and shipping contracts, among other things, for the citizens of Sagebrush ever since." He climbed a rolling ladder and ran his finger along a row of book spines then stopped. He tilted back the top of a book and snatched it from its place on the shelf. Taking his seat again, Nicholas Scoville placed it on the table.

Dr. Hoyle saw this as an invitation to relax again. As he sat, Scoville slid over the book, then reclined. "A gift, for an old friend."

Hoyle smiled as he beheld a volume on native herbal medicine. He thanked Scoville, and the two men continued exercising their bellows for the next couple of hours.

About the time Scoville gifted Hoyle the book, an increasingly aggravated crowd began to form in the lobby of the Sagebrush Grand. It was nigh on midnight and half the hotel had heard screaming off and on for hours. It seemed the only person who remained oblivious to the extent of Pearl's plight was the man responsible for her employ, and thus her maternal maelstrom, Martin Kelly. Martin had, at some point in the night, moved from the spotlight of the Parlor stage across the street, just up the way, to the Emporium. Dirty and covered in dry vomit, he passed out on the front bench still wrapped in the curtain he had ripped from the rafters.

The woman's veins were protruding from her neck and sweat was pouring from her pores when Lorraine's head popped up over Pearl's pregnant belly. "You're doing great, Pearl. You still with me?" she said. A grunt was the only reply.

"Oh, she's still with you," Rebecca said, gritting her teeth through her own pain, which she thought was best to not complain about at this time. Pearl had a death grip on Mrs. Turk's hand and showed no intention of letting go until she found her own relief. Mrs. Turk used her free hand to wipe Pearl's brow. The contraction passed.

"Mrs. Turk, may I have your assistance over here?" Lorraine and Rebecca stepped aside to refresh the towels. "Look," Lorraine said quietly, "Dr. Hoyle must have been delayed, and I am afraid we are out of time. If we postpone this any longer, I worry that it will put Pearl and her baby in excessive distress. This is a risky delivery because of the babe's position, but we have no choice. We must move forward, or it will endanger them both."

Lorraine made a few requests of Rebecca Turk, then the two lifted Pearl, standing her upright. After positioning her, Rebecca assisted in holding Pearl by the arms while Lorraine coached the women through the next steps.

"Pearl, look at me. I will not lie to you; I am anxious because of the dangers involved here. We don't have a doctor and you will be bringing this footling into the world upright; you understand?" Pearl nodded, fearfully but cooperatively. Her blonde follow-me-lads that once bounced gayly off her shoulders and seduced many a lonely man were now plastered to her face that was flush not from rouge, but strain. The next contraction seized her like a woman possessed. The severity of her cry chilled a trembling Rebecca who held on with every ounce of her might.

"That's it Pearl, do not quit on me now! Rebecca, hold fast," Lorraine said. Pearl was fatigued and quickly losing her strength. Lorraine grabbed the infant's ankles and applied steady pressure but failed to pull it free. "Pearl, the umbilical cord is pinched; your baby needs you to push, Pearl, PUSH!"

Slowly a euphoria began to creep across Pearl. She felt her breathing get lighter and the muscles in her face relax. The room spun as her vision blurred. Lorraine's voice seemed distant. Pearl was sinking into herself and could not make out the movements in the room that were now just a collage of colored light. She was vaguely aware of a soft cushion then a sudden sharp pain. The muffled sounds of panicked conversation were the last thing she heard before everything started to go black. Her eyes closed and the darkness was directly accompanied by an occasion of terrified clarity. Then, like a splash of ice-cold water to the face, a rush of adrenaline snapped her back into reality. Suddenly, her senses sharpened. Everything came into focus. She stared openly at a startled Rebecca Turk while desperately gasping for a long deep breath. Pearl mustered the very last of her energy reserves and gave one final push.

The sweet lullaby of an infant's cry attended her gradual descent into unconsciousness.

"Rebecca!" Lorraine exclaimed, "Pearl is losing a lot of blood! Can you try to stop it while I examine the child?"

"Right away." Rebecca made for the foot of the bed. The boy was starting to regain his color when Lorraine tied the umbilical cord.

"Hello precious one, welcome to the world. That's it, now just breathe." She moved toward the chest of drawers as she patted the infant down vigorously with a towel. A quick inspection of his eyes and mouth was followed by a good cleaning of his nose and ears. She counted ten fingers and ten toes then swaddled the boy and held him close to raise his body temperature. His wailing stopped and he settled into a slumber in Lorraine's arms.

"Looks like we've got mama under control over here," Rebecca Turk said at last. "I figure we'd ought to let her rest a while."

Lorraine nodded in approval, "Why don't you get some rest, too, dear. Take the sofa while I rock our new friend here." The three women enjoyed a well-earned repose.

The moon hung high as a hungover Martin awoke an hour or so after midnight on the bench in front of the Emporium. He sat for a time, content to do nothing but sulk. He felt ashamed but was too prideful to know it, and instead coped with his failure by projecting responsibility onto Pearl. He was embittered toward her. They had a good thing going, *how could she ruin it? How could she be so foolish, of all the girls?* Martin asked every question as though he bore no responsibility for the circumstances.

He was wide awake plotting what to do with himself now that he'd spent the past eight hours in a drunken slumber when he noticed a man departing the lawyer's place across the street. Dr. Andrew Hoyle, luggage in tow, was finally blundering toward the hotel.

The concerning banter in the bafflingly busy lobby caused Dr. Hoyle to inquire at the front desk if there was a Ms. Lorraine Baxter in house. Suddenly feverish with grave worry and embarrassment, he plodded upstairs with his medical kit to room 213 and knocked quietly. To his relief, Lorraine was pleased to see him and was proud to show off the healthy baby boy. With a fair amount of critical commentary and instruction from the seamstress, Dr. Hoyle addressed the needs of the post-partum paramour then left the child in her care as he and Lorraine made their way downstairs. There they noticed an injured man fumbling with a large hoop of skeleton keys.

"Please sir, allow me." Lorraine said to the man in the sling. She helped him open the double doors then inspected his patched-up nose with a smile that drooped to a frown. "Well, that won't do, will it?" Lorraine ushered the bandaged bartender into the Parlor and sat him down at a table. She requested Dr. Hoyle's medical kit and, after properly immobilizing Lawrence's sprained wrist, cleaned and dressed his wounded nose.

"There, that's better. Hey, I know you, don't I? Yes, I've seen you in here before."

"Ma'am?" Lawrence asked, not recognizing the unfamiliar face.

"I saw what those awful men did to you some days ago. What business do they have intimidating a gentleman such as yourself? Shame on them, causing you to spill their drinks then threatening you for it!"

Lawrence Hoak laughed, "Oh that? You were there? Why, ma'am, that was an accident! I dare say that Will Richardson does indeed have a temper to avoid, but he didn't go threatenin' me. And besides, that other man you saw, well that," he smiled, "that was Mr. Josiah Rush." Lorraine rolled his name across her tongue just to try it out. Lawrence continued, "Him and Will been knowin' each other since way back. And he's a good'n that weren't about to let no harm come to me on his account. He made sure to tell me it was all in fun that he got ole Will to let on he was upset. Did you know Josiah helped clean up?"

"Well, no, I-I . . ."

"Shucks, a little mischief on account of one 'nother's how folks 'round here keep from goin' plumb crazy. T'weren't nothin' to it," Lawrence said.

"Forgive me, it appears there's still so much I have to learn about this place." Lorraine thought about the awful look she had later given Josiah from the window of the Emporium and retreated into humiliation with these revelations because of another truth she had been avoiding. She quite admired Josiah for the restraint he showed, even in front of his peers and authority, before riding into conflict. He was not a man who seemed subject to the will of the mob or the badge, but carefully considered his own role in such events. He was hesitant for his own sake while others seemed eager for glory.

"Thank you for your kindness ma'am," Lawrence said regarding his wounds. "This one's on the house." He sauntered behind the bar to pour the kindly strangers a couple drinks.

Dr. Hoyle took a moment to appreciate the nurse. "I hate to see you so downcast, Lorraine. It's been a long night, you'll likely feel better tomorrow," he said as he patted her hand.

"Perhaps you're right, Andrew, it's just that people are so different here. My heart is at once inspired, but also deeply disturbed. Take Mr. . . . oh, forgive me, I don't believe I caught your name," she said as Lawrence returned to the table.

"Lawrence, ma'am. Lawrence Hoak."

"Pleased to meet you Mr. Hoak, I'm Lorraine." Turning her attention again to Dr. Hoyle she continued, "Take Mr. Hoak, here. Earlier this honorable gentleman suffered these injuries while in the service of a man who had completely lost his rudder." She turned to Lawrence and apologetically commented, "Dear, I was unaware at the time of the severity of your fall."

Lawrence gave a dismissive gesture then watched Dr. Hoyle finish his drink.

She continued, "but then just the other day, you would not *believe* how impertinent this old spinster became at the slightest inconvenience after a courier kicked up a bit of dust delivering what was clearly urgent correspondence." Her passionate indignation betrayed the stress she'd been veiling. Lorraine slammed back her drink then slammed the glass on the table. The noise was louder than anticipated, and it served as a reminder to regain her composure. Dr. Hoyle held his empty glass up to Lawrence inquiring about the propriety of another, but the bartender was already moving for the bottle.

"There, there, Miss Lorraine," Lawrence comforted her while this time pouring a double. "I know how tough it can be acclimatin' to new places. Don't you worry, though, I'm privy to all sorts of happenings and goings on 'round here. You just leave it to me, from now on, to help you feel welcome. Make yourself a regular in this place and I'll see to it that you meet any and everybody in this town the proper way."

It may have been the alcohol, but she hastily inquired, "Even that Josiah Rush?"

Lawrence chuckled, "Of course, if you wish." Lorraine took a drink, smiled, then laid her head dreamily on the table.

Dr. Hoyle swallowed hard, and the charm drained from his face upon interpreting her enthusiasm. Having lost the will to entertain, he stood up, meaning to retire to his hotel room.

"Well, Mr. Hoak, thank you for your hospitality. It is late and I'll now bid you a goodnight." He withdrew a pocketbook and handed Lawrence a slip of paper. "For round two. I insist." Lawrence studied the deposit receipt; a denominated bank note from Best's Bank and Trust. He stared curiously at Dr. Hoyle who said, "I do hope half an ounce will cover it."

"That is not needed, sir, but what am I to do with this?"

Dr. Hoyle gave a wry smile, "Do you mean to tell me that I, a newcomer, am privy to some 'happenings and goings on' in Sagebrush that you are not?"

Lawrence found it difficult to dismiss the insult that brought the doctor so much pleasure. "I suppose so," he replied. Lawrence stiffened his back, straightening up.

"I arrived this afternoon on a train with George Best, himself, with whom I have an account at Best's Bank and Trust back in the city. He shared with me that there would be a branch opening here in Sagebrush!"

"Oh?" Lawrence was puzzled.

"Well, with a branch in town I heard it from Mr. Best, himself, that such a proof of deposit would be redeemable as payment at any of his establishments without the hassle of first making a withdrawal."

Lawrence looked skeptically at the doctor. With one hand he folded the paper, though, and stuck it in his vest pocket.

"Very well, goodnight, sir," he said.

6

Josiah coughed, a result of the dust cloud he stirred up while hitting the ground on account of what he thought was a gunshot. Time seemed to slow. He scurried on his belly to the far side of the well in the center of Buffalo Junction. He sat up, with his back against the mortar, putting stone between him and a bullet. Scanning the windows of the buildings in front of him for movement, he drew his pistol. He made a point to simultaneously pat himself down with his free hand to feel for a bullet wound that, fortunately, was not there. His heart thumped heavy in his chest, testing the limits of his body's ability to contain it. Breathing was difficult in the dusty haze that still hung over him. Fighting to keep the sting from his watering eyes, he blinked out tears that trailed down his dirty face. Life came in flashes of disorienting still frames. Josiah took off his hat and tossed it away as a diversion. Immediately, he peered over the well and pointed his pistol toward the saloon, attempting to ascertain the position of the shooter as well as the status of his friends.

Upon cresting the stones, Josiah quickly realized that he was muzzling his own men. He raised his barrel and de-cocked the hammer. They all stood casually at their horses staring down at Josiah with a mix of pity, concern, and in the case of Deputy Butch Eaton, amusement. Levi Holdegel slowly walked over and joined Josiah on the ground at the well. Josiah slouched back down, dropped his head, and let out a long sigh.

Levi stared straight ahead, "Some ole pod tore out upon seein' the marshal. Clumsy lout kicked over a pine slat that crashed onto the boardwalk is all." Levi then turned his head to find Josiah looking at him. He gave a ruthful smile while Josiah offered a series of small nods. "C'mon now, don't be discomfited. Ain't a man here that wasn't surprised by it," Levi said. Josiah continued to nod away. "C'mon, pull yourself together inside over a drink."

Josiah walked to the saloon with Levi at his back. Cooper Emmons retrieved Josiah's hat, then he and Charles Crandall followed as Henry Olt secured the horses. Deputy Butch Eaton had an audience in Will Richardson and Jacoby Sutton, so he took the opportunity to comment on the situation to Marshal Felix Oglesby.

"That man is a liability," Butch proffered regarding Josiah.

"Had that been gunfire, that man would have saved your hide here today." The marshal gave a chirk and trotted off on his horse to join Olt at the hitching post. Will Richardson looked undiscernibly over to Butch, the corner of his mustache twitching ever so slightly, then joined the marshal with Jacoby in tow.

Josiah pushed through the unlevel batwing doors of the saloon. They creaked loudly, announcing his presence to the small handful of patrons in the long narrow bar. He paused to let his eyes adjust to the dim room. Josiah was a dark shadow backlit by the desert dusk. Though the wooden shutters on the windows were drawn closed, the sun still found its way through the cracks and a ray of light beamed through a bullet hole in the wall. The room was illuminated otherwise by a few candelabras placed sporadically along the bar emitting a demure glow. There was an old man behind the bar polishing a pint glass and whistling a haunting melody. He wore a faded sarape and had a face like leather. He seemed to be the only one who failed to notice the new guests as Levi, Crandall, and Cooper fanned out beside Josiah. The clunk of bootheels echoing off the rotting floor added percussively to his song as the four men approached the preoccupied barman.

"Pardon, mon frère," Cooper chaffed in a bastardized accent. His was the only laughter that followed. He looked around for a reaction but was met with none except from Crandall who seemed incredulous. Cooper widened his eyes briefly at the lack of humor from his associates.

The old man stopped whistling and set down his glass. In perfect French he replied, "Je parle Anglaise, monsieur."

That got quite the rise out of all the rest of the men as well as a few others at a table in the back. Cooper was perplexed. "What?" he asked. "What's so funny? What'd he say?"

At that, even Josiah cracked a smile. The tension in the room melted and with it, the tension in his chest. The bartender lined up a round as the marshal strolled in with Will and Jacoby at his wings.

"I see we're makin' friends. That's good," Oglesby said.

Will found his way to the bar and helped himself to one of the four shots. Crandall, being the man who missed out, leered at him and shook his head.

He gestured toward Cooper, then back at Will and asked him, "What am I gonna do with you two?"

Will replied with a loud, open-mouthed belch. The friendly bartender then took an empty glass and placed it purposefully into Crandall's hand and poured him a double. Crandall thanked him with a surprised smile, but also wondered if he would be expected to pay for the extra liquor.

"What's your name, son?" The marshal asked the bartender.

"What's your drink, sir?" he replied.

Oglesby smiled, impressed. "Okay. No names, then. We're searchin' for this man." The marshal produced the wanted poster with a likeness of the fugitive. "Here is his warrant and here is . . ."

"I know of him," the bartender interrupted. Marshal Oglesby straightened abruptly and turned his head to see if anyone else had heard this promising news. Josiah had.

"Well, that was easy," he said as if the outlaw had already been arrested. "Where can I find him?" he asked, spreading his hands.

"You will never find him if he does not want to be found."

No sooner had the marshal rolled his eyes, than in walked Deputy Butch Eaton dragging a man by his collar. Kicking and screaming in fancy new boots, the subdued suspect in custody was the outlaw Waddell.

"Welp," Cooper said, "I'm glad we *all* rode the whole way out here for that."

Will's mustache twitched and Jacoby adjusted his bolo. Josiah thought Crandall looked a bit disappointed, but he and Levi both shared a sigh of relief.

"You lyin' dog!" the outlaw screamed at the bartender. "You said you's gonna help me lay low and you done give me up!"

When the marshal heard that, he wondered aloud, "Well, Josiah, you think we've got room for two criminals on the ride back?" He asked this while focused on the bartender not Josiah.

"Ugh," the bartender acted hurt but did not look up from the glass he had resumed polishing. "You would arrest me on the word of a wanted man when I have so many witnesses to my good character?" He whistled and the locals at a nearby table stood up. From a room adjacent to the bar, a woman also emerged holding a scatter gun.

The marshal inclined his head toward the fearless fellow still polishing a glass. The bartender pretended not to see Oglesby point at him then tap his temple a couple times as if to say, "I'll remember this."

The marshal spun around and addressed the posse, "Gentlemen, we've got our man. Let's go home."

A couple hours out of town, they stopped to make camp for the night. They settled just outside the adit of an old, boarded-up mine because the natural berms provided some shelter from the windswept sandy soil. Waddell had sniveled and sobbed the whole way as he rode backwards, hands tied, and strapped to the saddle of a jack. The marshal had grown irritated with the man's incessant expressions of remorse so, upon reaching camp, he bound Waddell to a boulder separated from the other men, but still within sight.

The gang feasted that night. With Waddell already in hand, they had saved a good bit of time by forgoing lengthy interrogations and search parties throughout Buffalo Junction. As a result, they celebrated their success by indulging gluttonously in their rations.

When they had finished supper, they once again implored Deputy Eaton to tell the tale of how he came to best the butchering bandit. With animated volleys of dramatic movement, Butch agreed to indulge them and relived the harrowing ordeal in exaggerated detail.

"Well, Marshal Oglesby had just gone inside to make sure Josiah hadn't done nothin' stupid . . ." This line was beginning to annoy Josiah, not due to the personal slight, but more so the ridiculous way in which Butch used two fingers to imitate the marshal's walk. ". . . and I rode over to Mr. Olt who was investigatin' around back of the Tavern. We seent a pathway to a buildin' where we supposed the slippery sombrero musta run off to. So, we followed it real stealth-like." Butch was hunched over high stepping on tip toes around the circle of men.

"Well, when we came upon the buildin', we seent a differ'nt man what had his back turnt to us, so we asked if he know'd where our friend went. By golly, when he turnt around it was none other than our wanted outlaw hisself, just all smiles and helpful; said the man took off over yonder. I thanked him, asked his name, and when he went to shake my hand, I made my move." Butch grabbed at the air and pretended to put a man in a headlock and wrestle him to the ground. "Bastard's lucky he didn't put up much more of a fight. That's when I dragged him by his mane back to the bar where your lazy hind ends was merry-makin'."

Butch basked in their exaltations. He failed to realize they were not sharing his glory but laughing at his antics.

Josiah got up with a few bites left in his tray of beans and walked over to the dejected man behind the boulder. Gazing upon the creased face and the sunken eyes of the criminal, Josiah offered him a bite. The famished man initially accepted, but then in a fit of rebellion hardened himself against the kindness and spit the beans back out at Josiah's feet.

"C'mon don't do that." Josiah offered another bite, but the man grabbed the spoon with his teeth and ripped it from Josiah's hand. This time when the beans went flying Josiah stood and kicked angrily at the ground sending dust, dirt, and rock into Waddell's face. As he walked away, determined to let the prisoner go hungry, the sounds of whimpering compelled him to stop. He threw his head back having an attack of conscience and returned with his canteen.

Waddell was mumbling incoherently when Josiah crouched back down and barked, "Look at me!"

"I didn't mean to do it, I didn't mean to," Waddell cried. "That cheat, Reuben Ward, was holdin' my share of the profit hostage." Josiah listened as Waddell was now lucid. "We was to go our separate ways after the stockyards. I was headed further north for the line, but he insisted the agreement bound me further, to see him and his wagon all the way back home to his ranch. All I was doin' was takin' my share when he attacked me."

Josiah opened his canteen and washed the man's face. "I'm not your judge, Waddell. You'll have your day in court."

"Please sir, please. I abandoned my plans and done right by Mrs. Ward."

Josiah raised his eyebrows, "Careful, now. Don't you dare—"

"Wait, wait, wait, after defendin' myself Reuben lay dyin', you see. I feared for what would happen to the money for Mrs. Ward and the boy, so I took it all, and rode back at my own risk to make sure it would get to 'em."

"So, why'd you kill 'em?"

"Hex you for sayin' so! I was in love with Catherine Ward. I would never have hurt her or that precious child. I left 'em with that money like I intended, then hit the trail until I seen my face plastered across every town I come to. I don't know what happened with no fire, but a drifter like me has got no real chance against such accusations."

"Nah sir, you'll see a jury and you can tell them all about it." Josiah said, almost comfortingly. He heard a noise and peeked over his shoulder to find Levi standing there.

"I didn't want to interrupt; I just came to check on you is all," he said.

"We're just finishin' up here, anyway. Goodnight, Waddell." Josiah turned to leave with Levi.

"Wait, please, they'll kill me, I'm innocent! Please, just let me go-ho-ho," Waddell broke down into sobs.

Levi and Josiah moseyed slowly back to camp. "I think he might be tellin' the truth, Josiah."

"Might be, but I doubt it. You heard him; a desperate man will do anything for his freedom."

"C'mon, Josiah, what if he's right."

"Listen, I know it's better for a thousand guilty men to dodge punishment than for a single innocent man to suffer it. I've considered whether he's tellin' the truth, but my opinion on the matter don't count for anything. It's a jury he'll have to convince, not me."

"But are you convinced?"

"Nope. But I'm concerned that you are. See, the fatal flaw in Waddell's ploy was the glimmer of truth in his story. He claims he loved Mrs. Ward, and I think he did. With Reuben out of the picture it don't make no sense that he'd leave her with the money then try to proceed on with his other plans unless his affections were unrequited. In which case Waddell, whom we know ain't the shinin' example of emotional fortitude, killed her in a passionate rage for her rejection and because she could place him with Reuben. Waddell then killed the Ward boy, the only other witness to his crimes, and torched the house to make it look like an accident."

"Hmm . . ." Levi wondered. "You sure got a knack for thinkin' like a criminal."

"Tracked plenty of 'em. You seen them boots the hangman's gonna end up with? You think Waddell spent money on them from an honest share of that profit? Nah sir, he's got that gold he claims he left with Mrs. Ward stashed away somewhere, and he was tryin' to get back to it, get back on the run. I mean to find out where it is tomorrow and see it returned to the rancher, Reuben Ward."

The two men walked back to camp where Charles Crandall was poking at the fire. He smiled when he saw Josiah and patted a rock beside him. Josiah said goodnight to a bedroll-bound Levi, then took a seat next to Crandall. He admired the way his friend had thoughtfully constructed the crosshatch fuel logs in the fire pit. Josiah noted a channel underneath the ill-fated structure. It was dug to harness the breeze and give life to the flames from below. The light from those flames flickered off the splintered beams of the abandoned mine before them.

"A place like this has been good to you, Josiah. Does it bring back memories?" Crandall asked as he motioned toward the entrance to the pit.

"Well, yes and no. Reverend's Gorge wasn't quite like this," Josiah recalled.

"Oh?"

"Nah, this place seems sad and to be honest, a little scary. I've known men who spent a number of years in holes like this and if they surfaced with any minerals, it certainly wasn't worth the price of their health. Further northwest where I spent my time was different."

"How so? Come on, Josiah, tell me about it." Crandall leaned in.

"Well, you could follow the coldest rivers for miles. The water was so clear, the current so strong, an' it was just pregnant with all the trout you could hope for. Up, up, up, you'd go into the snow-capped mountains that seemed like they could never end. Then after weavin' through the dense evergreens, you'd crest a tree line and peer out over the largest, most lush green valleys you could ever imagine. I mean chock-full of grazin' bison as far as you could see, herds the size of armies, elk there, too."

"Sounds beautiful." Crandall said. The fire crackled.

"It was. You know, after the war, a cavalryman could make a good livin' workin' for various power brokers, so I spent a few years servin' at the pleasure of politicians. I encountered some real bad folks. Got to do some good, I suppose. After a while, though, I just needed a break but couldn't ever get it. I don't mean that people bothered me, but everywhere I turned some new bureau or other beckoned and just assumed I'd do their biddin' and track down their bad guys. Come to find out, you can start to lose sense of who they really are."

Josiah trailed off before abruptly stating, "So I quit. Until now, that is. I tried for so long to see if I could be left alone, no reputation, no endless struggles for power, no one stakin' a claim on the fruits of my labor. I quit and I headed west. I never intended to end up *mining*, of all the damndest things a body could do, but I traded my guns for a pick-axe and my name for a gold pan."

"But it was a success, I'd say. How was the work?"

Josiah shrugged, "I'd sift the beds of a deluge for days and days. Survivin' on trout, hardtack, and spring fed river water. I'd pocket every fleck and flake just to dig my hands in the earth and pull somethin' of value out instead of puttin' another body in."

Josiah searched the coal bed intently. "Then one day I just happened to stumble across somethin' that looked kinda like that," he pointed to a small glowing ember and his tone turned less severe and more optimistic. "I traced a line from the river up the side of the valley and just started diggin'. I'd dig all day, then sleep a while, and dig some more. I'd stop only to fish or hunt and eat. I could have dug a day or a year, I didn't know and didn't care it was just what I had to do. Every time I sunk my shovel into the dirt or my axe into rock, I was diggin' into myself. I'd drip sweat or freeze and I'd still dig. I wasn't beset by any troubles other than those I brought with me. I didn't realize it then, but I was tryin' to bargain with the ground to trade those troubles for its gold."

"It seems you struck quite the deal." Crandall said, thinking about the ranch that Josiah purchased with the success of his mining operations.

"Or maybe I had plenty of troubles to trade. One day as I hiked back up from the river, I passed all the destruction I'd left in my wake. Mounds of disheveled dirt and gapin' holes disturbed by my grief. I didn't feel ashamed, but I felt . . . recuperated. So, I weighed my gold and got a mind to fill my holes. I don't know how long it took, but with the same strength I used to attack the ground I then sought to restore it. When I'd finished, I just walked away." Josiah extended his hand from one side of the horizon to the other and held it there for a couple seconds then he added disinterestedly, "No tellin' how much of that yellow free-gold was left on the bench of that mountain."

"Well, I suppose I'll have to wrangle you into takin' me up there one of these days," Crandall said. After a few moments of silence, the fire popped, drawing attention to the lull in conversation and prompting him to add, "but not right now, because right now I'm off to the ole flea-bag." With that, he headed to bed. Josiah soon followed suit.

7

When darkness overtook the desert and the temperature dropped, the sinister forces that thrive in environments of death began to awaken. The moonlight offered a reprieve from the effect of the sun's oppressive rays on the painful, radiating sand. It was now cool on the belly of the cold-blooded devil cursed all its days to eat the dust of the earth. From the depths of the cavernous ruins left by the sons of Adam, the rattlesnake slithered calmly about, quietly weaving through the sleeping men who were oblivious to the immediate presence of mortal danger.

The rattler searched the heat of a soft warm nest abandoned by one of the men who had opted instead for the cold compact dirt. It moved on in its search for food to another man who emitted a scent of decay. It investigated a shiny object on the rising and falling chest of yet another. The rattler was not the only thing nightfall in the desert had awakened, however, and the snake at last picked up on the movement of prey. A lizard scurried up the berm and away from camp; the serpent followed. The peacefully snoozing men continued on in ceaseless dreams, ignorant of their peril.

The snake continued to stalk until the lizard disappeared under a boulder. It hunted the perimeter unsuccessfully until it rounded the side where Waddell was asleep, lashed to the massive rock. Still on the hunt, it climbed over Waddell's shins. When Waddell was brought to semi-consciousness by the movement at his legs, he reflexively kicked his boots, sending the snake soaring through the air. It coiled up and hissed when it hit the ground. Waddell's dream of dancing with a señorita to the rhythm of her maracas was interrupted by the nightmare of dancing with a viper to the rhythm of his rattles.

The blood curdling screams jolted Josiah from a dead sleep. He and Levi were up, guns drawn, before anyone. Back-to-back in their long johns the men circled in the dark scanning for any moving shadows as their eyes adjusted to the starlight. Josiah had both hands on his revolver while Levi rested his rifle in the crook of his nub. By the time the other men had roused, the two of them were already halfway to Waddell with Cooper Emmons on their heels.

"It BIT me! Ahh! That son of a bitch got me! Why-hy-hy-hy?!" Waddell cried.

"What bit you? Where'd it go?" the men asked as they frantically searched the ground.

"Ahh! Dear God! I'm sorry, I'm sorry, I'm so sorry. Ahh!"

"Waddell!" Josiah snapped. "*What* was it that gotchya?"

Then they heard it. The sizzle sent chills up Josiah's spine as he lifted his pistol toward the sound of the rattles. The rest of the posse stopped in their tracks and watched him. The shimmer of moonlight off his greasy hair made Josiah look just like the silver outline of an apparition. The trigger pull was textbook: even, steady pressure all the way through the break of the sear. The puff of gun smoke exhausting from the muzzle appeared to the men as though the ghostly figure had cast a spell that hung crystalline in the shiftless desert air. At the sound of the explosion, Waddell's cries stopped, as did the sound of rattling. In an instant, everything was still.

The silence was broken by Cooper Emmons whose shouts of disbelief were the man's way of blowing off steam. As Cooper danced through a cycle of pacing and cussing then crouching with his hands on his knees and pacing again, Will Richardson closed the gap. He walked over to the contorted and bloody lump of scales.

"Lucky shot," the big man said to Josiah as he investigated the gore. "Looks like you missed his head but caught half his neck just below it." He stepped carefully with his boot on the dead viper, drew his knife and finished what the bullet had started. He then removed the rattles from the snake's tail, intending them for Josiah as a token of their brush with death.

"Waddell wasn't so lucky." Josiah had turned to address the wincing man. Once he unfastened Waddell, and laid him down, Josiah fashioned a tourniquet from the rope used to restrain the captive. He applied it over the leg just above the bite. After the initial cinch, the pain left Waddell's face as shock set in. His eyes became distant and glassy.

"Will, hand me that knife," Josiah said. At this request, Charles Crandall turned and headed for camp.

"Forget that sorry bastard, serves him right," Will said.

Josiah whirled around and addressed all the men, but spoke to Will directly, "I know you're feelin' it, an' I am too; this saddle bum probably got what he deserved. But he's still a man. Besides, he ain't been to trial and I mean to see him answer for what he done. Now hand over that knife! Please."

Will accommodated the request but added, "Seems to me he's already answered for what he done."

Josiah wiped the snake's blood from the blade on Waddell's shirt. He cut the outside of the man's pants revealing twin red wounds, crusted and clotting. "Oh no, no, no," he said, "looks like it weren't no dry bite. What'd you do to piss that thing off so bad?" He took Will's knife and punctured the skin between the fang marks. He crossed the initial cut and made a second, deep incision in the swollen leg.

"Any volunteers?" Josiah surveyed the men shaking their heads. "Nah, can't bring myself to it neither." He, instead, grabbed Waddell's leg encircling the cuts and squeezed. Blood gushed from the mangled flesh. It poured out all over Josiah's hands, onto tattered pants, then swirled and mixed with dirt as it pooled on the ground. Waddell screamed as he sat up and reached for Josiah. Henry Olt was there to grab his shoulders and pin him back to the ground. Josiah squeezed again trying to bleed as much of the poison out as he could.

When it seemed like Waddell was about to faint from blood loss, the men carried him over to the campsite. Josiah grabbed his own knife and made for the fire, but Charles Crandall was already pulling a red-hot blade from the coals. Waddell's cries drowned out the sound of searing flesh and echoed across the desert as the men cauterized his bloody leg and removed the tourniquet. He passed out from the pain before the work was through.

There was an uncertainty in the camp in the immediate aftermath of the excitement. Deputy Eaton disrupted his sleeping arrangements in a paranoid quest to rid it of any and all other critters. The marshal lolled against a berm while everyone else just sort of poked around. It was clear that the men had already partaken in the best sleep they would find that night.

After washing up, Crandall and Josiah approached the marshal, curious of his intentions given the change in circumstances.

"What change? Did I say anything about a change in plans? Get some rest, tomorrow we ride out."

"Waddell can't ride, he's got to keep that bite elevated and he's already startin' to burn up with fever. A full day in the saddle under the blazin' sun ain't a good idea for him," Josiah said.

"Then he shouldn't have got himself bit like a damn fool." Marshal Oglesby looked carelessly at Josiah.

"What do you propose, then?"

"I propose we all get some sleep and talk about this in the mornin'." With that, the marshal tipped his hat low over his eyes and crossed his arms. Crandall nudged Josiah to step aside.

"Well, suppose it falls to us to figure out how to get him back to Sagebrush," Crandall said of the injured man.

Josiah thought for a moment, "No wagon, nothin' out here for a stretcher, the man sure ain't ridin' or walkin' . . ." Josiah shrugged as he let the words hang.

"Alright, I'll think on it. You best get some sleep, too, if you can," Crandall said.

The rest of the night the men all lay half awake. When they did sleep, it was less of a restful slumber and more of a delusional inability to consciously grasp time elapsing. There was constant shuffling as one or another struggled to get settled against the unforgiving ground. The temperature continued to drop. Besides suffering chilled bones, they also suffered from the sounds of phantom noises that alerted them to other perceived dangers the desert night might have had in store.

As the hours dragged slowly on, sleep continued to be elusive, but tempers were not. Will Richardson kicked at Deputy Butch Eaton who at one point had begun to snore. Butch in turn was ready to box the big man for waking him up. The two hotheads got a stern reprimanding from Marshal Oglesby for serving only to agitate Waddell.

Waddell was delirious and dripping sweat. His leg had swollen in the night to three times its usual size with discolored blisters occurring in gruesome pockets that ran from his hip to his knee. The man's groaning and shivering accompanied a congested Levi Holdegel who sniffled incessantly at the onset of a cold. Even the otherwise amiable Cooper Emmons tore off his covers and went for a walk to keep from losing his cool.

Cooper checked the condition of the horses, inspecting their shoes and searching for the onset of any girth sores. While at it, his foot had the misfortune of finding a fresh pile from Josiah's dysenteric mare. He slipped and fell, envious in that moment of the rough shod horse. While on his butt, Cooper noticed a little swelling around her worsening fetlock and thought he might mention it to Josiah in the morning. He left his soiled socks and sauntered back, unaware that he still carried traces of stool on his skivvies. As if the nerves and the noise weren't bad enough, now the men had to contend with a camp rich with the complex odiferous offerings of horse droppings in addition to the already acrid bonfire smoke and pungent body odor. Even after all else seemed to finally settle, Waddell continued in agony. His pleas for relief went unanswered and the suffering persisted through the rest of the night.

By the time dawn was pondering a presentation on the celestial promenade, the men were already stirring and packing up their personal belongings for the long day's ride. They would camp one more night before an early arrival back in town. Charles Crandall mercifully grabbed a canteen and made for the hallucinating man mumbling madness in a barely audible whisper. Waddell lay turned toward the opening of the mine and couldn't even take a drink; water poured over his lips and onto the ground.

"He's not gonna make it through the mornin'," Marshal Oglesby said.

"Perhaps not. I need to speak with Josiah." Crandall pointed to Waddell. "I plan to stay with him until he either passes or recovers enough to make the ride in another day or two."

"That's my fugitive," the marshal contested.

"Then you'll stay with us?" It was evident Charles Crandall was not giving Marshal Oglesby the option to take Waddell any further for the time being. For a moment, Crandall boldly received the glare he had evoked from the man, then nodded and sought out Josiah.

Deputy Butch Eaton wanted to satisfy a morbid curiosity and joined the marshal overlooking the grotesque display. After taking no more than a fractional glance he shied away and covered his mouth with a bandana and heaved. Staring horrified at Oglesby, he then took a step back, but the marshal grabbed his arm and pulled him close.

"You swear to me now, if it ever comes to be that I suffer as this man does, you'll afford me this same kindness," he said.

As Butch was still processing the request, Marshal Oglesby made for his peacemaker. Aligning the barrel with the back of Waddell's head he cocked the hammer.

"NO!" Josiah heard himself scream as he happened to see the marshal move for his gun. It was the kind of scream with which a man scares himself. The kind of scream that comes from an intimate familiarity with the trauma of death. The kind of scream that starts in the bowels and sends forth a spiritual power as the sound is thrust from one's throat out onto the world. The kind of scream that comes from a man exhausted by the exposure to—and experience of—killing, regardless of the arguments about the right or wrong of it. Josiah's scream was interrupted before the power it wielded could affect its intended audience.

The hammer dropped on the marshal's gun and ignited the primer of a chambered cartridge. Sulphur, carbon, and saltpeter erupted in the brass casing and let loose a .45 caliber projectile. It expanded under the heat of the explosion to fit the diameter of the heavy steel barrel as it scraped along the inside of the bore. The bullet found the light at the end of its tunnel, stabilized, and sailed through the air before colliding with its target. The lead shot penetrated the skull of the man who stared into a tunnel offering no such illuminative hope, and deposited itself into the ground with the other worthless, abandoned base minerals. The dead man laid there twitching in front of the dead mine. Marshal Felix Oglesby knew not what it was like to reach into the earth and pull something of value out, only what it was like to put a body in.

8

Lawrence Hoak set about sweeping the floors of Peregrine's Parlor. He dutifully moved all the tables and chairs and when he had finished, he returned the dirt to Main Street. Despite being encumbered by the loss of strength in his sprained wrist, Lawrence filled the oil in the sconces and trimmed the wicks. He put out new candles after wiping down every table. He polished the glasses and hung fresh towels for the patrons. He then inventoried beer kegs and liquor cabinets. Lawrence Hoak even rinsed clean the spittoons.

When he had finally finished, Lawrence reclined at a table savoring a cup of fresh black coffee. There was a fifteen-minute window prior to opening the saloon, and he planned to enjoy a break. Soon the bar would host a mixed array of bow ties, hoops and bustles, as well as clodhoppers and khakis. For now, though, he treasured the quiet rest. That was, until Perry exploded down the stairs in a flurry of motion, trailing loose sheets of paper behind him. Unable to contain his stress, Perry projected it onto his faithful employee.

"Mr. Hoak, is my money not good enough to merit your utmost efforts? Please sir, I'm asking nicely, find something productive to do while I'm paying you."

"So long as you don't pay me in these, your money is good enough to merit my 'utmost efforts' . . ." Lawrence defensively placed the bank note from Best's Bank and Trust, courtesy of Dr. Andrew Hoyle, onto a pile of papers Perry had set delicately on the table. Perry snatched it from atop his stacked ledgers, which were balanced only with regard to their towering architecture. Lawrence continued, ". . . but I'll be finishin' my break now if you'll 'scuse me." He sipped his coffee making a point to break eye contact so as not to invite a reply from his boss. He walked off and Perry slumped down in a chair studying the slip of paper bearing George Best's watermark.

"Uh, Mr. Hoak," Perry said at last, turning in his chair toward the bartender, "where exactly did this come from?"

"New doctor in town used it for payment last night. Hoyle, I believe his name is. Said it was good at all Mr. Best's establishments."

"Mr. Best's estab— Why, wherever would he get that idea?" Perry said to himself. Perplexed, he pinched the bridge of his sharp nose. He concluded that George Best was not in town to discuss solely the business of the Parlor and hotel but was there for other ventures to which Perry was not a party. Suddenly, he felt very small. Holding up the bank note in one hand, he then regarded the papers stacked on the table. Daunted, but undeterred, he resolved to inject himself at the first available opportunity into the middle of the affairs, whatever they may be, of Mr. Best and the fledgling local bank. Perry was still brooding over the paper he clutched when the voice of Mr. Best resounded from above.

"Why Mr. Page, it seems as though you've become acquainted with the latest instruments of financial innovation, my friend." The banker had been hovering with a sadistic grin over the indentured manager.

"Instruments of innovation, you say?" Perry looked up. A lock of black hair, oily from excess pomade, fell from its perfectly positioned place atop his head onto his brow. "This was given to my employee by another man as payment. Now, it was assumed by the customer that this was an acceptable method of settling the debt in *my* place of business." Perry stood and pulled out a chair for Mr. Best. He motioned for Lawrence to bring drinks. "Now, the arrogance of the patron can be forgiven, for he was under the impression that this form of currency was accepted at all of 'Mr. Best's establishments.'" Perry feigned confusion, "Mr. Best's establishments? Why wouldn't you extend the honor of acknowledging my ownership of this place?"

"Okay, Perry, look, I had hoped to talk to you about this first. The eager doctor must have mistakenly put two and two together. I never claimed ownership of your business, just mentioned that I hold your mortgage . . ."

"So what, I take this, yes?" Perry held up the receipt, "I drop it in an envelope. Entrust it for a week to some child on a pony or drunk on the tracks. Wait for it to arrive in the hands of a teller at your bank in the city. Then wait another week to receive my half ounce of silver for the liquor I sold two weeks ago that I've already since replaced? And this you call innovation?"

Mr. Best smiled at the amateur display of protest. "Well, not quite."

"Not quite because I am *not* going to have to wait for two weeks to receive my payment, am I Mr. Best?" Perry accepted the drinks from Lawrence and dismissed him with a wave. "Nor do I have to entrust anyone other than yourself with my money; not some young hot-shot rider, or some old railroad engineer—just you." Mr. Best hardened at the implosion of his, yet again, erroneous mis-estimation of his colleague.

"Okay, busted, but just stop right there . . ." Mr. Best was growing impatient.

"Mr. Best, let us speak plain. You are in town to purchase the Bank of Sagebrush."

"That's the last time you'll interrupt me, or your balance is due." Mr. Best was not talking about the mortgage, but the threat was lost on Perry. "Just relax, I got a proposition for you, too. Yes, the Bank of Sagebrush is for sale. No, you won't have to wait two weeks to get your coin. People deposit their gold, they get a paper receipt in the form of a bank note, then you give them liquor and they give you the paper. Now their gold is your gold, and the gold is always safe in that vault." Mr. Best pointed lengthwise across the intersection to the bank.

"Paper is not gold, Mr. Best." Perry struck a match and lit a candle on the table.

"Listen, I've been doing this a long time, okay? Initially it was only my own businesses trading in these bank notes, but then my other borrowers found it convenient to redeem them for their interest payments. Eventually, by not putting their hands on the gold at all, it was easier for them to spend. Later, I noticed people starting to use the bank notes amongst themselves and at other places which began to accept them as well. Next thing I know, I'm denominating multiple bank notes for a single deposit. What am I supposed to do?"

"Well, congratulations, sir, you have created something divisible, widely valued, and easily carried," Perry held the bank note to the flame and let the edges burn, "but paper is fragile, cheap and plentiful. Gold is not." He blew out the fire before it destroyed any meaningful transcriptions on the bank note.

"No, it is not, but the fact is, in the city wherever paper bears my name, it is as good as gold. You understand me?" Mr. Best gave Perry a look that he had seen only one other time. It was a look of risk and reward, of danger and riches. "I have something cheap and plentiful, now I'm inviting you to help make it valuable." Perry leaned in, skeptical, but curious. Mr. Best continued, "I'm no fool, Perry. I know of my soiled name in these parts, and I know of your responsibility for it. You run around here letting people believe the gossip that blackmail got you this fine structure out of which you hustle hooch." Best took a gander at the place. "What kind of man takes pride in his reputation as an extortionist?" Mr. Best rebuked.

Perry thought for a minute then said, "You want—no, you need my help . . ."

"I want it."

"Mmmhmm. So, you *seek* my help to establish the trustworthiness of the Best brand here in Sagebrush so that when your bank opens, people will store their gold in your vault and use your bank notes as currency in trade here locally."

"That's right."

"But you're not buying the bank with real coin are you, Mr. Best?"

"I'm not buying the bank."

"I'm sorry?!" Perry was flabbergasted and left waiting for an explanation.

Mr. Best grinned as he polished off a dram of whiskey. He used a towel to politely dab the spittle off his well-groomed whiskers and finally said, "I'd like to loan you the money to buy the bank. You'll make double what this place brings in, but you'll also get the privilege to run it under the name Best's Bank and Trust—for a small fee of course. This will ensure that you'll begin to repair my reputation and serve to facilitate a smooth transition into the latest economic advancement for a more convenient, safe, and efficient economy in Sagebrush."

"You sound like you're running for office. Okay, let's pretend for an instant that I agree to such an absurdity. Again, I'm not buying that bank with real coin am I, Mr. Best?"

"Not exactly. The payment has been arranged in bank notes."

"Bank notes that are fragile, cheap, and plentiful. Bank notes that are denominated and valuable thus far only in the city. Bank notes that are carried and traded by merchants and customers alike. Bank notes, though, that are not backed by any actual gold deposits, are they, Mr. Best?"

The banker adjusted his bowtie and gave a threatening smile. "This is capitalism."

Perry sighed and gave a thoughtful glance to the corner of the room. "No sir, this is not capitalism. This is fraud," he said.

"Oh, but it wasn't fraud burning down that blacksmith's place that was tied to your old building after he refused to sell?!" Mr. Best's taunting elicited a reciprocal threatening smile from Perry.

"Allow me to clarify a few things. First, that fire ensured financing for the Depot's construction, so don't sit there and pretend that it happened without your knowledge and consent. Otherwise, I wouldn't be right here in this magnificent building and that blacksmith wouldn't have his fancy new workshop down the way."

"You have to admit, it is a bit further from the livery," Best said.

"Second, the difference is that, other than a few matchsticks that once passed as a sorry excuse for a building, Cooper Emmons lost none of his critical and original investment in that blaze. His smithing tools, every day, see hotter fires than what we set, and he even re-used the same brick for the chimney at his new location. We did him a favor, really. And because I lost my place, too, they'll never suspect I had anything to do with it. As long as we can continue to work together in harmony, no one will ever know you did either. I'll see to it."

"Now that *is* blackmail, but so long as you'll agree to keep my bank notes rolling through and run that bank, I suppose I can accept that risk." Mr. Best gambled that Perry was not the kind of person to jeopardize his own livelihood out of spite.

"I don't know." Perry scanned the ceiling, ruminating on his next negotiating tactic. "That whole Depot business, well, that was hardly disastrous even for one man, but if this scheme of yours were to fail, it would be disastrous for a whole lot of folks."

"Look, Perry, as I said, I've been observing things for a while now and for every one person that actually claims their gold, there are two who make a deposit. Think of this as an incredible opportunity for the expansion of capital! So long as there is a revolving stream of customers entertaining business with my denominations, and I have a growing balance sheet under my care, who's to say I shouldn't leverage that power to provide further support to prospective industrial pioneers and proven entrepreneurs such as yourself? I practically feel I owe it to the people of Sagebrush to help them stimulate growth with such commodious financial resources. Perry, together, you and I can usher in a new era of unprecedented prosperity in these parts."

Perry found himself deep in thought. He was interrupted by the saloon doors slamming against the interior walls. The two men looked over to see a flop of red hair struggling to pull in an even redder curtain that was stuck on the stairs of the boardwalk. Lawrence appeared from the stairwell at the sound and offered his assistance to Martin Kelly, who was returning the stolen velveteen comforter.

"I laundered it for ye, Lawrence," Martin said. He showed off the work he had done to remove the biliary stains.

"Oh, well, thank you," Lawrence said. He then watched Martin Kelly drag the curtain across the floor of the Parlor leaving behind a thick trail of dirt brought in from the street. Martin ascended a ladder as the three other men observed. Perry crossed his arms and bit a knuckle.

After some coaching from the ground, Martin successfully re-attached the curtain and climbed down. While beaming proudly at Perry and Mr. Best, he carelessly leaned the folded ladder against a sconce. The oil font shattered, sending shards of glass scattering across the floor. Oil slowly dripped down the wall from the lamp, staining the paisley print.

With that, Best turned from the charade and addressed Perry.

"Peregrine," he said, "you have until tomorrow to let me know." He stole another sideways glance, looking down his nose at Martin Kelly and added, ". . . if I don't change my mind first."

Perry nodded, finished his drink, and set the smudged glass on the table. He grabbed his papers and proceeded upstairs.

Martin had begun to pick up pieces of the broken glass but was stopped by Lawrence, who insisted the man simply leave before he caused any other mischief. Martin obliged with a tip of the hat and walked backward out of the swinging doors. He nearly lost his footing as he tripped over the threshold.

Lawrence sighed and assessed the Parlor. He, once again, set about sweeping the floors and dutifully returning the dirt to Main Street. He replaced the oil font and re-filled the lamp fixture. He put out a new candle after wiping down the table where Perry and Mr. Best had been seated. He cleaned and polished their glasses and replaced the towel for the next patron. He was adjusting his inventory to account for Perry and Mr. Best's drinks when the first customer of the day strolled in and hocked into a spittoon before ordering.

9

Josiah Rush would have to sleep without a blanket. His became the burial shroud for the deceased Waddell who lay motionless behind the group of men who stood at the mouth of the mine. They had not buried Waddell deep, for there were no tools for such work. He was deep within the mine, however, free at least of the vultures that would be circling in a matter of hours.

Crandall used his boot to cover the marks left on the ground from where they had dragged the body inside. He made it a point to kick fresh dirt over the bloody spot where Waddell breathed his last, concealing the rest of what remained of the man.

Cooper squinted upon re-emerging from the mine into the late morning sunlight. "It's a shame about them boots, though, you know it?" he said to Levi. "I mean, I allow it's bad luck to steal from the dead, but they was real purdy."

Levi looked solemnly into the distance. "I don't know what we'd do without you, Cooper," he said.

The rest of the posse had not stuck around. The marshal was content not to afford the murderer a proper inhumation, and where the marshal goes, there too goes the deputy; likewise, where Will Richardson goes, there too goes Jacoby Sutton. The only exception was the tenderfoot, Henry Olt, who had turned back to attend the entombment but did not help.

A short while later, the men continued their ride back to Sagebrush. They looked forward to the comforts of home, not behind them to the macabre memory of the mine. About the time the horses began to exhibit a sheen of sweat they found themselves at a river crossing. There, parked in the shadows partaking in an afternoon nap, was the rest of the party.

The marshal stirred at the sound of hooves splashing across the water. "I wondered if you were gonna catch up today or not," he said, stretching.

Earlier that morning, Josiah had left camp while still in shock. After a couple hours on the trail, however, he had managed to achieve some tranquility. That was now disrupted. At the marshal's indifference, Josiah dismounted, then ground tied his horse without noticing her tense muscles and stiffened tail. Will and Jacoby arose from their slumber and wiped sleep from their eyes in time to see Josiah stomp toward the marshal with clenched fists. Deputy Eaton snored on until Josiah raised his voice.

"What in the *hell* is wrong with you?!" Josiah got up in the marshal's face. "That was *murder*! You murdered that man back there!"

"That was *mercy*!" Oglesby said, leaning into Josiah's advance. ". . . to which he was not entitled!" They stood brow to brow. "I did it as an act of mercy for these men and their morale, too," he said, pointing over his shoulder.

"That's *bullshit*!" Josiah shouted while the others fought to separate the two men. Levi and Crandall pulled Josiah back as he continued hollering.

"Don't mistake me," Josiah said, "I won't shed a tear for that swine; but that was the furthest thing from mercy I ever seen. That was an atrocity!" Josiah fumed, his face beet red. His temples throbbed to the tempo of his racing heartbeat. Will Richardson held back the marshal who attempted to lunge toward Josiah at the accusation.

"Hey! Hey! Hey! Okay now, okay," Crandall said, attempting to calm things down.

Josiah, however, did not let up, "Mercy is not shootin' a wounded man who's in no condition to object! Mercy is what these men are showin' *you* right now by not lettin' me whoop your ass!"

Marshal Oglesby held his hands up to Will, showing that he was composed. He popped his vest taut then retrieved something from his saddlebag.

"Look at this warrant, *look* at it. Says 'Dead or Alive.' Either way, justice was done." The marshal dropped the warrant and it fell to the ground in front of a still detained Josiah. Marshal Oglesby turned to the others, "Let's mount up. We'll stay just long enough for the late arrivals to water the horses then we're back to it. I'd like to see the pines at the end of this stretch before we make camp for the night, and we'll already be well into dark."

Only upon returning to his horse did Josiah notice Cooper's downcast face. He gently petted the beast. Josiah could now clearly see she was in distress; anxious and sweating but would not drink.

"You know, I's a little worried about her last night when I checked on all the horses, but I chalked it up to new waters and long rides. Now I don't reckon that's the case, I'm thinkin' there's somethin' here that's got yer pony in a bad way. It's prob'ly got to do with that." Cooper pointed to the infected cut on the animal's leg. Josiah met the observation with a pat on the shoulder and a shake of the head. In the span of no more than a minute he went from livid to languishing.

Between the sweat, blood, and the bullets of this trip, Josiah realized it had been ages since he remembered longing this badly for home. Not since battle fields under enemy fire in the sweltering summer heat, or since suffering through miles-long hikes with wet soles during the torrents of early spring had he desired his own bed as he did just then. Now, on top of everything else, this faithful horse was showing signs of agony. He wondered if she would be able to complete the trek back to the ranch. Although she had merely served as a work horse around Josiah's place for the past few years, he had taken a liking to the mild-mannered mare. The group was far from Sagebrush, though, and Josiah dreaded the decision he might soon face—especially since it would mean realizing a gloomy and probable outcome while still on the trail with the marshal.

"You know, Cooper, I'm beginnin' to understand how you felt after losin' Harvey," Josiah said. "Thank you for keepin' an eye on these animals. Let's just try to get her home."

Josiah transferred his things to one of the mules to lighten the mare's load. Upon resumption of their advance across the country, the team rode divided. At the fore was Marshal Oglesby and Deputy Butch Eaton followed by Will and Jacoby. Charles Crandall led the rear and trailing him was Levi, Cooper, and finally Josiah on his ailing horse. He further eased her burden by frequently going on foot for periods of time. Between the groups, like the coupler connecting two great rail cars, rode Henry Olt. Despite the heat and fatigue, the party was eager to get home. Well past the pine-rich river intersection for which they originally set out, the men made it within thirty miles of Sagebrush before finally settling on a place to stop for the night.

The tension among the men made for a hostile camp. Crandall dissuaded Josiah from attempting to go it alone and settle far from the others, particularly in light of recent events. For Josiah, sleep came in precious, vulnerable waves. It wasn't until he heard the heavy breathing of the marshal that Josiah allowed himself to doze.

Josiah found the point of utter exhaustion in which the novelty of delirium wanes and one becomes accustomed to the twilight of a restless semi-consciousness. In such a phase of transcendence between awakening and dreaming, it was difficult for him to discern actual from hallucinatory experiences. Natives had peyote and sweat huts, but Josiah needed no such assistance. His past was the vehicle for his ghostly visitations. As he lay entranced on a bed of pine needles taking in the midnight canvas of a hazy blue starscape pierced by the tops of the evergreens, he watched a meteor skate across the sky. Like a prophet, it ushered in a solitary blue-grey cloud. The sight of the cloud abruptly yielded to the presence of a man suddenly standing over Josiah, looking down upon him. The man was uniformed and affixed to his belt was a scabbard housing the gold encrusted hilt of a military sword. He seemed to be yelling something at Josiah, but there was no sound coming from his mouth. Standing, he waved at someone who then also appeared at once over Josiah. The smoky translucence of the figures did not affect their perceived authenticity as the second man studied Josiah then shook his head before turning away and disappearing again. Josiah tried to halt the departing specter but could not speak. Something caught the attention of the first soldier as he stood over Josiah and raised his rifle. The burst of gunpowder ascended to the sky and joined the solitary cloud drifting slowly across the treetops almost out of sight. The soldier dropped his gun, which dissipated before it hit the ground, and grabbed his hand in excruciating pain. Josiah bolted upright grabbing for the phantom soldier.

The man he actually tackled was Levi Holdegel in the flesh, whom he wrestled to the ground to keep safe from the illusory recollection of the assaulting enemy fire. Levi had heard Josiah's nightmare and roused him in an attempt to ease the man's torment.

"It's over, they've stopped shootin'," Levi said. "Josiah, you can let up now."

Josiah awoke confused to the sounds of his own grunts and cries. He rolled over and his aching muscles seemed to melt from his bones. He rested there a long while catching his breath. By the time his heartbeat slowed to normal, Josiah had gathered his wits. He peered at Levi with a darkly humorous grin.

"I don't remember that hurtin' as much the last time," Levi said, grunting to his feet.

"Well, last time you weren't such a lapper an' you'd just taken a bullet to your paw. Prob'ly didn't even feel it." Josiah accepted the good hand of the man he had once and again saved, and Levi pulled him to his feet.

Levi smiled, then asked seriously, "Does that happen often?"

Josiah shook his head, "It's been a long time actually."

Levi sniffled, "Well, if you can keep your act together until we get back, then we'll grab a beer just the two of us. We're overdo for relivin' old glory days. What do you say?"

"Fine, that'd be just fine." Josiah yawned.

The other men whose slumber had been disturbed by all the activity returned their attention to the back of their eyelids. Josiah and Levi sat up for a while tossing pine nuts into the dark to see if they could spook something. After an hour or so with no success, the two men drifted off to sleep.

In the morning, the travelers had a different energy about them. They would see Sagebrush by early afternoon, and they all anticipated the break from one another. Amongst the high-spirited rush to get on the go, there was a solemn revelation that halted Josiah. His injured mare with her swollen leg and rigid muscles had laid down in the middle of the night and rolled over. Her insides were all twisted, and she could not get up. Josiah saw that she was dying.

"It's a shame to see her suffer so," the marshal said from over Josiah's shoulder.

"Yes, yes it is." Josiah was dismayed.

"What are you gonna do, Josiah? Is it not inhumane to let the beast suffer any longer? She's surely beyond hope. Will you let her last breath be right here, sufferin', with us long gone, alone, frightened, watchin' the carrion crows gatherin' to devour her as their next meal?"

"Marshal," Josiah drew quick and dispatched the animal cleanly. After the echo of the gunshot subsided, he finished his thought, "a horse is a horse, and a man is a man, and a horse is not a man." Oglesby merely nodded then walked away while Josiah hung his head and mourned.

As the party packed, Josiah took off the mare's tack. He built up large stones around the horse to keep scavengers away and serve as a make-shift mausoleum. At last, when it was nearly time to go, Cooper Emmons strode over and shifted a few rocks revealing the lacerated hoof. He removed the horseshoe from the injured leg then replaced the stones carefully.

Handing the shoe to Josiah he said, "So's you don't forget the horse that saved you once," then added, "Course you wouldn't have needed savin' if weren't for her, and I mean really she was just savin' herself, but uh . . . ah, hell, here ya go."

"Thank you, Cooper."

Josiah placed the saddle atop a mule. The ill-fitting saddle was unsteady, and Josiah teetered in a continual balancing act for the next five hours.

Upon reaching town, the men came up Broad Street from the south and passed between the commercial docks and the stockyards. Sagebrush was lively with teams of men that traveled in from all over the territory for the quarterly auction. There were cowboys and butchers, buyers and breeders alike, all in a frenzy of wrangling herds, inspecting cattle, and sorting them among varied pens in preparation for the sale.

Josiah recalled the story of Christ riding a donkey into Jerusalem. The people praised him with palms and exaltation. As Josiah rode a mule into Sagebrush he was met with jeers and laughter. There was no glory to be found in returning empty handed among strangers who knew nothing of the posse's exploits. No admiration given to the sullen men whose service evoked no reverence. No ceremony to celebrate their valiance. Whether theirs was a tale of victory or failure not even they were of an accord.

One by one they reached the intersection in town and peeled off with no official conclusion to their commission. Josiah headed for the livery to return the mule while Cooper and Levi set out to collect their wages for the week's service from the attorney and treasurer, Nicholas Scoville. They were stopped along the way by a zestful man in a straw boater.

"Excuse me, gentlemen. Did you just ride in with that lawman over there?" he asked, pointing with his pencil, and holding a small note pad in his other hand.

Cooper perked up and nudged Levi in the hope of receiving some adulation he suddenly realized was desired. "Why yes sir boy I'll tell you it sure is good to get back in town you know it's been a rough week we was out there thirstin and sweatin' then freezin' and campin' and workin' to keep them horses in good shape I'm a blacksmith you see so that's what I do is keep 'em shod and well we was chasin' down this hardened man a thief and a murderer real tough big guy mean as a rattler well that's funny I put it that way actually you know . . . OUCH!" Cooper grabbed his shoulder then turned to see Levi's clenched fist. The curious man was not taking notes but was interested and leaning in, absorbing the energy of the rambling remarks.

"Just who's askin'?" Levi inquired of the stranger.

"Ah yes well Gentlemen I'm a newsman from the Gazette well not from the Gazette now I was with the Gazette for a number of years but I'm not with the Gazette any longer now I'm here in Sagebrush to begin publication of an entirely new paper a newspaper a new newspaper if you will I'm here to serve the citizens of this territory by reporting facts current stories old stories histories her-stories anything that might interest these folks and I'm chasing down any kind of information about . . ."

"What's. your. name?" Levi leaned closer with each word.

"Oh. Uh, Porter High, sir."

"Wait, so you're Porter the Reporter?" Cooper asked.

That particular combination of name and title had apparently never dawned on the journalist. "It would appear so, good sir. Thank you," he said with a smile.

"Well, that's rich." Levi spit tobacco on the ground between them, sending Mr. High a step backward.

"Ick," a resilient Porter held out the wanted poster for the late Colton Waddell, "I see that the marshal has been absent for—how long was it? And there was a thief, correct? Can I quote you on that? Is this the man? What was it you were saying about a snake, now?"

"You can go get your official story from the marshal. We got other business to attend to. Good day." With that, Levi dragged Cooper past Porter and up the boardwalk.

"Man, that guy could talk," Cooper said as they entered Scoville's office.

"Hello, gentlemen!" Scoville said, "I don't know that I expected you ba— whoa!" Scoville recoiled at their odor but remained diplomatic. "Let's step outside, shall we?" The little lawyer held the door. "That's better, thank you. I don't know that I expected you back so soon. Is everything alright?"

"So, do we still get paid for the full week?" Cooper asked.

"Pardon my friend here," Levi sat down on the bench, nearly looking Scoville in the eyes. "Yes, everything is alright, thank you."

"Well, so long as you ain't Waddell, anyway," Cooper said.

"What does he mean by that, Levi?"

Levi leered at Cooper as though he was going to kill him, then back at Scoville, "What my friend—who needs to be quiet—is sayin', is that everyone who left with the marshal is alright."

"I see."

"Now anyway, how are things around here? Been anything excitin' or eventful since we left?"

"Oh, sure, sure. Hmm, let's see. There is a doctor in town now, er, temporarily at least. Dr. Andrew Hoyle. Though, if I'm to be candid, you may be better off under the care of his nurse. Other than that, uh, Mr. Best has arrived. I thought you'd like to know; I understand you frequent his establishments."

"I do, and I'd like to head that way now, actually."

"Of course, wait here and I'll return with your full week's pay." As Scoville backed into the office he watched Cooper rub his hands together.

"Cooper," Levi said, "stop foolin' and look at me. We need to be careful; you can't be goin 'round blabbin' to folks all about Waddell."

"Huh? Why not? You heard the—"

"Shh."

While the men collected their money, over at the livery Dillon Turk ensured Josiah was apprised of the state of his ranch.

". . . and that pretty, brown gelding, Josiah," he whistled, "there is a special way about that one."

"That's Nero. I don't know how Levi come across him, but by the next auction I hope to have him trained up. He'll fetch a handsome profit, no doubt. Well thanks again, I know you got your hands full here and lookin' after my place kept you mighty busy."

"Don't thank me, it was my pleasure. Besides, it was the boys that done most the work, I just supervised." Dillon Turk tussled Cassidy's hair as little Jasper came trotting by on a broomstick horse.

"Long way around, Mr. Josiah, maybe someday they'll build you a bridge north of them lumber channels," Cassidy said. Dillon failed to notice the acknowledgment of the secret Josiah held for the boy that surely kept him from picking a switch. They shook hands and Josiah departed, at last, for home.

From the base of the hill that marked the boundary of his land, Josiah looked up past the long swaying wheat grasses. His gaze fell upon the timber frame of his abode as he ascended this final stretch on foot, carrying his saddle. The corrals were vacant. The cows and horses were as quiet as the distant mountaintops that were also shedding their winter coats, revealing more of their bald, rocky domes above the tree lines. These fixtures were a comfort because here, at least, was peace among the stillness of life. This was a place of healing, the prescription for Josiah's suffering.

At just past five o'clock, Josiah closed the front door behind him and collapsed face first onto his bed. Still fully clothed, he slept soundly clear through the night.

10

Birds chirped away outside his window, but it was the sun shining through that woke Josiah. Like a magnifying glass, an imperfection focused a beam of light onto his face nearly singeing the ends of his stubble. He rose, closed the curtains, then filled a wash basin. After bathing, he stropped a razor and shaved his face, finishing with a splash of spiced vetiver aftershave. Having retrieved from his wardrobe a fresh set of laundered denim and canvas clothes still crisp from the line, Josiah ambled to the kitchen. Making use of a heavy cast iron skillet, he fried up a hot breakfast. He slowly ate a hearty meal of maple bacon, peppered eggs, buttered biscuits, and coffee. When he had finished, he washed and replaced the dishes. Josiah pulled on his boots and ran a hand through his hair one time before placing his black hat, canted, atop his head. He made his way for the door but paused slightly to entertain an incomplete thought about the lifelessness of his living room.

Stepping outside, he was greeted by a bumblebee buzzing toward the blossoming springtime wildflowers that grew along the corrals. He paused with his foot on a fence to overlook a broad field, rich with masses of beef still on their hooves. He watched the solitary longhorn bull in the neighboring pasture. It was turned from the herd, provoked by some perceived threat or another. The bull grazed the entire pasture, but his usual paths were visible. He liked to cross from the gate to the river, strut up along the ridge, and then to the fence adjoining the other cattle and back. Josiah considered that this was a lot of field for one animal but could never bring himself to redirect the fences and close the beast in further.

Josiah took a walk to the stables where all the horses had fresh bedding and hay thanks to young Cassidy Turk; chores which were surely completed with, though not accelerated by, the assistance of his little brother, Jasper. The two plow horses looked healthy and would be ready for the first planting after the following week's auction. Next to them was the empty stall of the departed mare.

Josiah placed his hand on her door and remembered the gift from Cooper. He retrieved her horseshoe from his saddlebag, a hammer from the toolbox, and a couple nails. After hanging it up, he took a step back to admire his work and remember his companion. Nero whickered from the next stall and seemed to bow his head. Josiah approached him with some calming words and pulled an apple from a bucket on the ground near the stall.

Nero took the treat and Josiah asked, "Whaddaya say, young gun? How's about we get to work?" He petted the Morgan horse on his blaze and slipped on a bridle. Nero clopped around in a circle one time inside the stall then stood still and let Josiah throw over the saddle blanket. Once the saddle was cinched, he led Nero to the round pen.

"Alright, partner, let's see how much you remember." From the ground Josiah led Nero through a series of commands and he responded like any veteran steed.

"Okay, good boy. Let's see here." He walked along the side of the beast and placed his hands on its back. After applying some pressure, Nero seemed unbothered, so Josiah put a foot in the stirrup. The horse braced itself with an unsteady step but stood firm once accustomed to the weight. When Josiah kicked a foot over, Nero tensed and made a start, but did not buck. A simple tug on the reins and the horse stopped in its tracks.

"Shh, shh, shh," Josiah patted Nero's crest. "Well, if you ain't the darndest thing I ever seen. Let's see if you think I'm still the boss even outside this pen." He had the horse trot over to the gate and the gelding stayed still even after it was opened to him. Remounting, Josiah encouraged the horse to take a few steps, which he did, timidly. Suddenly, Nero unexpectedly took off in a full gallop with Josiah holding the reins in one hand and his hat in the other. Though the horse had not done so upon command, Nero ran cooperatively.

Occasionally Josiah would give directions to ensure he maintained control over the steed, but mostly he allowed Nero to simply run. Nero moved with agility and grace, gliding across the grasslands as though he never touched the ground. His swiftness was unparalleled for a horse with his power. His steady breathing under saddle told Josiah he could endure miles and miles without giving in to exhaustion.

When they had crossed into the wild country beyond the boundaries of Josiah's ranch, he let Nero run until the green pastures gave way to more rooty terrain. Afraid for Nero's footing, Josiah turned him toward the river and the two followed it back home.

By late morning Josiah felt comfortable taking Nero into town to see Levi.

At the river crossing by the stockyards, Nero was unphased by the cool water. He did not so much as flinch at the ballyhoo of the auction preparations. Strutting proudly up Broad, he passed the clanks and chimney smoke of Cooper's smithy, confident of his own presence among the muscle and meat that crowded the street.

Rounding the corner at the post office, Josiah turned up Main and headed for the livery where Levi would be supervising his prized pedigrees. For Levi, the Spring auction's lot of stallions and mustangs included a few quarter horses, a lineback dun, and the chestnut gelding, Nero, upon whom Josiah rode. Josiah hitched Nero to a post and greeted Levi.

"That's a mighty fine new horse you've got there, Josiah. Top stock. Just where did you come across such a purdy thing? I must have one, myself!" Levi said.

"Top stock, indeed, but boy I'll tell you whoever trained this horse done a mighty fine job. That's who deserves your regards." The two men laughed and shook hands.

"Ooh wee! Now that's what I like to see," Levi placed a hand on Nero as he examined the animal's general health. "What do I owe you?" He poked his head over the saddle and held his chin in his good hand while looking at Josiah.

"Half ounce of the yellow ought to do it."

"Josiah, don't sell yourself short or do me any charity. I'm just about insulted. You think I can't afford your services?"

"Fine, a half ounce and a drink down at the Parlor."

"Now it's a negotiation," Levi said. "Deal."

"Deal." The men shook hands, again.

"But as it turns out, maybe I can't afford your services, after all. Well, I *won't* be affordin' 'em, anyway."

"C'mon now, Levi, what are you on about?"

"Alright look, I got a good stock this Spring and interest in every pony I intend to bring to market. I'll be set. Now, I figure it's been a few days since we got back and you're in need of a horse. A good horse and not no finicky mare, may she rest in peace. I seen how Nero took to you so I think I'm just gonna sell him to you whether you're buyin' or not. Cheap, too. Say, the price of breakin' the steed? What was it? A half a round of yellow and a drink down at the Parlor?"

Moved by the gift, Josiah said, "Levi, if I didn't know any better, I'd say you was just tryin' to get a drink outta me."

"Well, *those* don't cancel each other out. Just means we're obligated for two rounds . . . plus one from the trail."

"Look, I appreciate your generosity, I do, but I can't let you take a loss like that on my account. You stand to draw at least three times what you'll get from me if you just take him down the road in a few days."

"Pleasure doin' business. Enjoy your new pony. I'll be down at the Parlor whenever you're ready to complete the transaction." Levi ignored any further refusals, walked down the street, and disappeared into the saloon.

"Well, Nero, how 'bout that, huh?" Josiah gave the horse a pat. "You wanna tackle the world together, boy?" Nero stomped a hoof. "Okay, buddy let's start by stockin' up on some supplies."

Josiah walked Nero across the street to Dodge's Emporium and Dry Goods. Martin Kelly was nowhere to be found, but behind the counter was a pale blonde woman holding a fussy infant.

"Good day to you, ma'am."

"Hello, sir. How can I help you?" Pearl asked.

"Well, the other day I started to ask Martin Kelly for an update on an order I placed a while back. We got interrupted by a—" the baby began to cry, "well, by a—" it burst forth into full brassy wails. Josiah gave a tongue-tied smile.

The gracious woman saved him the trouble of completing his thought, "I'll be happy to let Martin know you stopped by if you'd like me to take a message for you."

"That'd be wonderful, thank you." As Josiah spoke, an unseen Lorraine Baxter rounded a corner from the back, beckoned by the cries of the child.

"Alright, sir, your name is?" Pearl asked only out of courtesy, everyone knew Josiah.

"Josiah Rush."

At this, Lorraine paused and retreated behind the shelves to spy. She was interested in meeting the man, but she was suddenly stricken by an unfamiliar self-consciousness that took her by surprise.

"Very well Mr. Rush, is there anything else I can do for you while you're here?" Pearl asked over the baby's cries.

"Well, yes, a few sacks of flour and oats back there, but I hate to bother you for it now, you've obviously got your hands full."

"No bother." The affable Pearl shoved the infant into Josiah's unexpectant hands and turned to the shelves. After a moment of hesitation, he held the upset babe and soon found himself naturally bouncing the child in his arms.

"What's his name?"

"Carson," Pearl said from over her shoulder.

Josiah tucked in the corners of the tiny blanket, tightening the swaddle. He began to pat Carson on the back. The baby promptly burped then spit up all over Josiah's shoulder.

He chuckled, "I bet you feel better, don't ya, son?"

Josiah had turned by this point to peruse the Emporium and cradled Carson in his arms. He gently bounced the boy and soothingly patted his back. Carson settled down. After a few moments of pacified cooing, he fell into a shallow slumber.

"You're brand new, ain't ya now?" Josiah smiled down at the boy and ran his thumb calmly across the fine-haired, faint red eyebrows.

Josiah failed to realize how long he had been humming a lullaby to the child until he turned around and saw two women behind the counter staring at him. Lorraine had stacked his groceries neatly after emerging from hiding to lift the heavy bags for the carefree and convalescing Pearl.

"Oh, I'm sorry," his face flushed as he shied away, "I didn't realize you were ready for me."

"No problem, Mr. Rush," Pearl sang. Walking over to Josiah, she swung her hips as though she was working. Upon relieving him of the boy she shot a wink at Lorraine then took off for the back, leaving them alone to settle the bill.

"Goodness, me!" said Lorraine approaching from around the counter, "I'm terribly sorry about this." She grabbed a rag and walked behind Josiah. As she was dabbing away the stain on his shoulder he reached up and took her hand.

"That's . . . quite alright, ma'am. Thank you," he said. Josiah turned around to face her. He let go of her hand slower than she expected, but not so slow as to ensure his intent. It was, however, sooner than Lorraine would have liked to admit. She stood there unmoved until he spoke again, "I'll just . . . take another. You can add it to my bill if it's all the same."

"Oh, of course!" She shied away, abashed upon realizing how close she stood to Josiah whose backside pressed against the counter. He gave a smile and fled between a rack of clothes and the far wall.

That was odd, he thought. *The last time I saw this woman she looked at me like there's no way I'd want her on my jury. Now, though . . . now . . . now what?*

Goodness me! thought Lorraine. *What has gotten into you? Get a hold of yourself.* She set about editing the bill.

Josiah, unable to help himself, looked around the corner to behold the woman again. Lorraine was a misfit in his vision, a splash of color and life among the earthen tones of stained lumber and burlap. She wore a dress of elegant blue with a white apron and her scent was a mix of salt and juniper that still lingered in his head. Her voice echoed across his memory, "Goodness me! Goodness me! Goodness me!"

Lorraine sensed eyes upon her and glanced toward the far wall in time to notice Josiah watching. He quickly ducked behind the clothes.

Was he staring at me just then, or am I imagining things? She asked herself. *Goodness me! Why do I hope he was staring at me?*

What are you? A child? Josiah mused. *Is this the schoolyard? Pick a shirt, stay composed, and just pay your bill.*

Josiah did pick a shirt, but he could not maintain his composure. He was a soldier seasoned by war, trained to perform under the direst of circumstances when his body was flooded by emotions that would disorient another man. During those moments he was able to cut through the fog and focus on his objective, a talent that had been nurtured on bloody battlefield after bloody battlefield, honed into a masterful skill set. But here, his poise failed. At the present he was defenseless against Lorraine's stunning barrage of confusing and contradictory signals.

There, behind a clothes rack in the midst of the Emporium, Josiah unbuttoned his soiled shirt and commenced to change. Lorraine had become curious after she noticed him staring, but mistakenly concluded that he needed some assistance, so she walked over to help. The canvas shirt dropped from Josiah's brawny shoulders as Lorraine rounded the corner. Confronted by the tan backside of the half-dressed man in the aisle of a store at which she was not employed in a town which she was not yet settled, Lorraine gasped at the impropriety. Josiah turned around surprised to see the woman staring at him.

"I'm sorry, I'm so sorry, I didn't mean—goodness me, I must have—" Lorraine stammered. She did not, however, avert her eyes.

Josiah glanced down as though confirming he was, in fact, shirtless. Then without moving his head, his eyes climbed slowly from Lorraine's stockings up to her blushing face. Upon his own was drawn a crooked smile.

"Allow me to take that. I'll see that it gets washed." She grabbed his dirty shirt and bit her lower lip as she turned around, paused, then skittered away. Josiah untied the twine price tag from his new shirt and walked it to the counter. In no time he was met with the teasing smile of a baby-free Pearl who finished the sale.

"She new here?" Josiah asked.

"Who, Lorraine? She doesn't work here silly," Pearl leaned across the counter, "and she's not one of Martin's girls either, if that's what you mean." She winked.

The color drained from Josiah's face, "Heavens no! I wasn't askin' if she was a—" then realizing that Pearl *was* one of Martin's girls he said, "I mean not that, well . . . I didn't mean to . . ."

Pearl giggled then once again saved the man the trouble of completing his thought, "She's a nurse, Mr. Rush. Here in town workin' for some travellin' doctor. She helped me bring that child into this world and she's here now lookin' after us is all."

"Well, I suppose that explains a thing or two," Josiah said. Just then the bell above the door chimed.

"Oh, and speak of the doctor, here he is now!" Pearl was beaming, "Hi, Dr. Hoyle!"

Dr. Andrew Hoyle closed the door behind him, then turned and straightened his jacket. The doctor offered only a furtive wave to the woman upon realizing they were with company.

"Pleasure seein' you again, sir!" Pearl said, louder.

Dr. Hoyle cleared his throat and uncomfortably asked if Lorraine was present.

"Oh, she's here alright," Josiah said. He watched Pearl for her reaction rather than regard Dr. Hoyle who leered at the stranger. Pearl stifled her amusement with a forced frown that fooled neither of them.

"Excuse me?" Hoyle said. "And just who might you be that you would speak of her with such casual familiarity?" Hoyle stepped forward and scowled. Josiah turned and matched Hoyle's step. He stared down his nose at the doctor.

"Someone who needn't answer to the likes of you," he said.

"Oh boys, boys, stop that now. Josiah Rush, you've had your fun, go on, git!" Pearl playfully waved him away. "Doctor, what can I do for you?"

Josiah loaded up an armful of his merchandise and made for the door, but not before noticing the doctor shoot him an especially dirty look and then withdraw for Pearl an especially unique piece of paper from a coin pouch.

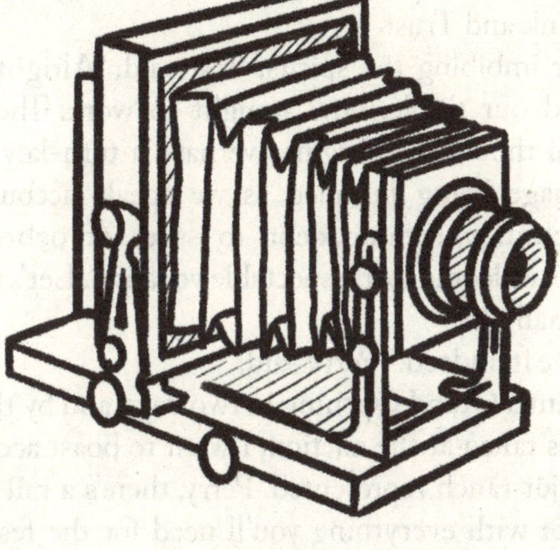

11

"Gentlemen, it's been an honor. Best of luck to you on your enterprises back east. I wish you good fortune." George Best shut the door behind them. "Suckers." He practically danced back into the office where Peregrine Page and Nicholas Scoville awaited his return.

"Hehe! Now folks, *that* is what you call a steal!" Best said. He bowed triumphantly then spun his cane and took a seat in one of Scoville's leather chairs.

"And that ain't even the half of it, now is it Mr. Best?" Perry dared the allusion to the duo's unscrupulous efforts in the presence of Scoville. Best's face lost its delight for a terrifying instant before he burst forth with obnoxious laughter. Perry helped himself to Scoville's whiskey and poured a celebratory round for the three of them. The exchange was not lost on the attentive Nicholas Scoville. He had always had men like Best underestimate him; it was a reality he had learned to use to his advantage. Scoville was hosting these men to administer the transfer of the Bank of Sagebrush to Peregrine Page d.b.a. Best's Bank and Trust.

After imbibing the spirits, Best said, "Alright good sirs, we've had our tipple, now straight to work. There are five days until the auction begins, we have a turn-key bank with new signage being installed as we speak, accounts to roll over, accounts to sign up, debts to issue, and debts to collect. Peregrine, welcome to a respectable vocation. Let's make some money, shall we?"

"*Make* it, indeed." Perry said.

"I want a Grand Opening in two days, and by the time the first bid is taken at the auction, I want to boast accounts with every major ranch represented. Perry, there's a rail car held at the Depot with everything you'll need for the festivities. I'll have a reporter at the bank on the big day and you'll pose for a fancy photographic portrait with the mayor, a local judge, and some other business owners from here in Sagebrush." Best grabbed his suit jacket. "I'm heading over to the hotel now to begin distribution of our enumerated bank notes. Soon they'll be used all over town to settle debts and accelerate trade."

"Or . . . to redeem for a withdrawal, yes?" Scoville said. He sought clarification, but there was an edge of accusation in his voice.

"Obviously, sir," Best said. His assurance was quick and flippant before turning his attention again to Perry. "Your Parlor's next, and later I'll stop by the Emporium, the Depot, and the Feed Store to do the same. I need you to talk to the folks over at the Lumber Mill. With them on board we should have enough leverage to revolutionize commerce in Sagebrush."

"That is a tall order," Perry said, "but very well. Let's get to work."

George Best stuck out his chest, buttoned his suit, and peered down at the lawyer. "Mr. Scoville, thank you for your assistance once again. Here is what I owe you for having officiated this, my most recent marriage of interests." Best withdrew from his pocket a blank deposit receipt and on official letterhead filled out the amount due to Scoville.

"Mr. Best, excuse me, sir. I must respectfully insist that my fees be fulfilled by weight of assayed or minted coin."

"Indeed. Here," Best thrust the slip of paper to Scoville, "Good as gold."

Scoville blinked.

"You can take this to the bank," Best said.

"Your bank. I am a rather busy person, Mr. Best, perhaps next time you're there you can make the errand of withdrawing money to fulfill this debt to me, sir. Until then, trust that no interest will accrue, and I shall do you the courtesy of a regular invoice as a friendly reminder."

"Scoville, you're being ridiculous. I'm not your errand boy and I have no intention of making any extra work for myself when you may simply accept this, and your remuneration is sitting in the bank, yours to do with as you please—if you'd only claim it."

"Perhaps I've been unclear, sir?"

"Scoville, don't play games. If you refuse now, I'll have to assume that you've denied the payment entirely."

"That wouldn't withstand scrutiny."

"I should hardly think anyone would believe it unusual for me to have received such generosity after you've profited for years from my faithful patronage."

"For years you have faithfully paid my fees with agreeable means. What has changed so suddenly, and without my consultation?"

Best pretended to be disappointed. "I've never known you to be such a difficult man. I'm done having this conversation, I've indulged you plenty. Deny me now, but you cannot deny the shifting tide, Mr. Scoville. There will come a day when every one of your clients will seek to settle their accounts with payment bearing my name. The inconvenience of gold money will drive away your customers until you become a relic, sidelined from all economic activity." Best dropped the paper on Scoville's desk, turned and walked out of the office with Perry close behind.

The next two days saw yet more arrivals as Sagebrush spilled over with activity. The Sagebrush Grand Hotel had completely sold out and the Parlor stayed open around the clock. Will Richardson and Jacoby Sutton began to notice pots containing Best's bank notes right alongside copper, silver, and gold bets at the gaming tables. Horses and wagons lined the street as Dillon and Rebecca Turk at the Livery Stables had reached capacity as well. The cattle pens at the stockyards were sloppy and crammed. As a result, many of the cattle drivers who had registered for the auction chose to camp out with their herds in the western grasslands beyond the river, awaiting a final push until it was their time to sell. Scoville sent word to his managers at the Auction House that as they completed transactions over the next week, under no circumstances would bank notes from Best's Bank and Trust be honored as settlement for the house's commission. At first, most of the ranchers failed to see it as an issue. Over the course of the week, however, some of them became aggravated because Best's Bank and Trust had insisted that people and businesses found these bank notes suitable for trade "all over town."

By and large, the statement was true, though. Perry had been able to convince the folks down at The Mill to not only accept the notes for payment, but he also secured for them a loan to purchase a steam-driven machine that would turn their excess wood pulp into a paper printing operation. Perry procured the first order in advance, for the bank, of course.

Martin Kelly, already indebted to Mr. Best, had no option but to begin accepting this new money; nor did he bother, as a business owner, to redeem the notes he accepted. Rather, he incorporated them into his ledgers and stored them in neat stacks next to the slowly dwindling supply in his coin pouches.

The Depot's owners, beholden to Best for the mortgage on the new building, assented to the adoption of the bank notes as well. After all, they figured, back when circulation first began in the city, they had noticed an appreciable increase in profits at their primary station. They were more discerning than Martin Kelly, however. After daily settlements, they redeemed their bank notes. The Depot's success, shrewdness, and subsequent additional principal payments would eventually cut into the bank's future interest profits, but that was no longer a concern for Mr. Best as business at the Sagebrush branch was already booming by the grand opening.

Peregrine Page found himself at the Depot on the evening before the ribbon cutting ceremony awaiting an incoming train. He had been tasked with transferring the contents of Mr. Best's railcar to the bank and overseeing preparations. Anticipating a very busy day, Mr. Best had also sent for a few of his brightest employees from the city branch. They, too, would be arriving to assist Perry and provide some expertise over the next week, ensuring new operations ran smoothly.

The brakes squealed as a steam engine lurched to a stop. A hiss resounded from the release of the piston pressure as the last of a black plume of smoke arose from the chimney. The engineer checked his pocket watch and marked down the time while two men who had been tending the furnace sat down on the floor of the locomotive, smearing soot across their brows upon wiping away beads of sweat. The doors of the passenger cars creaked open. Assisted by the railway attendants, one by one the finely dressed ladies and gentlemen stepped over the small gap between the steps of the railcar and the platform of the Depot.

Perry, feeling dapper in a fresh suit tailored by Mrs. Turk, watched his new employees disembark and was smitten. Three gorgeous young women emerged from the train wearing uniforms displaying the Best's Bank and Trust name. Perry seemed to almost dance as he strolled down Main Street at their side. They each walked in lockstep, arms intertwined, and Perry felt fulfilled. He was now a man of wealth and influence in the company of beauty, and soon he would command the same veneration that Mr. Best evoked. Behind the party, a small wagon team carrying decorations followed them to the bank.

The trio strung up a series of colorful flagged banners across Main Street, all attached to the same point at the bank's balcony. They directed the construction of staging for the upcoming theatrics and skirted the platform with patriotic themed ruffled fabrics. They draped curtains and set up gift tables in preparation for the pageantry.

Finally, as the last light of day disappeared beyond the horizon at the end of Main, they tied the large red ribbon between the posts of the bank's primary entrance. Upon completion, the young women popped the cork on a bottle of champagne. They pranced across the dirty street and into the Parlor, led by an uncharacteristically confident Peregrine Page.

The morning of the grand opening, George Best awoke early in his suite at the Sagebrush Grand Hotel. He dressed hurriedly, anxious to see the arrangements and review his schedule for the day. For Best, this was bound to be one of merriment. His profits were up, and he had made his way into the good graces of the political figures in the territory. They could soon boast of unprecedented prosperity under their leadership. Best didn't mind them taking credit for the fortunate circumstances he created, though, because he understood that a politician's only concern is re-election after all, and the quid pro quo relationship with government officials was valuable and alluring. Once he straightened his bowtie and donned his top hat, Best stepped out of the lobby into the sunny day.

The banners hung neatly and the stage appeared inviting. Everything was just as it should be, right down to the way the red bow hung dead center in front of the bank. Best amused himself by watching the puzzled looks of passing cowboys who scratched their heads, befuddled by the spectacle. He entered the bank and inspected its dusty wooden counters; his top lip curled with disapproval. Back in the city, Best's Bank and Trust was the pinnacle of sophistication in architecture with marbled columns and decorative glass work. He suffered through the simple surroundings, though, and found his way to that central object of his desire: the safe. The heft of the steel fortress made it seem intimidating and impregnable. It was black as coal with a palm sized silver dial and a large wheel that could have belonged to a sea-faring vessel. Best retrieved a piece of paper from his vest. On it was the combination for the lock. The dial was smooth as it spun to the left and right, tactile under the pressure of Best's anxious fingertips. He turned the wheel which spun two full revolutions before giving an audible pop as the multiple hardened dowels retracted into the mass of the door. Heavy on its hinges, the safe swung open with a slow creak, revealing a darkened, air-tight vault.

Best lit a candle and entered the crypt-like coffer. The faint glow of the firelight illuminated portions of the room, gleaming off the lustrous assets and reflecting in the eyes of the banker. *Just can't trust the audit*, he thought. Best pulled a scale from beneath the table in the center of the room and began a new ledger. With every fraction of an ounce, he seemed more enthralled with his work. The quill's nib coasted across accounts, trailing ink with calligraphic serifs; numbers, after all, deserved the adornment of an artist. Compared to the scales swinging against gravity, time became an insignificant measurement as one ignored hour after another passed over the face of the clock in the lobby. It was not until one of his arresting arrivals from the city appeared in the doorway that Best broke his concentration.

"Say dear, what brings you here this early?"

"Early, Mr. Best? Why, it's eleven a.m.!"

Unconcerned, Best closed the ledgers and locked the safe. He straightened his bowtie and looked to the woman who clapped rapidly and gave him an enthusiastic cheer. Adorned with a crooked smile and oozing artificial charm, the banker surfaced from within his newest branch location to the reception of uproarious applause. A small ensemble of musicians struck up a cheerful march and streamers garnished the pathway to the stage. He shook the hands of those he knew and those he didn't, just the same. A polite word here and a gracious affirmation there were all accompanied by ardent pats on the back. He saw an array of suits and skirts, cowboy hats and corsets, tailored hems and baggy chaps, but the faces all seemed porcelain. To George Best, people were not real; they were resources. Their savings did not represent the precious hours of their lives—baptized by sweat—which they traded to meet the material needs or desired services of others; hours often spent away from their homes and loved ones developing the reputations of their ventures. Rather, this was all sport to George Best. One in which the wealth of others was the object. To succeed, he need only take advantage of their initial trust.

The steps creaked beneath Best as he ascended the stage and found the podium. The event's emcee held up his speaking trumpet and introduced the banker to the crowd of onlookers. George Best stared out over those porcelain faces and sold them all on the heights of prosperity, indifferent to the dangers which could cause them to shatter.

"Ladies and gentlemen, thank you for being here on this grand occasion. I am delighted to support your very own Mr. Peregrine Page in his newest undertaking, the next chapter of the Best's Bank and Trust legacy. You'll hear from him in just a moment, but I have a special announcement to make first." Best cleared his throat then looked over at a puzzled Perry who stood nearby. "Folks, I'm going to be candid with you. Sagebrush is dear to me; I love this place, its locals and pilgrims alike. As a man with investments in this town, it has been a sincere pleasure to see it develop. Look around you, Sagebrush is growing fast. Unfortunately, however, faster than it can accommodate the demands placed on her, and folks believe me, as a businessman, I hate to see any of my clients leave money on the table."

From the corner of his eye, Best saw Porter High in his straw boater furiously taking notes. "So, I am here today to tell you that I am committing to a plan of further capital investment to advance the inevitable destiny of this town to become the economic center of all westward expansion. I envision a sprawling Sagebrush able to meet the changing needs of her residents and guests. I'd like a future where every person has the opportunity to take part in successful and productive trade unhindered by inability to access the means to begin."

Best expected clapping. Instead, he heard murmurs ripple through the crowd.

Someone from side stage shouted, "He's got money for you!" This elicited the response for which Best had hoped as the crowd cheered.

"In addition," Best continued, "I wish to extend a hospitable welcome to our travelers here today who are in town for the upcoming auction. I am aware that many of you make Sagebrush your commercial destination with regularity and I want to help each of you establish a financial garrison, if you will, here in town. As a thank you for your hard work, when you register a business account with us today, we are offering a short-term, interest-free thirty percent advance on your auction proceeds. To claim your money now, you'll need only see one of our employees, then after a speedy appraisal of your livestock, you'll have *your* money in *your* hands for *your* share of *your* future sales!"

As if on cue, the employees scattered among the crowd began to cheer relentlessly and soon those in attendance were caught up in ecstatic applause. Best waved, said inaudible thank yous, and bowed graciously to the people. He took a step to the side of the podium soaking in the attention and motioned for Peregrine Page to join him. Best shook Perry's hand and brought the crowd to another wave of ovation by raising it triumphantly overhead. Perry, holding the ceremonial scissors in the other hand, stood on stage basking in the publicity. One of the employees encouraged some of the esteemed guests and local business owners to join them, and somehow Martin Kelly found his way onstage, too. At the sound of a drumroll and yet more clapping, the gang posed for Porter's picture then cut the red ribbon. Perry made his speech as the bank's employees were already signing up new accounts and giving away gift baskets. George Best casually strolled back to the vault, whistling while returning to his ledgers.

Flush with paper representing value still in their herds, the folks in town for the auction unleashed a frenzy of economic activity on Sagebrush over the two days following the grand opening. Sales at the Parlor continued to surge. Both the Emporium and Feed Store found it difficult to keep their shelves stocked, each unprepared for the advance demand.

Some of the vendors, intent on offloading their equine at the sale, were craftier with their business and sought to utilize the advance from Best to increase their profits. After many miles and weeks over rough terrain en route to the markets of Sagebrush, they paid a visit to the local blacksmith. Cooper Emmons, a dedicated tradesman yet not a current economic events analyst, was baffled to see bank notes used to settle for his farrier services, but reluctantly agreed to terms on account of there being a new local branch of Best's Bank and Trust.

Dillon and Rebecca Turk were also perplexed by the gall of some of their customers at the Livery Stables who became insolent after having their assumptions about the universality of Best's bank notes challenged. Seemingly overnight, the landscape changed, and the Turk's thought it sensible to exercise caution engaging with this new currency. The Turks sought the counsel of Nicholas Scoville concerning the matter and had their reservations validated.

"This is getting out of hand!" Scoville said.

"Well, sir, we didn't bring this to your attention to get your anger up," Rebecca Turk replied.

"You are a kind lady, Mrs. Turk. Never you bother with my well-being, I believe there are things in this world that deserve our ire. This preposterousness of Perry and Best's is fraught with the opportunity for abuse, and I will not stand idly by as good people like you two are bullied into the schemes of swindlers. Have any other business owners voiced their concerns to you?"

"You know Cooper Emmons, sir?" Dillon asked.

"I do."

"If he's askin' questions, I couldn't say for sure, but there must be others, too."

"How soon can you find out and get me a list of their names?"

"We'll get on it today, sir. Hope to let you know by dark." Rebecca said.

"Very well, thank you. Good day, to you both."

Dillon and Rebecca immediately made their way to the smithy to inquire whether his concerns were indeed shared by others. They approached the stone furnace where a hammer was punishing a red-hot iron rod and were startled to see Charles Crandall wielding the tools.

"Mr. Crandall, hello sir! We didn't expect to find you here, where's Cooper?" Dillon asked.

Crandall smiled, "Every now and then someone's got to remind Cooper how it'd ought to be done! You might find him 'round back!" Crandall pointed the hammer over his shoulder to a doorway.

Behind the smithy they found Cooper Emmons dominating conversation with Josiah, Levi, and Martin Kelly.

". . . and that's how I knowed it to be a rattler. You shoulda seent it, Martin. Josiah picked up the sixer blind then, BLAMMO! No mas la serpentino."

"That's quite the long bow ye draw, Mr. Emmons," Martin said.

"Shoo fire, then what happened next was . . ."

"That's quite enough, Cooper," Josiah said. "Thank you for the generous account, though." Just then, he noticed Dillon and Rebecca heading their way. "Alright, quit talkin' about 'em, here they come!" The jape was not lost on Dillon and the two shook hands.

"Good to see you, Josiah. Look, I wish this were a social visit. We came here on business with Cooper, but we'd do well to talk to all of you if'n you got the time."

"Very well," the rest of the men nodded in agreement.

"Well, it seems to me that we may have a problem developin' with our newest neighbor here in town. I think that George Best fella may have misunderstood our small-town hospitality and taken advantage of our good graces by meddlin' in our business."

"Go on." Josiah rubbed the scruff on his chin.

"Well, you see, for some reason he's got a lot of folks believin' they can settle their accounts with us by usin' his bank notes. We've talked to Scoville, and I think we need to have a meetin' of the minds about this."

Martin Kelly spoke up, "Now Mr. Turk, I don't understan' what the fuss is about. Mr. Best seems a good man and he's drivin' a lot of business our way."

"Truth is," Dillon said, "I don't know the man all that well. At the risk of soundin' like a gossip, I've heard rumors that he's got secrets which may or may not have already been used against him."

"Now, Dillon," Josiah said, "I've heard such talk and it's just that—talk. You expect us to confront this Best fella on account of some hearsay?"

"You're right, I beg your pardon. I don't mean to spread lies about the man, but imagine you take your cattle to auction in a couple days—"

"Ah, I ain't bringin' any this go-round."

"Now hear me out. Imagine you take your cattle to auction in a couple days and instead of placin' money in your hand, the buyer slaps a receipt down and tells you to retrieve the coin yourself. Seems a little rude, but it don't stop there. Now just to settle I gotta involve someone else. Let's say I don't have any business with this Best's Bank and Trust, well now I gotta pay a portion of my earnings to open an account and for what? The hope he's got my gold when I go to collect? Again, I say, I don't know this man. Why should I trust him with all my money? He's lyin' to folks already, Josiah! Tellin' 'em these notes are good all over town without so much as consultin' us. Not only is it insultin', but it don't inspire the kind of faith to earn my business. When too many folks start to believe this liar, what option I got but to go along to keep tradin'?"

"This true? Is this happenin'?" Levi asked.

"Oh yeah," Cooper said, "Why just within the past three days folks been tricklin' in here lookin' to swap iron for that stuff. At first, I told 'em 'no' and they pulled out they silver, but then these folks start sayin' all kinds of nonsense about havin' they silver up at Best's and 'this here paper's proof' and 'don't I got business set up with the biggest bank in the West' and all this other bully so finally I says 'fine' and start collectin' from the bank at the end of the day. Well, 'cept for yesterday, I been meanin' to get up there, but I got busy."

Charles Crandall had appeared from his toils at Cooper's anvil and Josiah noticed him nodding along in agreement.

"Alright, fine, tell Scoville I'll hear him out," Josiah said. Dillon and Rebecca appeared visibly relieved, but Martin balked.

"Ye can't be serious, Mr. Rush. Most folk in town don't share Mr. Turk's alarm. Ask Mr. Emmons if he's ever had a problem gettin' the gold and silver he's owed from one of these bank notes." Cooper shook his head at Martin's inquiry. "'Tis but a small convenience fer the customer and it has great benefits fer our bottom lines. Cooper has no doubt seen an increase in his business. Sagebrush is goin' ta need the genius of a man like Best to lead her into da future."

"Perhaps a man like Best can have my gunpowder kegs here in a timely manner, too?" Josiah said.

Martin tilted his head and pointed a finger in Josiah's direction. "Now that's not my fault." The man was embarrassed and sought to save face. "Ye see my supplier had a bit o' trouble wit—"

"It's fine, Martin, just don't give my refund in no bank notes," Josiah said.

Martin watched the gang walk away, and in no time he stood in the lobby of Best's Bank and Trust demanding to see Peregrine Page.

"Perry, listen to me. Right now, ye need to be seekin' legal support fer the adoption of these bank notes fer use in trade." Martin Kelly considered Perry reclining comfortably behind his new desk.

"What kind of nonsense is this? People are free to trade whatever they want, are they not? Why would we need any legal help?" Perry asked.

"Not everyone has taken kindly to the adoption of Best's plans."

"Don't be so dramatic. Why, even the mayor and that Marshal Oglesby have both opened accounts here. They're spending bank notes just as easily as coin, too. Tomorrow is the start of the Auction and after that, there won't be anyone left in Sagebrush, not even that contrarian Scoville, that would be crazy enough to deny the benefit and prosperity we bring to this town. Thank you for your concern. Good day, Martin."

As Martin left the bank, a group of citizens gathered at the law offices of Nicholas Scoville, Esq. concerned about the false claims of Best's Bank and Trust.

12

Josiah made it home from Scoville's late. He stayed awake a great deal of the night, troubled by the abruptness with which an idea like Best's took hold. When he finally awoke due to a knock at the door it was well into the morning. Stumbling out of bed, he shimmied on his pants and grabbed his revolver. Having lost his head in the void of the folds of his shirt, he tripped his way to the door. Disheveled and dirty, he cracked it open half expecting trouble, half expecting Levi. Instead, radiating in the glory of the morning, Lorraine Baxter stood at his threshold. She moved slowly to not alarm the dumbstruck man staring blankly back at her and casually lowered the barrel of Josiah's firearm. When his offense suddenly occurred to him, he apologized profusely.

"It's quite alright, Mr. Rush. I'm sorry to have disturbed you," she said. "I can return some other time."

"No, no! Uh, please. What can I do for you, Miss Lorraine?"

"I've come to return your shirt." She held out the clean folded fabric procured earlier in the week at the Emporium.

"Well thank you." He tossed the shirt onto the table behind him. It slid off and crumpled into a chair. "Awful long way for such a simple errand, no?"

"It's no problem, Mr. Rush, I'm terribly sorry about the other day."

"Quite alright," he smiled, "and please, call me Josiah."

"Very well, Josiah, have a good day." She gradually turned to leave.

"What's it been? Five days? Take you that long to work up the nerve to come see me and bring this back?" He raised an eyebrow.

"It *has* been five days. Have you not worked up the nerve to come see *me* and retrieve it?"

"I've got others," he said.

"And I fear how long it would take me to launder them. It required multiple washes to cleanse those deeply soiled threads, and I'm not referring to baby Carson's contributions, either."

Embarrassment surprised Josiah. "My, you're as courageous as you are breathtakin'." When the words fell out, they both stood there disarmed, figuratively.

Josiah watched for her response as he slowly moved to unbutton his shirt. Despite covering her mouth, Lorraine's laughter was evident.

"What are you doing? You crazy fool!" she asked.

"Reckon it's time for a clean shirt, apparently been wearin' this one almost a week now." He retrieved the button up from the chair and began to change.

"I don't see why if, as you said, you've got others."

"Well, aren't you clever? Come on in, I'll make us up some breakfast."

"Mr. Rush, I'm— "

"Please, just Josiah."

"Right. Josiah. Well, I'm not sure that's entirely appropriate."

Josiah poked his head through the doorway. With a hand to his forehead, he scanned the empty corrals, the vacant stables, and the cow pastures.

"Ah," he shrugged "I don't think the cattle will care."

He swung the door wide and walked away headed for the kitchen. Lorraine paused. She keenly considered the amount of trust he placed in her, noting the revolver abandoned by the open door. She straightened the front of her dress and took a step into the house where her bootheel clopped against the hardwood floor. At that, Josiah closed his eyes, one corner of his mouth curled up into a smile.

"Dirty shirts and dangerous weapons strewn about . . ." she said as Josiah lit the stove. ". . . a soldier with a conscience, tender with a child, and hospitable to a guest . . ." she hesitated and sat. ". . . troubled, maybe."

"You think you got me figured, huh?"

"Haven't even begun to know."

Josiah stopped whisking their eggs. "You're right about that," he lied. Josiah felt vulnerable at hearing her accurate insights, but also quietly comforted in knowing he was understood.

"Forgive me, I've been too assuming," she said. Lorraine put her hands on her lap and smoothed out her dress.

"Let's see," Josiah said, returning to the eggs. "A woman with skills, smart and independent, bored with small talk. Kind to the workin' girls. Moody, maybe?"

Lorraine's mouth dropped to a gaping smile, at once flattered by the attention and offended by his accusation.

She managed an exasperated "Asshole!" and then cocked her head to the side, her eyes reflectively scanning the ceiling, ". . . but guilty as charged."

Josiah chuckled and poured the eggs into a sizzling cast iron skillet. "That new mom down there at the store tells me you're a nurse, that right? Says *you* delivered her boy, not the sawbones. What's the story there?"

"Well, Pearl was in labor and Dr. Hoyle hadn't yet arrived; it was just me and Mrs. Turk. Sometimes you have to do whatever it takes."

"I see."

"She's a brave girl, that Pearl. I do worry about her, though. She's awful young and well, I think Rebecca is willing to teach her to be a seamstress. It would be an honest way to provide for the child."

"Rebecca is a fine woman, heart of gold."

"I consider her a dear friend, already."

Josiah prepared their plates and sat down to enjoy breakfast. Throughout the meal, Lorraine shared how she had come to be a nurse in the war and how the experience led to her current appointment assisting the traveling Dr. Hoyle. Josiah spoke freely of his dislike for the man, which amused Lorraine.

When they finished, Lorraine grabbed the empty plates and made for the sink. She washed as he dried and put away the dishes. Upon completion, Josiah offered a tour of the ranch so the two set off to see the grounds.

"I had the main house built with timber from the mill," Josiah said. "You can see from out here that some of the logs are book matched. They harvested all these just northwest of the property and they float 'em down the river, I'm sure you've seen 'em from town. They drive 'em all the way to the docks where the mill workers pluck 'em, dry 'em, and cut 'em up for sale. A lot of good lumber like this is makin' its way back east nowadays."

They strolled down the hill to a smaller place by a tributary that intersects the river at the edge of the property. "The guest house is more of the same. I had it built when I thought I might hire some labor if I ever grew the ranch past the point of what I could handle myself." He crouched down for a hand full of dirt and scattered it on the wind. "These days though, I'm content. Got quieter ambitions. Been reflectin' on why I'm drawn to this kinda life. Ain't got all the answers, but I do know that it ain't for the sake of growth and the hassle it brings."

"Josiah," she gently touched his shoulder, but said nothing else.

"Anyway, over here's the corral," he stood abruptly and began walking. "You mighta heard it called a paddock where you're from. On occasion I still relive my time with the cavalry by trainin' horses."

Lorraine wondered whether shyness or defensiveness drove him from the tenderness of her gesture.

"Come on, I'll show you the stables, introduce you to a few of 'em. I've got two that help me with that crop field over yonder past the cattle. Also got Nero in there, thanks to my friend Levi. You'll have to meet him."

Josiah had Lorraine feed the horses and found her enthusiasm for the team that drew the plows impressive. He excused himself to check on a water trough just outside, and when he returned Lorraine was braiding the mane of one of the giant Percherons.

"Strong," Josiah said. "The loggers use 'em to transport felled lumber. They'll pull a plow with relative ease."

"They're absolutely enchanting. I've never spent much time around horses."

"No? Well, they're like us in some ways, not so much in others. These two belong together; there's a safety they feel in the company of one another. Keep 'em fed, though, and they're happy. They don't show signs of longin', and they don't need freedom like we do."

"That's it then? Forever happy conformed to the will of men?"

"Hmm. Ain't a man alive that won't conform in some way to the will of another. Otherwise, wouldn't nothin' ever get done. Men cooperate with each other until we don't. That's the song and dance of human history, but I never seen a horse wield a rifle."

"No, I suppose not."

Josiah found himself at the empty stall of his mare, "They just serve, even unto death. Suppose that's as noble an example as any."

Lorraine let the braid fall against the horse's neck and walked confidently over to Josiah. She reached up, fixed his collar, and let her hands rest on his shoulders.

"Say, cowboy, why don't you take me for a ride."

No sooner was Nero saddled than the two sat atop the steed. Josiah felt the warmth of Lorraine's arms as she wrapped them instinctually around his ribs. She pulled herself close.

The additional rider did not seem to bother Nero. If anything, Josiah thought Lorraine's presence conjured some manners in him. The three followed a creek north into the rockier pines at an unhurried pace. After a while, Josiah turned from the trail to ascend a hill.

In a clearing at the top, Josiah stopped and dismounted. He offered a hand to help Lorraine down. Instead, she kicked a leg over and fell, dead-weight, right into his arms. He caught her but stumbled a step before securing his balance. The spontaneity aroused a dangerous, wild laughter from deep within her. Josiah found it as thrilling as striking gold. He had discovered something just as rare and precious and could not imagine ever growing tired of the sound. In fact, he suddenly feared a life without it.

The occasion revealed to Josiah his incompleteness; he wished for a way to capture her laugh—to revisit if ever he felt alone. He wished more so not to possess that piece of her, but to strengthen the bonds that were forming so he might continue to enjoy those little moments as they naturally occurred. Josiah treasured Lorraine's laughter because he treasured her. Even if he could capture the moment, he would still crave her essence.

The world around them erupted as he held her; every blade of grass and every rock, every gust of wind and ray of sunlight joined in their chorus of joy. There was no occasion, no pomp, no bravado, or spectacle of human action, but there was a celebration all the same. It was pure, absent of the corruption that decays and strains human connection. It was the salutation of the newest regeneration of an amaranthine power, ancient and holy.

Lorraine wiped her watering eyes as she calmed down and finally looked up at the face of the man holding her; a face that had changed, it seemed, in the ephemeral span of her plunge. His once fatigued eyes offered signs of relief from their burdens. There now shone a tenderness in them. The concern once evidenced by his clenched jaw had given way to rest. The strength of his arms secured more than her body as they effortlessly cradled her against his own. As she nuzzled her head into his shoulder, she harbored a newfound appreciation that gravity was not the only force, just then, that caused her to fall.

Josiah took a few steps toward the edge of the hillside and sat down next to Lorraine.

"Look there," he said. Beyond the winding tree line following the stream across rolling hills was a town nestled in a pocket created by a much larger river. Sagebrush appeared, from their perspective, to be as unmoving as the mountains. Down below, however, the town would soon be abuzz with the fervent activity of the first day of the auction.

Lorraine clasped her hands and brought them to her chin, "I would have never thought that in such a short time this place and its people could have grown on me as they have. But I sit here looking out over everything and I think about all those people down there. Rebecca, how tough and good she is, and sweet Pearl for all the mess that seems to follow her. Even Lawrence." Lorraine turned her attention from the town up to Josiah. "It feels like I'm already finding roots here with purpose and people that I care about. Even the mean-spirited joker from the Parlor turned out to be a thoughtful, honorable man."

"Don't you go about town spreadin' lies about me now, Lorraine."

She playfully slapped his chest, then in the same motion hugged his arm. "Lawrence certainly came to your defense. You're a good friend. Even when you sic your dog, Will, on him."

Josiah chuckled recalling the event. "That was kinda mean, huh?" He liked that Lorraine saw him not just for who he was, but the man he could be. Without commanding him, she inspired Josiah to hold himself to a higher standard. He reckoned any man would be lucky to benefit from the care of a woman like that.

"Josiah, you are a man admired by so many, including men like Lawrence. How does that not provoke some pride in you?"

He fell silent for a long time. Josiah would take a breath as though he was about to speak, but his chest would deflate without so much as a sigh. It puzzled Lorraine, she thought it was a rather innocuous question. She meant to flatter him, even. To see Josiah hesitate, to struggle as he did, meant that she had somehow struck a nerve. She regretted asking the question and was about to retract it when he finally broke the silence.

"No, the admiration of men for things no one should glorify does not provoke pride in me. In fact, I carry a mess of regret."

"Josiah!? What are you talking about?"

Lorraine had referenced his character, but Josiah spoke of his past. Realizing his mistake, he deliberated whether to broach the topic further. By the time he concluded that he should have changed the subject it was too late as he found himself already answering her.

"Well, I was in the war; you know that much. What you don't seem to know—what everyone else does, thanks to Levi and company—is that I got some accolades for it, some medals and whatnot. Afterward, spent some time with a badge. Maybe for my part I think too little of people, but despite their praise, despite the affirmations that what I done was right and good, no one else can see the eyes of the . . ." Josiah stared off into the distance. ". . . they tell me otherwise. Accuse me. Haunt me. So no, I'd trade all their admiration for a clean blade and a clean bore."

Lorraine found his account sobering. She crawled in front of Josiah and sat on her heels to disrupt his withdrawn gaze.

"Make no mistake, Josiah Rush. You are admired not for the sins you have committed, but for the man you have become. You don't understand the effect you have on others—on me. You carry guilt and I'll not deny you that, but guilt does not condemn us, only teaches us the things we no longer wish to do. It leads us to seek and accept forgiveness. Now, you go on and carry that shame if it keeps you humble. It's a powerful thing to be honest about your capability to make mistakes, if you believe they were. But don't be hampered by the past, let it help guide your steps forward in this life."

Josiah removed his hat and ran a hand through his hair. He shifted against the hard ground and said, "I've learned how to make peace with the sins of my youth. I just have to do it over again every day."

Lorraine thought less about the words he spoke, and more about how his heartbreak affected her. She was overwhelmed by the desire to nurse his invisible wounds.

"You are an honest man," she said at last. "Troubled, indeed."

"Is that troublin' to you?"

"We all have our grief, Josiah. Will you find *mine* troubling?"

Josiah shook his head, "I'd share in the worst of it, if workin' through it meant hearin' your laughter again. Why, I believe I'd sacrifice any hope of ever findin' my own, just to see you in another moment of pure joy."

"A warrior and a poet. And to think, everyone said you were so guarded."

"So you been askin' about me, huh?"

"Don't flatter yourself, cowboy."

"Ah, I ain't guarded really, mostly I find I can overwhelm folks, so I try to keep to myself. Though most times I find that keepin' to myself gets me all bound up so when folks do inquire of me, I end up meaner than I mean."

"I see."

"Forgive me, though, I have shared much more than I ever intended." His tone abruptly changed, becoming upbeat and inquisitive. "Enough about me, you were a nurse in the war, right? I'm curious to know what kind of spirit let's a woman see the worst in humanity and still hunger for the kind of adventure that makes her board a train and move, by herself, into the wilder parts of this world. You runnin' from somethin'? Someone?"

"Mmm, you were closer with the hunger for adventure. If I were running, I'd say I was running *to* something," she glanced up at Josiah, but did not speak all that she thought. "I suppose I have my regrets, too, if I'm to be forthright, but they *inspire* that spirit, as you put it, not smother it. There are certain things I can't stand the thought of, like wasting this fleeting spark of existence. I try, not always successfully, but I try to embrace my moments of despair because once I've dealt with them, there's more room for that joy you seem to be missing." Lorraine poked his arm.

"But aren't you afraid?"

"You mean, do I have my concerns about life out here? Sure. I'm concerned about homesickness and loneliness; I'm concerned about being in over my head trying to care for people, like with Pearl; other concerns, too, but my *fear* is missing out on actually living! I dare say, I think facing that fear requires a certain measure of boldness and adventure. Wouldn't you?" Lorraine put her hands triumphantly on her hips.

"Whatever brought you to this hill right here, sharin' this view right now with me—whether it was boldness or somethin' else—I'm glad of it."

"Me too."

Josiah and Lorraine stayed on that hill until well into the afternoon. They sat side by side watching great herds of cattle moving in and out of Sagebrush like swirling eddies in the river. The locomotives made their way through the Depot in predictable intervals. Some headed for the mountains to the east pulling as many as twenty cattle cars at a time. They saw mule deer prancing in distant meadows and red-tails diving after field mice. The rustle of windswept leaves and the chirp of the occasional squirrel decorated the passing time; time that could not have been better spent by either of them doing anything other than the nothing-at-all they were doing just then.

"Well," Josiah said at last, "Suppose we ought to get you back before dark. I'm curious to see how Levi made out today, anyhow. What do you say I take you into town and we grab a drink at the Parlor?"

"That sounds lovely."

Josiah retrieved Nero. As they rode past the house and beyond the great bend in the river, Josiah explained to Lorraine that Sagebrush had been a thriving town prior to the railroad, but once that came through the town truly blossomed.

"Ah!" Lorraine said. "So that's why the auction is now such a big deal. That Mr. Scoville sure has a keen sense for the needs of these pioneers."

"So, you've met Scoville?"

"Yes, what a charming and delightful fellow. I think his foresight with the Auction House was nothing short of genius."

"Have to agree. I have every reason to believe he is among the best of us."

Upon reaching town they made their way through the sea of mud and leather to the Parlor. They happened upon Levi and Cooper just outside.

"Well, how'd she go boys?" Josiah asked.

"Ooh wee!" Cooper hollered. Levi Holdegel just smiled and gave Josiah an aggressive clap on the shoulder. He produced a money pouch that was half full of silver and half full of bank notes. Lorraine gawked at the proceeds.

"Not a bad haul, friend. Congratulations!" Josiah said. "Levi, Cooper, this here's Miss Lorraine Baxter. She's a friend of mine and a nurse that's here in town a while. Lorraine, meet Levi Holdegel and Cooper Emmons."

"Howdy," Cooper said.

"Pleased to meet you, ma'am. Rebecca Turk speaks highly of you." Levi tipped his hat.

"It's a pleasure, gentlemen. Give Mrs. Turk my regards."

"Levi," Josiah said, "you better get outta them bills tomorrow, ain't nothin' good can come from them bankers' schemes."

"Yeah no shit," Levi looked at Lorraine, "Pardon ma'am. Josiah, you missed the stink at the Auction House when Scoville's guys first tried to refuse them bills to settle commissions."

"First? Wait, you're sayin' Scoville caved?"

"I did no such thing," Nicholas Scoville appeared from behind Cooper and gave the blacksmith a fright. He recoiled, and Scoville said, "Don't worry, I'm used to it."

"I didn't mean to insinuate . . ." Josiah said.

"Never mind that. Earlier, Best sent a representative down to the Auction House after people complained that *he* lied.

It was a whole ordeal, silly and needless. A childish display intended to make me look ridiculous in front of that nosy reporter. They literally acted as an intermediary, accepting payment in bank notes, then closing the sale with me in real gold money. It was humiliating the way they were apologizing to customers for *my* unreasonableness. MINE! Do you believe that?!"

"But it seems like everyone got what they wanted, what's the problem?" Lorraine asked.

"The problem is, my reputation has been smeared and my transaction records now show a day's worth of business with Best's Bank and Trust, not our neighboring ranches. I don't like it; I don't like the leverage Best has."

"Don't get ahead of yourself," Lorraine said. "You're not beholden to the man in any way and you've got four more days of business ahead of you. He's the one bearing the extra expense of having a representative at your place of business, not the other way around. Take some comfort in that."

Scoville smiled at Lorraine then said to Josiah, "How's a toad like you end up with a treasure of a woman like her?"

Lorraine was tickled by Scoville's presumption, but even more so to see Josiah squirm at the awkwardness it created.

"Oh, uh, no we're not, I mean . . ."

"Mmm mmm," she shook her head at Scoville. Cooper rolled his eyes and Levi groaned.

"Well, if you're expecting an apology for the mistake then you'll be left wanting. You two are strutting around here like autumn whitetail," Scoville said.

Levi and Cooper laughed, "Hey Josiah, we'll be inside. Save y'all a seat."

"Josiah, there's another thing," Scoville said. "It wasn't just that lady that showed up from the bank, today. She was there, to add insult to injury, with security. Not just some cowboy with a six shooter, but a badge." Josiah squinted as Scoville continued, "Marshal Oglesby, himself, for reasons that make no sense to me, was overseeing our transactions."

"What?"

"Josiah, listen to me. I am a cautious man, a careful man, and I like to know who I'm up against. I notice things, and folks have been off since returning from that little bounty hunt a couple weeks back." Josiah was subconsciously shaking his head. "Yes, yes they have. I know something happened to Waddell, but I can't get a straight answer about what it was."

Lorraine picked up on the passionate intrigue of Scoville and the strong reluctance of Josiah to answer his inquisition. With an embellished yawn she interrupted, "You boys and your silly talk, always so serious and boring. You're putting me to sleep. Josiah, would you please see me to my room? I'm afraid I simply can't manage to stay awake any longer. Mr. Scoville, it has been so great to see you again. Do be safe getting home." With that she grabbed Josiah's hand and walked away, practically dragging the man through the Parlor doors as he waved goodbye to Scoville.

"Treasure of a woman!" he heard Scoville shout as they rounded the corner out of sight.

Inside the Parlor, Philippe La Brune sent the cheerful notes from his piano sailing on the smoke that encircled the card tables where men drank and gambled away their profits. Levi and Cooper had found accommodations at a poker table with Will Richardson, Jacoby Sutton, and their new friend Henry Olt. On the stage was a company of dancers in red and black ruffled skirts. On the floor was a company of Martin's girls getting handsy with the travelers, lifting loot from those who refused their advances. Martin Kelly sat with Dr. Hoyle and watched his girls while Dr. Hoyle watched Lorraine lead Josiah by the hand, shamelessly, through the middle of the saloon and up the stairway to the second-floor rooms.

"Well, this is it," Lorraine said as they arrived at her door. She turned around to see Josiah staring off into the distance.

"I've had such a wonderful day," she said, moving her head to meet his eyes.

"Me too," he said, "It's been the best I've had in as long a time as I can remember. It's been an honor to share it with you. Goodnight, Lorraine." He tipped his hat and turned around.

"No," she said quickly, grabbing his hand to stop him from leaving, "Josiah Rush, I would forever hold your secrets if that burden were the price to, just once again, hear the sound of your voice. Now, you're carrying a weight you were never meant to carry. What happened to that Waddell fellow?"

Josiah's eyes dilated and sweat began to form at his temples, his heart rate increased, and his breathing became heavy.

"You don't have to face this alone," she said. Josiah moved his shaky head around to see that the hallway was clear before he spoke.

"Official story gonna be a snakebite. Ain't a lie, but it ain't the truth. Waddell may have been a dead man already, but he was helped along. Oglesby killed him. Some folks would see it as a good thing," Josiah's top lip curled and he held back the tears forming in his eyes, "but it was murder. No trial, no judge," each word became harder to say, "no jury, no doctor, no nurse," his eyes met Lorraine's, "he might've deserved it, but not that way."

"I'm tired of seeing men die, too," she took off his hat and pulled him into her shoulder. She felt his hands wrap around her lower back as she ran her fingers through his hair. The two stood there, affectionate and exposed, for a long time before they were startled by a door closing and the footsteps of a stranger.

After saying goodbye, Lorraine pushed closed the hotel door behind her. She slumped to the ground inside the room, exhausted, framing her face in her hands. With widened eyes she desperately searched the fabric of her petticoat as though on it she would find a written explanation of her heart. Josiah left unseen through the hotel lobby.

13

Porter High placed the final piece of tin onto the stereotype and carefully transferred it to the cylinder. He took a step back to appreciate the intimidating piece of iron clad machinery residing in his workshop. There was some mystery to its engineering, a magic to its function, but Porter was well versed in the routine operations of the printing press. Large rolls of blank news sheets occupied much of the remaining real estate in the room. Their distinct scent blended with the oily aroma of the ink to create a fragrance that, to Porter, smelled like money. He started the steam-powered engine and watched the conveyer spin. Porter High then fed the paper into the machine, creating the first copies of the inaugural edition of *The Sagebrush Sentinel*.

Outside, Cassidy Turk used his sleeve to clean a dirty window and peer in on the process. Little Jasper wasn't tall enough to see. Before long, he had dragged over a wooden crate, climbed up, and stood on his tiptoes. Even still, his eyes barely crested the window frame to which he desperately clung with the tips of his fingers.

Dillon Turk had given his approval for the boys to start working for Porter. For a few coppers a day, they would soon be delivering the *Sentinel* all over town. Little Jasper intended to spend his earnings on the candy he liked at the Emporium, but Cassidy had other plans for his wages. Porter had told him to keep his eye on the paper, there was a spectacle coming to Sagebrush and he would want to buy a ticket.

The printing press ran, and the paper was cut, folded, and tied. The boys delivered on their end of the bargain and were richly rewarded as promised. Rebecca Turk beamed when she told of her enterprising young businessmen and was grateful to Porter for the opportunity.

"You see the paper, today?" Levi asked Josiah. They leaned against a railing out front of the Livery Stables with Dillon Turk. "Apparently the auction last month brought in quite the tally for this here town. Why, accordin' to that Porter feller, people all over been seein' record profits. I know I can attest to it; shoot, all my accounts will be settled once I collect on a drink and a visit with my oldest friend." He stared at Josiah, "Be a shame to take that horse over the price of a beer and old times."

"Alright, alright, I get it," Josiah said. ". . . and that horse's *name* is Nero."

"Right, well, you been almost as inseparable from Nero as you have Miss Lorraine for weeks now. Suppose you ain't got no time for a poor cripple like me, I guess."

"Poor, you say?" Josiah referenced a brand-new hat atop Levi's head. "Guess the first round is gonna have to be on me."

"Wonderful! After that you can buy me the round I'm owed!"

"Dillon, what d'you say? Join us?" Josiah asked.

Dillon Turk hollered for Cassidy to look after things for a while and the three men set off for the Parlor. On their way, Levi stopped by to invite Scoville. After his collegiate acquaintance, Dr. Hoyle, had neglected to bid farewell before leaving town for business elsewhere, Scoville was heartened by the offer. In his haste, he failed to lock his office until the men asked if he was forgetting something. Scoville then rummaged for his keys, visibly excited to have been included.

They were almost to the Parlor when a voice rose from across the street, "That's the ugliest bunch of ruffians I ever seent in these parts, y'all'd back a buzzard off a gut-wagon!"

"Okay old man, how's about you just get on back to learnin' them hens to cluck!" Levi yelled back to Crandall.

"How's about a drink instead?" Crandall flipped the sign on his door and did a little saddle-sore shuffle across the street. He greeted the men, and they all made their way to a table inside the empty saloon.

"What's new, Lawrence?" Josiah said.

"'What's new?' you ask. Why beseech me, we have a paper for that now, sir." Lawrence tossed a copy of the *Sentinel* on the bar for Josiah to see.

Levi leaned over to Crandall, "What's his problem?"

"Apparently our friend Lawrence here ain't happy about bein' replaced as the town gossip," Crandall said.

Lawrence waved his hand dismissively. "Laugh it up, gentlemen!"

The men took a seat and Josiah grabbed the paper. He joined them while glancing over the headlines.

"Didn't think you cowboys could read," Scoville said.

"Let's see," Josiah flipped a page, "Ah yes, here they are—obituaries. RIP Nicholas Scoville. Apparently, his big mouth got him pummeled."

"Ugh, it's Nicholas Scoville, *Esquire*. Do I get no respect, even in death?"

Suddenly Josiah sat straight up, intrigued by what he had truly been reading. There on page three, buried between an advertisement for an attraction in the city and an opinion piece on the latest in women's fashion, was the public statement from Marshal Oglesby on the fate of the outlaw Waddell.

"Well, gentlemen, we all seen this comin'," Josiah slammed the paper down and drove his knife right through the article into the table. *SNAKE BITE CLAIMS LIFE OF WANTED CRIMINAL* the headline read. A silence fell among them. Scoville gazed inquisitively at a confused Dillon Turk. Suddenly, from outside, they heard someone yelling. Levi and Josiah exchanged a worried glance and stood up from the table.

"Gentlemen, order three whiskeys. We'll be right back." Levi said.

The two men burst out of the saloon doors and stepped into the dusty intersection just as Cooper Emmons emerged from around the post office. Still wearing a blacksmith's leather apron and gloves, he was waving the first edition of *The Sagebrush Sentinel*. All worked up, cussing and spitting, he was bound headlong for the courthouse.

"Oglesby!" Cooper shouted, "Oglesby, what is this?! This ain't at all what happ—" Josiah and Levi each hooked their arms on either side of Cooper and dragged him into the Parlor trailing pieces of the newspaper in their wake. Deputy Butch Eaton watched with squinted eyes as they disappeared into the saloon.

"Enough! Let go of me, would ya?" Cooper shook free and adjusted his twisted clothes. "I don't understand what business you got interferin' with the truth. I seent the look in your eyes when we buried Waddell, Josiah, so why you lettin' the marshal get away with this?!"

"I *knew* it!" Scoville said.

"Cooper! We are tryin' to look out for you!" Levi threw up his hands. "For your own good."

"Scoville! Not a word of this to anybody, do you understand me?!" Josiah said.

"Not yet, I don't! No sir! You've got some explaining to do!"

Dillon Turk turned green as Charles Crandall shouted for silence. He pointed at all of them, snapped his fingers, then pointed to the table. They each took a seat and Lawrence brought over a whole bottle of whiskey.

"Thank you, Lawrence. Give us a minute, please?" Crandall asked.

"Of course." Lawrence returned to the bar.

"Here's how this works," Crandall said to the group. "Scoville's got questions, Cooper's confused, and none of us . . ." Crandall gestured toward Josiah and Levi, ". . . have made the effects of all this very clear. That changes right now." Everyone nodded. Crandall yielded to Scoville who inquired about what exactly transpired in the desert. Josiah described in detail the detainment, the snake bite, and Oglesby's actions as well as their own. When he finished everyone affirmed to Scoville that the statements were true as they were told.

"Why in the hell haven't any of you come forward with this testimony?" Scoville asked.

Josiah held his hands out, palms up. "See, none of us make it a habit to regularly meddle in the affairs of law enforcement. We mostly steer clear of activities that would find us unfavorable in the sight of the law, don't we? Well, then it's got to be a matter of timin' if something's to be done. And I still ain't sure it'd ought to be."

"How can you say such a thing? *Of course* something ought to be done. What are you waiting for?" Scoville said.

"Well, let's say for a minute you're right. I don't imagine the marshal would take too kindly to us testifyin' to some higher authority about it. I don't know about you, but the idea of puttin' a target on my own back just don't seem a wise thing to do presently."

"Josiah, I thought you were better than this, thinking about saving yourself instead of standing up for justice!"

"Watch it. A man can't stand for justice where it don't abide. He certainly can't stand for it if he's lyin' in an abandoned mineshaft next to a dead suspect. Waddell wasn't able to see his day in court and the man that made sure of that won't see his, either." Josiah's attention turned to Cooper. "Look, the marshal is a representative of the capital and to hold him accountable legally takes a capital prosecutor to review and report evidence against him. Scoville will tell you that much. The victim's party don't even have the privilege to see that the evidence gets rightly presented. That prosecutor would just as soon, in this case, protect one of his own instead of seein' him hang for the death of a piece of shit like Waddell. See, when the government investigates the government, it's gonna find that the government done nothin' wrong; in which case we'd have only made an enemy. We'd find ourselves, in the court of public opinion, guilty of sidin' with a known rustler and murderer. I don't know about you, but that don't sound like the wise thing to do. We can't right every wrong."

Josiah was surprised that there were no protestations from Scoville. Crandall was nodding and Cooper hung his head.

"Cooper, we aren't made to endure death, but it is somethin' we gotta deal with. I wish we could unsee the whole thing. I'm angry and I know you are too; I think we got every right to be. I know you wanna reason with Oglesby and for the truth to come out, but I don't wanna see any of us ruined for it. This is a stand we can't make, it ain't like Waddell was one of us. Murderers make for poor martyrs."

Crandall was stern as he placed his fists on the table. "This is the last time we discuss the matter, agreed?"

Scoville mulled over Josiah's words and reluctantly agreed, "It's as you said, this must be a matter of timing and now, at least, is not the time."

Dillon Turk waved a hand as though to say he wanted to hear nothing more of the topic of Waddell's death ever again.

"Well, I think I've had about all the fun I can handle for one afternoon." Levi stood up from the table. "I'll see you gentlemen later."

"'Fore you go," Josiah said, "There's somethin' else. We've already made one pact here today; I'd like to propose another." The group scanned tentatively amongst themselves.

"What have you got in mind?" Scoville asked.

Josiah leaned in, "There's a lotta good folks at this table. We got our quarrels, sure, but we're more alike than not. Right now, things seem to be changin' fast. We got a lawman we can't trust, I think we got a banker who's up to somethin', and we got a mayor that ain't fit to keep this train on its tracks. I'd like us to keep an eye on things in town as they develop. Maybe take a look at what this Porter feller has to say in his paper and meet up once a week to share any other news."

"I don't think that's such a bad idea," Levi said.

"I agree," said Dillon and the rest of the men assented as well.

"Alright then. That's all I got for you." Josiah pried his knife from the table and re-sheathed it. He pointed to the paper, "Rest of that's just auction news, an ad for some travelin' show, and talk of the grand openin' over at the bank. Take a gander if you'd like but I think I'm gonna make my way back to the ranch 'fore long."

"Yeah, sounds good. I should prob'ly get back to work anyway," Crandall said. "I'll see y'all here next week then?"

The men nodded as they finished their drinks and gathered their belongings. They said their farewells and most of them trickled out while Levi met Lawrence at the bar to settle the tab. Josiah joined them and ordered another round.

"Lawrence, this one's on me," Josiah said.

"Yeah, that's what Levi tells me! I'll leave you gentlemen to it, just let me know if you need anything else." Lawrence wandered off.

"Been meanin' to catch up since Buffalo Junction," Levi said to Josiah. "How you been?"

"Good, I've been good. I hate that I ain't been around much, though."

"Ah, I understand. Got a woman now, huh? It is good to see you soften up a bit, maybe now you won't be such a prick."

"Ha! Well, you're right that Lorraine and I have been spendin' some time together, but it ain't like what you think. I mean she's a mighty fine woman, don't get me wrong. We're definitely fond of one another, but things are a little more complicated."

"How so?" Levi asked.

"I mean, I got the ranch and she's here for now, but who knows for how long. We ain't makin' plans for the future. Mostly we just sit, enjoyin' each other's company and watchin' the sun set."

"You're kiddin', right?" Levi's jaw dropped.

"No, why?"

"Man alive, you got fools all over this town fakin' sick to see her and you're tellin' me you ain't so much as got a—"

"Levi! C'mon now, that ain't really anybody's business."

"Even your best longtime friend?"

"Especially."

"Alright fine. Last I'll say on it is she seems like a rare bird, so don't be fiddle-headed and foul it up." Levi threw back a shot, "Hey, I was hopin' you could tell me when you was gonna come inspect the mortar 'round my well?"

The jest drew a try-me glare from Josiah. Levi was the only one who could somehow get away with pressing his buttons. It had been over a month since Buffalo Junction and Josiah hadn't spoken about the incident at the well.

"You know what pisses me off," Josiah said, "is that I just don't understand how you can be so cavalier about that after what all we been through. I mean, don't you feel *any*thing?"

"Just some gallows humor, relax."

"You're right," Josiah said. ". . . but hear me out. I mean, in spite of all we sacrificed, all we deal with as a result, I look around and I see corruption and the abuse of power, and I think, 'this ain't what I fought for.' I'm bothered by it. Why aren't you?"

"How can you say that? Like I ain't got a heart just 'cause I ain't mopin' about all the time?"

"Oh, is that what you think I do?"

"I *think* what you're doin' is finally startin' to come around. I *think* you hate that you realize you need other people but they ain't all good to each other. While you've been off for years on your little quest for peace, I've been livin' life and dealin' with actual problems." Levi held up what remained of his arm. "If I don't seem as bothered by 'em anymore it's 'cause I learned a long time ago to manage, is all. So don't criticize my cover if you're just now rejoinin' the fight!"

Lawrence Hoak appeared at the sound of raised voices and rebuked them. "I don't know what you two are thinkin', but if you don't stop this bickerin' there ain't no way we'll ever keep the wolves from the door."

Intrigued, Josiah said, "Go on."

Lawrence's voice dropped to a whisper. "Your hunches 'bout Best ain't without merit. I overheard a lot 'tween him and Perry. That's all I can say right now."

Levi straightened up, "I suppose folks underestimate you, don't they, Mr. Hoak?"

"What else you overheard?" Josiah asked.

"Nothin' about the marshal and Waddell if that's what you mean. Nothin' at all."

"That is what I mean, and I thank you for keepin' that under your hat." Josiah finished his drink and dropped payment on the bar. He said to Levi, "I suppose you may be right. I'll think on what you said, but don't let your knack for bearin' the misery of this world make you so callous you accept what's wrong as normal."

"Whatever you say, Josiah." Levi walked off.

14

"Lorraine, I can't stand it." Josiah sat a cup of coffee down on the kitchen table and took a seat.

"No one likes to see trouble on the horizon. You're a good man, Josiah." Lorraine rubbed his shoulders.

"Then why don't I feel like it?"

"You expect folks to be good to each other. When they aren't you want to act, but when you step out you feel all alone. That's a scary place to be." She took a seat across from him. "Darlin', I think Levi was right, there is a part of you that hates that you need others. If you didn't, then making your stand would be a whole lot easier, there'd be nothing to sacrifice. No relationships, no business, nothing. But it would be a sad and lonely world. Listen to me, there are others who share your concerns, and they need someone to be brave enough to risk all that first. It helps inspire them to find their own courage and join you."

"I regret the way I left things. I hope to make it right when I see Levi this afternoon."

"I'm sure you will. Don't forget you need to pick up some supplies today, so if you're meeting the guys you'd better get going."

"Suppose you're right. Thank you, Lorraine."

"Hey! Don't be so hard on yourself, cowboy."

Josiah saddled Nero and rode peacefully down the tall grassland pastures of his homestead. He passed the clear, wide river waters and made his way into town and up to the Emporium. From inside came the muddled sounds of shouting. Josiah paused at the door debating whether to enter. Pearl and Martin Kelly were bickering over what sounded to Josiah like living arrangements, and when it escalated to the point of shattering glass, Josiah decided to step inside. The heated squabble suddenly ceased as the bell above the door jingled. Martin turned his head in shame as Pearl retrieved a broom and pretended it had been an accident. Josiah apologized for the interruption and asked if there was a better time he could return, although the question was obviously one of propriety, not sincerity.

"Not at all, Mr. Rush," Pearl said, "we're done here." Martin Kelly stormed off to the back.

Josiah gathered his order and was outside loading up his saddlebags when Martin Kelly reappeared from the alley beside the store.

"Friday, Mr. Rush. Yer shipment will arrive on Friday. Save ye ten percent for the long delay, it's surely not the way I like to treat me customers."

"Very well. I thank you." Josiah added, "Got yourself a handful now ain't you, Martin?"

"Aye, that Pearl's a pistol."

"You two were really goin' at it in there, I reckon it likely ain't the first time either. Am I right?"

"Oh aye, things were fun for a while, but e'er since that boy she's got mad ideas about us becomin' a family. I just want me rent."

"I see. Well how *are* you takin' to fatherhood?"

"Fatherhood, Mr. Rush? I'm sure I don't have any idea what ye mean. There's no way of knowin' who dat child's father is."

Disappointment settled on Josiah like the heavy-laden bags on Nero, not unbearable but undeniable. He cinched a strap and led the horse away without acknowledging Martin's denial.

As Josiah headed down Main Street, he saw the opportunity for which he hoped when Levi stepped out of the bank tossing a coin pouch in his good hand. The two of them stood silent for a minute as if to judge the disposition of the other before finally shaking hands.

"You know I've been thinkin' about last—"

"Me too,"

"I'm sorry about—"

"Me too. You know I said some things that I really didn't—"

"Me too."

"Ha! Alright, then." The two men turned and headed for their weekly meeting at the Parlor.

Josiah tied Nero to the hitching post and waved to the old men rocking out front. Levi spat out the plug of tobacco he had been chewing and wiped the dust from his face with a handkerchief. The Parlor was busier than normal, but Crandall and company sat around a large table joined by Henry Olt. The friends had a few copies of the latest edition of *The Sagebrush Sentinel* spread out and were discussing train tickets when Josiah and Levi joined them.

"Afternoon, gentlemen," Josiah said. "Anything interestin' this week?"

"Ride the Rails, Josiah! You'd ought to see the latest promotional offer from our beloved Depot on passenger tickets to and from the big city!" Scoville tossed a copy of the paper across the table.

"Fifteen percent discount on train tickets when paid with Best's bank notes. Crafty."

"Turns out, the bank's loan program ain't limited to auction advances either," Crandall said. "Want to expand on that pretty piece of land you got out there north of the river? Well, don't worry about savin' for it, have it now and pay Best back a little at a time—for a premium of course."

"So instead of savin' with the goal of buyin' land, now folks will be driven to work by the fear of losin' what they can't afford in the first place. Sounds like tradin' a dream for a nightmare," Josiah said.

"Folks are free to make agreements as they see fit, Josiah," Henry Olt spoke up. "Ain't nothin' new about a land loan."

"I don't deny that; folks are free to do a whole lotta things that ain't wise. But heaven only knows where all that capital is comin' from."

"You're so suspicious and skeptical, why can't you see plainly that Best's methods are *savin'* people money?" Olt added.

"It may be savin' 'em money on a train ticket, but not on interest. You watch, it'll end up costin' 'em elsewhere, too, as prices start to climb."

The men bantered on for a while about the cost of feed and fencing, the shipments of ore and other exports from the territory. There was rumor of some civic project or other that was underway and following the railroad westward. They guffawed over the debut of a comic strip in the *Sentinel* portraying the mayor as a bloated man stuffing his pockets with tax revenue from auction transactions. A few whiskey drinks and family inquiries later, the men said their goodbyes and agreed to reconvene the following week.

They did so and continued in fashion over the next three months. Another season came and went as the buds of cool, early spring blossomed into the flowers of an oppressively hot summer. Another auction came and went, too. Another representative from Best's Bank and Trust exchanged bank notes on the spot under the watchful eye of the marshal. Another herd of ponies made their mint for Levi, and this time Josiah participated in the ordeal by selling off some of his cattle as well. A week after the knocking of the final gavel signified the last sale at the auction, the men gathered once again at the Parlor for drinks and debate.

"Well, Scoville," Josiah said, "that Auction House of yours is probably goin' to see you retire from practicin' law before too long on account of all that coin you're pocketin'!"

"Are you talking about all that coin I'm passing on to the crew running things down there?" Scoville said.

Josiah frowned with consideration as his eyes found the Parlor's tin ceiling. "Suppose it ain't cheap, is it?"

"No sir, but it is worth it. What do we have today?"

Crandall spoke up, "Front page story: *LOCAL ECONOMY BOOMING!* Don't I know it, too, my head is achin' from all that hammerin' they're doin' next door to me at the Emporium. Martin's got a mind to renovate them old crumble sticks into a respectable establishment. I believe the man aims to win the approval of Best by borrowin' whatever he can."

"The Irishman's got a *couple* money-makin' businesses already," Cooper said. "Shame he can't take pride in 'em around Best. You'd think he'd tire of tryin' to impress the man."

"Only thing those two got in common is that in their lines of work, successful don't mean honorable," Josiah said.

Cooper slouched down in his chair and lowered the brim of his hat triggering laughter from Henry Olt.

"Well that ain't the only thing interestin' this week," Olt said. "You 'member when I got hired on down there at the Lumber Mill a couple months back and I told y'all payroll came in the way of them bank notes? Now Best and them got an arrangement to just move that money into our accounts at the end of the week. Pretty handy if you ask me, they callin' it the payroll model of the next century!"

"I hope that works out well for you, Henry," Dillon said as Scoville and Josiah exchanged a wisened glance.

Crandall popped the paper, "Anyway, at least givin' has increased along with all this growth. Looks like there's gonna be a little white church with a steeple goin' up at the end of the road. They've been meetin' in a tent down there by the river for what seems like ages." He read on, "Oh wait, maybe givin' ain't gone up, says here land prices are on the rise and they got a construction loan from Best. Well, property values are up, that there's good news."

Scoville hung his head.

"Scoville, when you do that after news about your Auction House goin' up in value, you have me concerned," Josiah said.

"Gentlemen, gentlemen, if indeed people are willing to pay more for land, of course that is a good thing for landowners, but I fear it is a little more complicated." Scoville took the paper from Crandall and skimmed through the article.

"Mmmhmm, I see." He took off his spectacles and took a drink. "Let me try to explain it like this. I don't think land values are up because of the reasons mentioned in the paper. Sagebrush hasn't seen an influx of population dramatic enough to account for these numbers. It's also not as though the land is somehow suddenly more replete with desirous resources, and people aren't necessarily becoming more cunning with the implementation of those resources at the moment, either. Undoubtedly, demand *is* on the rise and industry is growing and innovating, but these factors alone are not sufficient to explain this rapid inflation.

"I think this 'good news' is in fact a result of the manipulation of the money supply. People now have access to more of these bank notes to borrow and are misled by claims of their integrity, the belief that they represent the qualities of gold money. I fear that the purchasing power of the supply is being compromised by the mistaken belief that they are a secure store of value, safe from the exploitation of profiteers. This isn't good news at all, in fact, for anyone who works hard and tries to save their money because their savings are constantly being diluted by outside forces.

"This happens to hurt a lot of people because labor rates are almost always the last thing to rise along with the money supply. By the time they catch up, Best will have already printed and loaned his way to more and more inflationary ventures. I'm concerned, gentlemen, that rising land prices, while good for speculators, is not good in terms of real growth as measured by any meaningful metric. I'm sure what Best is doing, although I can't prove it, is creating circumstances where the citizens of Sagebrush will be left financially devastated when people realize that Best has circulated worthless bank notes and overextended credit."

"Sounds like some nonsense," Henry Olt said. "Folks, I got to be makin' my way back to work. I earn my money with sweat and muscle and as long as it's still good at the store where I buy my food, I'm gonna get back to makin' more of it."

Dillon Turk shook his brother-in-law's hand but did not share his enthusiastic disregard for the admonitions of the lawyer. Olt dropped a bank note on the table and walked out.

"Gentlemen 'scuse me for interruptin'." Lawrence Hoak suddenly appeared from behind the bar. "I try not to make a habit of eavesdroppin', but I think it's time you hear what I got to say. I do hope you'll forgive me for not speakin' up sooner, but I also hope you can understand the predicament I been in about riskin' everythin' I got." Lawrence sat down and lowered his voice. He proceeded to explain to the men in detail the conversation that he had overheard between Peregrine Page and George Best prior to the Grand Opening of the Sagebrush branch of Best's Bank and Trust. He told them about the bank notes used to purchase the business, about Perry's involvement in the deposit receipt fraud, and about Best's threats. Finally, after checking over his shoulder a few times, Lawrence Hoak spilled his guts about the real estate scam that led George Best and Peregrine Page to conspire to burn down the original Parlor and the smithy of Cooper Emmons.

"I'll kill them!" Cooper shouted. He stood up abruptly and drew his pistol. Levi and Crandall stopped his departure, but Cooper was enraged.

"Come on now, Cooper, settle down. Your business is back up and running, it was just a building." Scoville's attempts to reason with Cooper only angered him more. Josiah placed a hand on Scoville's shoulder and subtly shook his head.

"Let me go! I'm gonna find 'em and kill 'em!" Cooper continued.

Josiah leaned over to Scoville, "That fire claimed the life of Cooper's blind old mutt, Harvey. You don't know how much he loved that dog."

15

Josiah splashed water on his face and took a deep breath. He observed his reflection in the mirror and saw the stress evident in the lines on his forehead and the bags under his eyes. He shook droplets from his fingertips and dried his hands on a towel hanging by the basin. Josiah had not been sleeping well so the prospect of a steaming cup of coffee comforted him. Stepping out into the kitchen to begin breakfast, he was sidetracked by a knock at the door.

Lorraine stood outside with a basket of fresh greens and a loaf of bread. When Josiah opened the door, she grabbed a fold of her skirt with her free hand and gave a deep, slow curtsy. Things weren't so bad for Josiah when she came around.

"You're wearing your serious face today I see. That simply won't do," Lorraine said as she brushed past him and entered the kitchen. "If there is a time for war, Josiah, then today is a time for peace; if there is a time for mourning, then today is a time for dancing!" She sat the basket down and twirled over to Josiah throwing herself into his arms. He caught her and lowered her into a dip, from which she looked up and with childlike delight said, "Today is the circus!"

All over Sagebrush, folks' anticipation energized their efforts. They buzzed about hurriedly to accomplish their daily tasks in order to make it across the tracks to the fairgrounds and join in the festivities. Among the bustle, Cassidy Turk cut through the crowds determined not to be delayed by the congestion. Little Jasper lagged behind under the weight of a stack of *Sentinel* papers. He carried them by the twine that tied them all together. Cassidy's pockets jingled with the savings from the past three months of deliveries while Jasper wiped chocolate from his mouth, smearing it across his face.

The bell above the Emporium door chimed as the boys made their way through a sea of wool, buttons, and belts to the register. Cassidy heaved both stacks of papers onto the counter and grinned widely at the pretty Ms. Pearl. She swatted at his cap then shooed the two Turk boys back outside where they sprung for the tracks. A gentleman picked up a copy of *The Sagebrush Sentinel* from the stack on the counter and read the full front-page ad for Macomb's Museum, Menagerie, Caravan, and Hippodrome.

"Mesmerizing Attractions," it read, "Superb Displays of Unimaginable Feats! Strange and Unusual Oddities! Witness the World's Greatest Show!" Such boasts were accompanied by images on playbills of big tents and clowns, dozens of riders standing atop rushing horses and acrobats. There were also pictures of fortune tellers and sideshow curiosities. Intrigue and imagination had gripped the citizens of Sagebrush, and in a tiny corner of the front page were the words, "made possible by Best's Bank and Trust."

Conspicuously absent from the town's flurry of excitement was Nicholas Scoville, whose dark office had been shuttered with a "Closed" sign on display. Levi was inspecting a few investment Filly's just up the road from Scoville's at Dillon Turk's Livery Stables where he inquired after the lawyer.

"Ah, I gather a man can only take so many jokes about whether he'd be a feature at the circus before callin' it a day. I believe he mentioned he was headin' home for the afternoon to read," Dillon said.

Meanwhile, down at the smithy, Cooper Emmons helped the traveling circus' farrier with an order of shoes. The bizarre man was gruff, tattooed, and dirty, but adamant about impeccable quality in his purchase, which Cooper respected. The large bald customer smiled with approval at the delivery and tipped Cooper two tickets to the show.

"Be sure to stop by my *own* exhibit, while you're there!" the man said, heaving three burlap sacks full of iron, one hundred fifty pounds each, over his shoulder before departing.

Down at the Parlor, Lawrence Hoak had been pouring drinks when in walked two gentlemen he thought peculiar: one in white tights and the other in a top hat holding up a handful of tickets. The man in tights worked his way through the crowd and helped himself up on top of the bar where he proceeded to balance a customer's drink on his chin while juggling three expensive bottles of liquor. The outburst caused raucous applause as Lawrence chased down footprints with a bar rag. The other man in costume swung the curtains to the stage wide open and teased the crowd with free passes. Through sleight of hand tricks, however, they would mysteriously wind up missing from the pockets of lucky patrons and back under the hat of the magician.

"More! More!" the crowd exclaimed. "Again! Again!"

"Ladies and Gentlemen, this is but a mere glimpse at the sensational offerings we have in store for you this weekend! Come satisfy your fascination with the macabre, see death-defying stunts, and marvel at the vast array of the world's most exotic species . . . of beasts and men!"

As quickly as they had arrived, the performers were gone, leaving everyone to unsuccessfully inquire about who ended up with the free tickets.

The sun continued its arc across the sky, drawing closer the start of the circus. In preparation for the event, Lorraine found herself down at the Emporium. "Pearl, isn't this going to be so much fun!?" she said, reading the playbills.

"I suppose." Pearl rested her head disinterestedly in the palm of one hand.

"What am I to do with you? You and Josiah both, so glum for such a joyous occasion!"

"Speakin' of, where is your beau?"

"Oh, he'll be along directly."

"I'm so happy for you, Lorraine," Pearl said. "They say envy is a sin, and it should probably be the least of my worries as far as any preacher would be concerned; but I must say I wish I had someone to look at me the way Josiah looks at you."

"Oh, Pearl!" Lorraine said. "I hope you find all the love and happiness your heart can handle; you absolutely deserve it. You're a very brave girl. I admire that in you." She patted Pearl's hand just as Josiah poked his head in and called Lorraine away.

Shortly thereafter, Pearl still minded the register at the Emporium when the bell chimed. A man with sharp features and sure footing strolled through the door. He approached her directly, seeking assistance with items for his travel bags. Pearl found his accent alluring and wished to hear more, so rather than pointing she escorted him to the products. She struck up a conversation with the attractive acrobat.

"You must be in town with the show."

"And you must be the most beautiful woman in all the west," he said. "A lone rose among thistles and thorns." At his directness, Pearl blushed. Unaccustomed to the receiving end of such confident flattery, she fanned herself. An hour later,

Pearl was on an exclusive behind-the-scenes grand tour of the three-ring circus.

Also touring the fairgrounds in a less official, or in fact legal, capacity were the Turk boys. Crouching behind barrels and crawling under wagons, Cassidy and little Jasper snuck their way into the staging area for the caravan. They saw lion tamers feeding raw cuts of meat to their friends and monkeys rattling their cages. They found themselves awestruck as a carriage splashed by carrying two passengers that shared a lower half. Jasper gasped at the morbidity and began to cry which led Cassidy to slap a hand over his younger brother's mouth, but it was too late. Dragged by the ankles out from under their hiding place, the Turk boys screamed "Werewolf!" The monstrosity led them by the collar to the office of the ringmaster.

"Found these two in our back yard, sir," the man with the face full of whiskers said.

"Looks like the dinner flag's up. I'll handle it from here, thank you," the ringmaster replied. The dog-faced man exited, and the ringmaster turned his attention to the boys. Wide-eyed and trembling, Cassidy asked if they would still be allowed in to see the show that evening.

"Allowed in?! Why, you've already *been* in!"

"Yes sir, sorry sir!" Jasper squeaked.

"Well, I see plainly that you know you shouldn't have been back there, so lesson learned. Don't worry yourselves about that anymore. You two are bold and daring and that's the kind of people we celebrate here! I'm Preston Timothy Macomb and tonight you will have special front row seats to the World's Greatest Show! Come, follow me!"

Macomb led the boys the long way around the big tent introducing them as his guests to trainers and performers alike. When they had reached the top of the bannerline, Macomb knelt, withdrew two tickets from his red tuxedo coat, and handed them over. As the boys scampered away down the sideshow corridor of curtains and barkers, Macomb heard a voice from behind him.

"Giving away tickets to my customers, are you?" George Best said.

In his most effectual ringmaster tone, Macomb replied, "What's two passes for starry-eyed youth when our sell-out awaits?" The two shook hands and withdrew into the big tent as engineers were performing final inspections on suspension points. The grandstands lay staged for a packed house with heralds on every seat all the way up to the blues. Candy Butchers were packing straw on the floor for extra seating. In the middle of the center ring was a red and white striped platform. Macomb ran to it and spun around on one foot atop the show box with his arms outstretched. George Best removed his handkerchief and held it over his face in disgust as a whiff of the menagerie trailed in from Clown Alley.

"I've paid you for the right to sell those tickets, Mr. Macomb. We agreed, six performances in three different towns. Now I hear reports of your . . . freaks . . . giving away passes to my potential customers here and I'm not happy about it. How much have you cost me everywhere else you've been?"

"Relax, Mr. Best!" Macomb said, "You haven't paid me yet, only given assurances of payment."

"We have only one weekend here in Sagebrush. At thirty percent of the take, every ticket counts, Mr. Macomb."

The ringmaster pitied the banker, "As you wish," he said. "And you're sure that no one is wise to our big surprise? You've left that reveal to us, yes?"

"I haven't said a word. There have been suspicions raised regarding the infrastructure development but nothing has hit the papers so most folks will be caught unawares."

"Excellent! I do appreciate your efforts to ensure this coincides with our brief residence. I live for such thrills!"

As the afternoon waned, the townsfolk arrived in droves for the event. Ranchers and their families surrounded the hippodrome to watch stunt riders and sharp shooters mounted upon decorated horses perform in the gun show. Josiah and Lorraine leaned against the barricade encircling the dirt track. There was a man in the field standing on two different stallions balancing a woman on one hand while holding a pistol in the other. When the rider shot the cap off a bottle from fifty yards away, Lorraine looked at Josiah as though issuing a challenge.

"I don't think you got it in ya, cowboy," she said. "Think maybe I'll just try my luck with him!" She raised her eyebrows and grinned.

"Go on then, if you think you'll find happiness with an actor shootin' blanks at a rigged target. I'll be over here buyin' candy."

"Ooh, what kind of candy?!"

"Uh huh," Josiah laughed, "That's what I thought." Lorraine hugged Josiah's arm and the two headed for the concessions.

"Besides," she said, "I already know you can shoot; I want to see how you stack up against the World's Strongest Man!"

Candy in hand, by happenstance they did wind up at the World's Strongest Man exhibit, only to find a familiar face on stage. Cooper Emmons, sweating and straining at an arm-wrestling table, attempted to pin down the tattooed hand of a bald man who was preoccupied making eyes at the ladies in the crowd, evidently unphased by the efforts of his opponent. Josiah watched Cooper's shoulder drop as he gave his adversary a frustrated frown. The instant he let up pressure, SLAM! went his wrist down to the table. The bald man stood triumphantly with his fists on his hips. The crowd cheered as he and Cooper then shook hands.

As the last rays of dusk descended beyond the western horizon and the late summer twilight revealed the night's first visible stars, a crowd with starry eyes of their own funneled into the glow of the lamplit Big Tent. Ushers collected tickets and shuffled folks down narrow makeshift boardwalks to their seats. Townsfolk made awestruck comments about the three great rings in the middle of the floor, the curious glass orbs strung along the inside of the canvas roof, and the various swings, cables, and nets of the aerial team. Josiah and Lorraine settled in just as a hand found Josiah's shoulder. He turned and gave a quick greeting to a gentleman bearing the scars of an infantryman whom Josiah did not recognize.

After the man had returned to his seat Lorraine said, "I know sometimes it's difficult for you, because of the way you feel about your past, but I have noticed you're much more gracious with people lately."

"Thanks," Josiah said, recognizing the ring of truth in her comment. "I'll be more careful next time," he joked.

She frowned and punched his arm.

"You gonna box him, you better straighten your wrist," a voice said from behind Lorraine. Will Richardson took his place next to them on the wooden bleachers and delicately adjusted her technique. "There, now give him a wallop." Lorraine, with a devious grin, offered Will a thank-you nod. Josiah was still shaking his head with disbelief at Will when the next punch landed on his shoulder.

"That one stung," Josiah said, "Good to see you, too, Will."

The big man laughed as Jacoby Sutton's head popped up over his shoulder, eager to ascertain what had happened. Just then, the sound of a drumroll filled the tent and dozens of ushers, in unison, snuffed out the lamps. Josiah was caught off guard; he immediately crouched down in the pitch black and tugged on Lorraine's shirt with one hand while the other found the handle of his gun which stayed holstered. Confused, he blinked furiously hoping his eyes would adjust to the near total darkness. He was preparing to lead Lorraine by the hand off the bleachers away from the crowd and out of the Big Tent to safety when he realized she was trying to sooth him by rubbing his back.

"Not now," he barked over the murmur of the muddled congregants, "with me on one, two . . ."

"And now, ladies and gentlemen, the moment you've all been waiting for!" the ringmaster announced. "Welcome to the World's Grrreatest Show!" The audience's cheers were louder than the POP! from outside the tent where someone flipped the switch on a giant breaker which, for the very first time in Sagebrush, opened the flow of electricity. It traveled through the wires and illuminated hundreds of bulbs throughout the red and white striped tent, soaking everyone and everything in a rich amber glow. On the center platform the ringmaster, Preston Timothy Macomb, relished in the sudden collective gasp that captured the breath of the attendees who then erupted with rapturous applause.

When the lights came on, Josiah realized that a few folks, including Will Richardson, stared down at him. Misinterpreting Josiah's preparation to evade for cowering, Will snickered condescendingly.

"Afraid of the dark, are you Josiah?"

Josiah let the insult slide as he collected himself from the fleeting sense of alarm. Standing, he tried to scan the crowd, but was too captivated by the series of humming globes strung along the tent converging in the center above the middle ring. Josiah found the ringmaster, arms outstretched in his red tuxedo tails, then scanned the faces of the people before the lights once again lured his attention to the center. He noticed the Turk boys on the front row with Dillon and Rebecca. The joy spread across their faces made Josiah long for the days of childhood innocence. Suddenly, while beholding the miracle of artificial light, a long-forgotten sense of wonder set upon Josiah as though a rediscovered sentimental relic of the dusty past. For a magical moment, his desire had been pure enough to merit satisfaction; Josiah felt joy.

On the ringmaster's cue, a small brass marching band began to play and prompted a long train of circus performers.

An overture of talent flooded into the arena, winding its way around the three rings and showcasing a glimpse of the features that awaited the audience. Clowns with painted faces in oversized clothes fumbled their hats and tripped over one another as dancers and contortionists gracefully maneuvered about. Acrobats followed, clapping their hands and creating a fog of white dust. As one such chalk cloud dissipated it revealed a man with sharp features who scanned the guest's section looking for Pearl. When their eyes met he blew her a kiss, leaving white residue in the shape of his fingers across his face. Before she could even giggle he was ascending a rope ladder with other members of his troupe.

Next into the parade, an unusual woman spewed flames and her companion taunted the crowd with the hilt of a sword protruding from his mouth. By the time the jugglers entered, bodies sailed through the air on the trapeze, and someone balanced a long pole on a tightrope high above. Levi walked in with Nicholas Scoville just in time to hear the roar of a great lion. It startled a juggler who nearly impaled himself on a dropped knife but recovered seamlessly by using his foot to fling the blade up into the air and back into rotation. The lion's car was followed by a similar caged cart which housed the show's rambunctious monkeys. As the camels were making their appearance, the deafening trumpet of an elephant drowned out the music. High upon the slate gray concrete hides of the hose-nosed animals rode scantily clad beauties with white feathered plumes adorning their headwear.

"Oh Josiah! Look!" Lorraine said. She bounced up and down, clapping her hands quickly. Josiah could see that she was captivated by the experience and was sharing in that effervescent glory grown folk are privileged to entertain with ever waning frequency. She looked his way and her wide eyes revealed that she, too, was spellbound. When Josiah Rush realized that the resplendence of the grand event paled in comparison to Lorraine, he placed his hands on her hips and pulled her in close. The breaker's switch was not the only thing that sparked for the first time that night; Josiah Rush kissed Lorraine Baxter, completing a circuit of a different sort. Like the lit filaments within the glass bulbs above, a current of passion electrified the two of them.

Lorraine was slow to open her eyes. After a hesitant silence between them she said, "I thought we weren't doing this, cowboy," but she kissed him again.

16

Arriving once again at the Depot upon his return to Sagebrush, Dr. Andrew Hoyle stepped off the train and flipped a copper to Cassidy Turk who was on the platform selling copies of the *Sentinel.* He sat down and opened to a review of Macomb's traveling show. Once again, Dr. Hoyle was perturbed that he had failed to schedule himself in the same place at the same time as the circus. He peered across the tracks into the fairgrounds and watched as the Big Tent was being packed up.

"Surely some of those deformed accidents of nature would prove the most shocking skeletal subjects to study," he said to himself. His revulsion was matched only by his intrigue.

He read the review. "'A splendid and enchanting evening with the most magnificent of displays!' I'm quite sure that was the case, Mister," he scanned the page, "Porter High."

Dr. Hoyle had been waiting for an attendant to carry his bags to the Sagebrush Grand Hotel. When the young man arrived, he remarked on the pearl handle of a polished steel sidearm that newly adorned the Doctor's hip.

"Do no harm, huh?" the attendant said.

"It's '*first*, do no harm,'" the doctor corrected. "And that is, to those who would not harm you. Though, I must say that the number of baser miscreants in these parts inclines one to believe there aren't many of those people for miles."

"Maybe it's 'cause you seem to got a big mouth." The young man dropped the bags at Hoyle's feet and walked away despite Dr. Hoyle's appeals.

Dr. Andrew Hoyle shouldered a bag and lifted two other large pieces of luggage which he struggled to manage on his walk to the hotel. After checking in, he established a presence in the room by setting up a small chemistry set on the desk, inventorying his equipment. He then requested hot water for the basin and sent a suit with the staff to be pressed. After bathing, Dr. Hoyle shaved, then applied an expensive cologne acquired on his travels. He ate a small meal, dressed, and made for the Parlor just after six o'clock in the evening. He was joined by Lorraine.

"Dr. Hoyle, dear, how are you? It's so very good to see you again!" she said.

"Wonderful, wonderful! Great to see you as well. My, I have so missed having you around. Do tell me, how has it been adjusting to such lowly conditions as these?"

"Oh, Sagebrush has become just dear to me. As you said, there was an initial adjustment, but really these people are quite hospitable."

Lawrence arrived with drinks for the two of them. "Good to see you again, Doc. I hope you been managin' alright."

"I'm sorry, and you are?"

Lawrence flushed and Lorraine was baffled, "Why, Doctor, this is Lawrence Hoak! Surely you remember us tending to him the night Pearl delivered sweet baby Carson."

Hoyle smiled unconvincingly, "Why sure, how do you do?" he said to Lawrence. "Now, Lorraine, darling, I don't have a clue who these other friends of yours are, but I'm happy you're settled. How is business?"

"If you mean the health of these kind people, why a mixed bag to be honest. Of course, with the resilience of youth, minor coughs and such are common-place and easy to address. There are those aging souls, though, who are battling more sapping ailments. Poor Ms. Eudora is having quite a difficult time in her garden this year because of her knees. And—"

"Oh, that's too bad. Well, um," Hoyle cleared his throat, "yes, well, about the, uh—"

"Business accounts, Doctor?" Lorraine said.

"Yes, but please, just Andrew." He smiled and patted her hand. She withdrew it, but graciously grabbed her glass and took a sip.

"There's a lock box at the bank. There you'll find medical billing records, and a schedule of appointments I've taken the liberty to make for you during your stay. You can also request assistance with an audit of the accounts if you so desire."

"It's not that I distrust . . ."

"Not at all, Doctor! I understand that managing a practice is detailed and I'm simply trying to be helpful."

"Indeed, you are Lorraine. Thank you."

As the evening progressed, Lorraine did update Dr. Hoyle on the condition of Ms. Eudora and half a dozen other patients requiring extra care. The two laughed as Hoyle recounted exaggerations of his adventures across the west, and an attentive Lawrence Hoak dutifully delivered multiple rounds to the colleagues. The later it got, the louder it got; the louder it got, the closer Dr. Hoyle got.

"I'm sorry," he slurred, "Wha' you say?"

"I said, '. . . that's when she jumped into a tiny pool of water from a platform near the top of the tent!' It was spectacular!"

"You know wha' I think? I think you're spec-ac-ular!" He said.

"Oh, I uh, thank you."

"I mean it," he leaned further in, uncomfortably close to Lorraine who shied away from the strong odor of alcohol on his hot breath. "You're spec-ac-ular." Dr. Hoyle tried to kiss Lorraine.

She abruptly turned her head and said, "It's getting late, perhaps you've had a bit much, I think I'll just . . ."

"Wha' is it? Look at me, wha' is it? Spend time with me, Lorraine, I know you're lonely. You must crave the company of a civilized man. I've been longing for you."

"Excuse me, sir! This is entirely inappropriate! No, I'm not lonely, and the only uncivilized person here right now is you!"

"You're lonely for a man, I can tell," he tried to grab her arm, which she jerked away.

"Not that it's *any* of your business, but I have someone who's ten times the man you are!" Lorraine stood up just as Lawrence arrived to offer aid.

"Is there a problem, Ms. Lorraine? Would you like me to send for Josiah?" Lawrence said.

"Josiah!?" the drunken Doctor scoffed.

"No, Lawrence, I was just leaving, thank you," Lorraine said.

The Doctor continued to ramble as Lorraine exited to the hotel lobby. "Only a stupid trollop would forsake the pleasure of my company for that of a savage."

"Alright, that's enough, asshole! Time for you to get out!" Lawrence Hoak picked the doctor's pocket, withdrew enough to cover the drinks, then tossed back the wallet. Hoak kicked the chair to emphasize he meant immediately, and Dr. Hoyle staggered off to his room. The patrons in the saloon returned to a revelrous mood after the embarrassing outburst and Lawrence stuffed the bank notes in the register drawer.

As Lorraine and Dr. Hoyle were having their ill-fated meeting at the Parlor, Cooper Emmons and Nicholas Scoville passed the evening at Scoville's office just up Main Street.

"Cooper, thank you for joining me."

"Sure thing, Mr. Esq."

"Cooper, you do know that's not . . . you know what, nevermind." Scoville poured a drink for Cooper and one for himself. "I extended this invitation for a number of reasons. First, it has been enriching getting to know you over the past few months and I'm glad to call you a friend. Second, I wanted to check in to see how you've been doing. The rumors levied against Mr. Best and Perry concerning your business, I mean . . . after consideration, I wanted to say that I'm sorry for failing to understand the importance of your original smithy and everything you lost."

"I 'preciate that. S'pose there's gonna be a reckonin' one of these days, but so long as the law 'round here is crooked as a sidewinder I'm just gonna bide my time. Far as I know, Best and Perry ain't awares I know what they done so if'n it comes to it, they gonna be blindsided when they answer for it."

"Just be careful, Mr. Emmons. Make sure you have the legal and moral authority to take any action against them or it will not go well for you, I promise. We are still a land of laws, even if it seems they only apply to citizens these days."

"Ah shoot, I figure with this kinda corruption, a man ain't gotta worry about what's legal to do what's right. I ain't willin' to do nothin' I can't live with, so don't you worry about me."

"Well, I do, my friend." Scoville smiled and sipped his whiskey. A silent moment passed before he changed the subject to a more cheerful topic, "Anyway, did you happen to make it to the show? What did you think? Enjoy it?"

"Shore did! Man alive, I tell you, they got some hardscrabble folk to handle that kinda life, huh? I's glad to get to see it all together, love them elephants—wouldn't wanna smell 'em all the time though. They make horse droppings smell like perfume. How 'bout you? You go?"

"It took some convincing, but Levi was able to drag me from the den. I'm truly glad to have gone, too. It was really quite charming. I always thought that kind of life was exploitative, but everyone seemed so dignified; perhaps I could be persuaded from my bias, after all."

"Uh huh, but how 'bout them elephants!?"

Scoville laughed, "Yes, they were quite marvelous."

"Shore was." Cooper stood and helped himself to another drink. "Well, anyway, had that circus snagged you up, you wouldn't have been the only one gone with it from 'round here." Scoville stared curiously at Cooper who took a swig of his whiskey.

Across the street, all alone in a small, quiet apartment above Dodge's Emporium and Dry Goods, little baby Carson lay swaddled and sleeping soundly in his bassinet. The moonlight shone through the window covering and illuminated the room with silver beams of light which reflected off a metal pin that secured an envelope to Carson's blanket. That envelope had nothing but a single name on it, written by an unsteady hand with ink that bled slightly, the result of a single teardrop.

As dawn broke, Lorraine crossed the street and ascended the stairs outside the Emporium up to Pearl's apartment. She softly knocked a few times and waited for an answer. When none came, she knocked louder. Inside, Carson began to cry. When there was still no answer Lorraine pounded on the door.

"Pearl! Pearl! C'mon open up!"

Fearing something had happened to Pearl, Lorraine tried to turn the locked handle. She was kicking at the door when Martin Kelly arrived at the Emporium to open for business and rounded the corner upon hearing the ruckus.

"What're ye doing, Lorraine!?"

"Oh Martin, quick, do you have the key to this door?" she asked.

"Of course I have a key, dis is my store, is it not?"

He ran up the stairs and opened the apartment. Carson cried in a crib in the corner of the dark room, but there was no sign of Pearl. Lorraine dashed to the helpless babe and cradled his cold little body against her own. Panic set in as Martin examined the empty vanity and drawers.

"She's gone," he said.

"No, there's no way! Somethin's happened."

"What happened is she packed her bags and left, Lorraine. Look around ye, do ye see any of her day-to-day things left here that she would have needed?" Lorraine explored the vanity; there was no brush, no powder, and in the drawers there were no garments.

"Impossible!" The denial in the word was accompanied by a flash of anger in her tone. "There's no way a mother could ever do such a thing! It's *not* possible. Something's happened." She sank down against a wall and held Carson closely. They were both crying.

"Why are ye here dis early, Lorraine?"

"Pearl asked me if I could look after Carson first thing this morning, she seemed distraught, but I assumed she just needed a break as mothers often do."

"Or she planned to leave town in the night and if she couldn't be a mother to the child, she needed to make sure someone could." Martin hastily retrieved Carson's blanket to cover Lorraine when he felt the sting of a paper cut. He ripped the envelope from the pin and handed it over.

"Looks like dis was left for ye. Let Pearl speak fer herself, den yes?" he said.

"Why is that addressed to me? And how are you so calm about this, Martin? Shouldn't you be a little more upset about the fact that she's left you?"

"Left me? We weren't together, and it seems she's done me a favor openin' a room to rent."

Lorraine was appalled and snatched the envelope from Martin. She tore it open and read the note with her mouth gaping in disbelief.

Lorraine,

I tried. I can't. I must start over. I'm sorry.

—Pearl

"She's really gone," Lorraine said after a long silence. She dropped the note and interrogated Martin. "How on earth do you plan to raise this child by yourself?"

"I'm afraid I dunno wha' ye mean. Why should I be raisin' Pearl's boy?"

"Martin!? This is *your* boy, clearly, and everyone knows it!" Martin was shaking his head. "Yes!" she pleaded, "Yes he is! We all indulged your denial praying one day you would come to your senses and acknowledge the boy as your own, that you would grow to love him. That *has* to be today, Martin!"

"Yer out of yer mind with shock."

"Don't be absurd, look at his hair! Martin, it's as red as your own!"

"You knew of her work, and plenty of men travel through these parts."

"You're absolutely unbelievable! Have you no heart at all!? Just look at this darling child!"

"Quite fond of him are ye? Perhaps Pearl knew what she was doin'. You'll take care of him, then?"

Stunned by his callousness, Lorraine was unable to proffer any further arguments.

"You drove her away. You drove her away with your cold heart and your rejection and now you'll see your son raised by another. You're a failure, Martin Kelly, shame on you! If I am all this child has in this world, then I will see that he becomes a better man than his father." Lorraine was screaming and Carson was crying when a sharp sound—SLAP!—echoed across the wooden floors of the apartment. As Lorraine stumbled backward, Martin felt immediate remorse.

"Oh Lorraine, I'm sorry. I just got so worked up that I..." He wasn't sorry, though. Martin was, instead, suddenly overcome with fear of the repercussions Josiah Rush would impart.

Lorraine stormed past him and descended the stairs with Carson. From the small balcony, Martin watched her run with the child until they were out of sight, then turned around and slammed the door to the apartment.

Once back at the hotel, Lorraine headed upstairs to her room. She closed the door and scanned what had been her home for the better part of four months. Now with the immediate concern of caring for a child, she began to question the duration of her commission and whether more permanent accommodations would be appropriate. Lorraine spent the next five hours swinging wildly between cleaning, eating, sobbing, adoring Carson, and convincing herself that a remorseful Pearl would come bursting through her door at any moment.

When the clothes were folded, the windows were washed, and the rest of her room was immaculate, Lorraine could no longer put off her unavoidable desire to go see Josiah. As she passed through the hotel lobby carrying Carson in her arms, there was an upheaval coming from the Parlor. Men shouted and cussed, glass broke, and a crowd gathered. Spilling out onto the street cutting off Lorraine's path of travel, the group of onlookers quieted in astonishment as two dark figures occupied the center of Main Street. They began counting paces. Lorraine took cover in the threshold of the hotel and peered out. To her disbelief, one of the men was her employer, Dr. Andrew Hoyle. Lorraine watched dumbstruck as Dr. Hoyle stood trembling, glaring back at the cold stare of a man whose composure betrayed him as a veteran gunfighter.

Lawrence Hoak exited the Parlor from behind the bar into the lobby and crouched down beside Lorraine whose cutting look demanded an explanation. "He showed up first thing this mornin' still drunk from last night," Lawrence said as he guided Lorraine further inside by the shoulders. "By the time this other fella come in with his buddies, your friend here . . . well, acquaintance anyway . . . Dr. Hoyle, he was well into the sauce and actin' quite spiteful to be honest. Started runnin' his mouth and here we are."

The occasional jeer was heard from the crowd as their anticipation grew. Lorraine watched Dr. Andrew Hoyle fold over and retch. An onlooker threw something at him from the crowd. She was too far away to hear what was said, but Hoyle's bravado and resolve was apparent when he hobbled to his feet then pounded his chest.

"It's like he wants to die," Lorraine remarked. "Someone needs to put a stop to this."

Lawrence prevented her from leaving and gave a stern look. He glanced at Carson then shook his head. "Don't be foolish, you can't go puttin' Pearl's boy in that kind of danger."

Upon hearing "Pearl's boy" in reference to Carson, Lorraine was surprised by how foreign it already sounded to her ears. She was still pondering the strength of her emerging maternal connection to the child when the clock above the courthouse struck high noon.

The two shots came quickly, but there was audible evidence of terror from only one man. Lorraine recognized the voice. She handed Carson to the bartender and pushed her way through the crowd to find Dr. Andrew Hoyle clutching his chest with bloody hands. The other shooter mounted up with the rest of his gang and rode off before the marshal made it out of the courthouse. Lorraine applied pressure to the wound, but it was only for show. She watched as blood trickled from Hoyle's lips.

"It's you," he whispered. "I'm glad it's you."

Lorraine was silent but managed to force a smile as a last gesture of mercy right before Dr. Hoyle coughed up more blood and breathed his last.

17

Sweat dripped from Josiah's saturated clothing as he worked the plow yoked to his team of Percherons. In the high summer heat, he was cultivating the crop field beyond his grazing pastures when he noticed a figure in the distance. He removed his hat, wiped his brow, and squinted in the sun to see who was careening up the pathway toward his house.

Tucking his gloves into his belt, Josiah led the team to water and decided it was a good time to break for the day. He sauntered back at first, but when he heard Lorraine's pleas and knew something was wrong, he broke out in a full sprint. Rounding the corner, he caught Lorraine and the baby as she collapsed into him. She tried to muster an explanation, but her words failed. Lorraine simply held up a hand that still contained traces of dried blood. Josiah exhaled and dropped his head.

"C'mon, we'll get cleaned up inside."

"I'm sorry to have—I-I know you're—"

"No, no, no," he said, "I'm here, I'm right here."

He took Carson in one arm and hugged Lorraine with the other. They limped inside where Josiah heated water for the tub. He left a new bar of soap and a fresh towel for Lorraine. While she bathed, Josiah cared for Carson. He changed the boy, then changed out of his own sweaty clothes. Before settling down, he attended to Carson once again, for the boy had immediately soiled himself.

When Lorraine finally emerged wearing one of Josiah's button-down shirts, she found him asleep on the couch holding Carson. She curled up on a small corner of the remaining cushion with one leg under her, resting her head on the back of the sofa admiring them. Josiah sensed the movement and cracked an eye open, then a smile. Upon realizing that his living room was no longer lifeless, he brimmed with gratitude. It was as though an unsaid prayer had been answered. Lorraine nodded toward the door, so Josiah carefully transferred Carson to a pile of blankets on the floor and the two stepped outside to talk.

"Pearl's run off," she said.

"That so?"

"Pearl's run off and left me to care for Carson. Martin won't have him."

Josiah sighed in disbelief. "What a shame."

"Only, how am I supposed to care for a child, Josiah . . ." Lorraine stared off at the horizon. ". . . when I no longer have means of employment?"

"Wait, what do you mean?"

Lorraine stated matter-of-factly, "Andrew is dead."

He closed his eyes and nodded slowly, "Ah, Lorraine, I'm so sorry."

"Don't be. I'm not. I'm relieved. For all the good men in this world, there sure are some bastar—" She interrupted herself, suddenly sensitive to the term. "Josiah, he got physical with me last night when I rejected him." Lorraine stopped short of telling Josiah about her altercation with Martin.

"What?!"

"Get the details from Lawrence if you must, but he got angry and picked a fight with the wrong man. The fool spent four months out here and thought he was a gunslinger. Thought he was you."

"Hmm. You saw it, then? You gonna be alright?"

"I've seen worse, Josiah. Seen death arrive for better men than him. You're familiar with how it still shakes you, though. I'll have time for all that later, but first I have to figure out what to do next. My room is paid through the week. I suppose I can claim what's in the account at the bank seeing how Andrew left behind no kin. Pearl's position at the Emporium is out of the question after the exchange I had with Martin this morning." She held her tongue again.

"Stop. Don't get ahead of yourself and don't go jumpin' into somethin' that ain't right for you just 'cause you're frightened. You're here now, with me. We're gonna make sure that baby has what he needs and we're gonna make sure that you take care of yourself so you can keep takin' care of these folks. But none of that has to be figured out right now, today."

Josiah moved closer and held her tight, sensing that her spirit had become distant. He understood her withdrawal and did not take it personally, despite his own pain watching her suffer. Knowing intimately his own struggle to reclaim his heart after such events, he offered nothing further in the way of words, but continued to hold her for a long time.

Later, when Carson awoke and began to cry, Josiah made him a mash of boiled vegetables. Lorraine watched from her couch cushion as he danced about the kitchen with a rag over one shoulder cradling the boy and feeding him small bites of peas and carrots. It lifted her spirits enough that she stood up and walked to them. She hugged them both, then Josiah and Lorraine shared another kiss.

"Here," he said, "If you can take over, I'll go make up a bed for you two, and you'll stay in the guest house tonight."

"Oh, Josiah, are you sure? You know how this town can be. I don't want to invite a scandal."

"Lorraine, I worry about my conscience, not their gossip. You'll stay?"

She nodded, continuing to feed the baby as Josiah donned his hat and headed down the hill to prepare the room. Upon returning a short time later, he found Carson babbling pleasantly in Lorraine's dozing arms. She was sprawled out on the couch, so he covered them both and retreated again to his own guest house to spend the night.

18

After a long string of continued successful engagements across the west, Preston Timothy Macomb, the circus tycoon and ringmaster of Macomb's Museum, Menagerie, Caravan, and Hippodrome, stepped onto the tile floors in the lobby of the marble clad premier city branch of Best's Bank and Trust. The profits from their original venture had thrilled George Best, so he and Macomb extended their agreement for another series of events. As a result, Macomb was bursting with bank notes bearing the Best name.

Macomb's subsequent ambition was to take his circus across the sea to foreign lands far beyond the influence of local commercial norms. To fund his operation further, he found himself at the bank redeeming the receipts from months of touring profits.

"You'd like to do what, sir?!" the teller asked.

"Yes ma'am, you heard me. I'm here to trade the whole lot of it, and I'd like a discount on the premium for assayed coins please," he said.

Some of the bank's other customers there that day became disconcerted after witnessing the initial scramble of managers flurrying about seeking various approvals from unseen accountants. The savvier observers requested to redeem the bank notes they had on hand as well. Soon after, they returned to the bank to redeem the entirety of their saved notes and encouraged friends and colleagues to do the same. This set in motion a series of events over the course of the following week that led to the delivery of a certified letter addressed to Peregrine Page at the Sagebrush branch of Best's Bank and Trust.

The letter prompted an alarmed Perry to audit the reserves in the vault and compare them with Sagebrush's last estimated liability in outstanding bank notes. When Perry realized that an influx of liquid capital from the city had outpaced local lending and his branch was over-extended by as much as forty percent, he sent a panicked correspondence to George Best. To Perry's distress, it was met with a flippant dismissal of his concerns as well as a demand for the transfer of all Sagebrush's gold and silver holdings to the flagship branch, thus centralizing the deposits for an entire territory in the city vault. The townsfolk in Sagebrush were none the wiser, though. Truth be told, no one would have ever questioned the contents of that midnight train out of Sagebrush the fateful evening all their savings became eastbound freight, had it not been for the timing of an incident that unfolded the very next day when someone else attempted to steal all the savings as well.

It was midday when Josiah Rush and Levi Holdegel were at the smithy commissioning a set of hinges that Cooper was to forge for a new gate. Suddenly the sound of stampeding hooves was accompanied by shouts and gunfire. When they witnessed people fleeing past the shop down Broad Street, the three of them grabbed their weapons. They peered out to see a gang of six men brandishing long guns in the middle of the town's intersection. Two of them dismounted and entered the bank carrying bags.

As the remaining men busied themselves scaring off bystanders, Josiah maneuvered to concealment behind a couple barrels stacked on the boardwalk next to Crandall's office. The postman soon joined him in hiding and sought an explanation. Josiah could only shrug and gesture toward the brick building. At the same time, Levi and Cooper crossed the street unseen and took cover behind the bank. As this choke point cut off one avenue of exit, and the river beyond the hotel cut off another, Josiah surmised there was a fifty percent chance this would erupt into a full-fledged gunfight, depending on the actions of the men in the bank and the route they would try to take out of town.

Quickly, Josiah peeked over the barrels to assess the positions of the four men outside. He drew fire from one of them. The thief missed, and the bullet pierced a barrel. Water spilled out onto Crandall who cussed the circumstances but did not dare move. Josiah could not return fire because beyond the shooter, Marshal Oglesby and Deputy Butch Eaton emerged from the courthouse. They posted up behind a wall flanking the gang. Their presence would deter the bandits' evasion westward down Main Street, leaving the only escape east across the tracks. Josiah glanced toward the railroad which lay in that direction beyond the Livery Stables. To his horror, he watched the brothers Cassidy and Jasper Turk hazard into the road; the elder boy twirled a slingshot.

Josiah instantly sprawled out prone beside the barrels and took aim at the trigger-happy lookout who was drawing a bead in the direction of the boys. Just as Josiah was about to dispatch the robber, a voice prompted the gunman to stand down and he retreated from view.

The gang whirled about on their horses in confusion as the two men that had entered Best's Bank and Trust reappeared with empty bags.

"Money's all gone," one of them said.

"What?"

"Money's gone, let's move. Hyah!"

As they bickered, Dillon Turk darted across the street. Lifting a boy under each arm, he cut across into the alley to safety. The gang spurred their horses and hurried east across the tracks. When the dust settled, it revealed Josiah and Crandall, Levi and Cooper, Marshal Oglesby and Butch Eaton all standing shoulder to shoulder once again in the middle of Main Street. Will Richardson and Jacoby Sutton soon arrived from the Parlor and joined them.

The marshal was first inside the bank where Peregrine Page was consoling a hysterical teller. The vault door lay wide open and inside its only contents were a table with a leger. No copper, no silver, and positively no gold. The men streamed in with wide eyes and gasps of disbelief.

"Perry, you two alright over there?" Marshal Oglesby asked.

Perry's anger flared, "What are you doing in here?! Get after them!"

"Peregrine. Where's all the money?" Oglesby asked.

"With the people of Sagebrush! Where else?"

"Don't play me for a fool, Perry. Where's *my* deposit?"

"I've just been robbed and you're questioning me?! Unbelievable. Well, as fate would have it, we just had a safety audit," Perry said. "It was determined, and rightfully so I might add, that this branch posed a certain degree of liability. Perhaps due to the state of regional law enforcement? Anyway, all reserve funds have been transferred and are secure in the city branch of Best's Bank and Trust as of yesterday."

Cooper's lip quivered, face to face with the man responsible for the demise of his dog, Harvey. Although provoked by the lies dripping from Perry's mouth, he restrained himself as it appeared the marshal might be inclined to pursue an investigation.

"We'll see about that," Oglesby said. "For now, shut that safe and close the bank for the day. Your employee, send her home and then come find me." The marshal turned around and walked toward the door, spurs clinking against the wooden floor. "The rest of you, thank you for your help. That'll be all."

It did not take long for word to spread and a crowd to gather at the bank. Upset customers pounded on the door, demanding Perry let them in to redeem the bank notes for their gold and silver deposits. What they held were receipts, after all—or so everyone had been told. When it became apparent that their efforts would not be satisfied, they turned their attention across the street and began to demand justice at the courthouse.

"Theft!" they shouted. "Fraud!" "Where is our money? We want our savings!"

Their pleas went unanswered. Inside, Marshal Oglesby was exacting an explanation from Peregrine Page.

"Look at them out there, Perry! Just what were you thinkin'?" He paced from one corner of the room to the other.

"Well Oglesby, bank notes, deposits, and withdrawals—they cycle through the bank with regularity. There's a predictable pattern and so long as that pattern persists then the bank can extend credit to those looking for expansion opportunities. Why, that crowd out there has hardly any right to riot as half of them owe us more than they had stored in that vault anyway."

"But now they don't trust you anymore, Perry!" The marshal sat down rubbing his temples. He opened his desk, withdrew a bottle of whiskey, and poured himself a shot. Then another.

Perry began to sweat. He swallowed hard before finally speaking again, "That trust has not been broken, but they don't see that. The deposits are in the city being reinvested by George Best himself."

"And you don't see a problem with that?!" Oglesby slammed his fist down. "Loanin' out other people's money, gamblin' with what they delivered to you for protection, endangerin' trade by printin' bank notes as you see fit?! Jeez Perry, is that why the price of grain is through the roof around here?"

"All of which we have well in hand, none of which is unusual!"

"Alright look, I got a mess on my hands and a pocket full of worthless paper thanks to you. This is your problem; how are you gonna fix it?"

"Well sir, for that I'd need to speak with the mayor."

By the time a special edition of the *Sentinel* hit newsstands the next day, the bank was teeming with people, nearly boiling over into a mob. Porter High sent Cassidy and Jasper Turk home for their own safety and delivered the papers himself. Disbelief rippled through the townsfolk as the headline, rather than announcing charges against Peregrine Page and George Best, instead announced a series of emergency edicts issued by the mayor in response to recent events. The first announcement repeated Perry's claim that a safety audit had revealed vulnerabilities in the security of the Sagebrush branch and, as a precautionary measure, the town's savings had been transferred to the city by rail.

"When's it comin' back?" the people grumbled. "Perry's got plenty of money for new suits," they said, "why ain't he spendin' it on security?"

The second edict the mayor implemented was a demand that any business within Sagebrush and the immediate surrounding territories, including the auction, be conducted solely with the use of bank notes in circulation. While this was done in the attempt to stem the contraction of economic activity, a certain segment of farmers, cowboys, and business owners saw this as an outright ban on the use of gold currency.

"Folks been tradin' in gold forever," they complained. Not only were they cynical of the mayor's balm for their current financial ills, but they scoffed at the idea that anyone who refused legal action against a crook had any right governing business between free and good men.

"There's gonna be a shortage of gold pans, rockers, and sluice boxes all across the west," they predicted.

As if the mayor's first two edicts weren't provocative enough, the final regulation had citizens stomping the paper into the dirt:

As a result of the increase in violent crime on the streets of Sagebrush, after the murder of our beloved doctor and the brazen assault on our trusted financial institution, it is hereby ordained that the use and carry of firearms within the limits of Sagebrush is strictly prohibited.

19

Henry Olt finished a shift on the docks of the Lumber Mill. It had been weeks since the ordeal at the bank and months since his arrival in Sagebrush. His sweat stained clothing had worn thin from hard use. He was hungry. He was tired. He was sore. Knowing his food stores were low, he set out for a bag of flour and figured he would pick up a new shirt while he was at it.

Olt shook the rain from his hair in front of Dodge's Emporium and Dry Goods. The store was deserted except for Martin Kelly behind the counter half-asleep. The bell above the door did little to rouse the morose shopkeeper whose greeting was no more than a grumble. Helping himself to a rack of clothes, Henry found his size. He placed the plaid apparel on the counter along with a cut of beef jerky and was taken aback upon hearing the cost. *Sure*, he thought, *things have been a little tight lately, but how's a man supposed to live with prices risin' like this?*

His shock must have been apparent to Martin Kelly who offered an explanation, "Those bank notes just don't go as far as they used to."

"Ain't that the truth? Now would you believe they're tellin' us we *have* to use 'em!" Olt said.

"Yer not the first to be complainin' either, people are a bit tight these days. Dat journalist feller calls it a recession."

Olt hesitated, then laid the last of his bank notes out on the counter. He grabbed his things and left.

The next day Henry Olt requested a meeting with the foreman at the mill. The foreman listened to Henry go on and on about how hard he worked and how he was giving so much and not receiving enough in return. When he had finished pleading his case, Henry was led by the shoulder to one of the table saws. The foreman showed the measurable wear on the blades and the loose bearings on the rollers. Then he shared the invoices from the railroad for shipments between Sagebrush and the city. The costs of maintenance, shipments, and other expenses were all on the rise. It seemed like everything was going up except the profits. This, the foreman argued, left no room for an increase in labor expenses. The company, he claimed, was doing well just to maintain wages despite the difficult circumstances it was now facing.

Later that week, Olt boarded his horse with his brother-in-law, Dillon, at the Livery Stables. As he saw the horse gorge itself on fresh hay, Dillon commented that it looked pitiful and emaciated. Olt shrugged and pulled an empty pocket from his pants. Dillon boarded the animal free of charge and filled Olt's belly with a hot meal, which was all the charity the man would accept. Defeated, he walked down the street to the mill. He passed Scoville's office just as the lawyer was exiting. The two walked together for a while.

"Scoville, I don't get it. Things were great earlier this year. Everything was busy. I could pay for a place and pay for my beans no problem. Now though, I don't know, I'm feelin' pinched."

"And didn't I warn that this would happen, Mr. Olt?"

"I reckon so. I just don't understand how that Perry guy seems to be the only one that's doin' alright for himself."

"Well Henry, you see, there's nothing supporting these bank notes anymore. The treasure that gave the paper its value was pulled out from under the local economy. The bank has begun to boast on the notes themselves that they can legally be used to settle a debt, but since they can't be redeemed here in town for real coin, they aren't actually worth anything anymore. Their value is just an illusion."

"What's that got to do with that Perry fellow?"

"Well, by law Perry—and really it's George Best, but Perry benefits too—since by law they no longer have to worry about ever making good on those receipts, they just print all they want. They have the advantage of spending the money they create while its purchasing power is still high. By the time you see it, well that's a different story now isn't it? That's why your same wage once seemed adequate, but now finds you feeling—how'd you put it?—'pinched.'"

Scoville stopped at the intersection where their paths would diverge. Henry Olt held his head low with his hands in his pockets and stirred the dirt with the scuffed toe of his boot. Scoville waited patiently for Olt to consider his position and say something, but he never did. He only continued to sulk.

"Look, give yourself a break," Scoville said. "You've faced some trying circumstances. Don't deny yourself that, but don't be defeated by it either. Trust me. When you're ready to move beyond the way you feel about your situation, to change it, you just let me know."

Scoville departed and Olt proceeded to the Lumber Mill for work. He was late that day and the foreman let him know that he certainly wasn't getting a raise if that behavior persisted. Henry was used to being patronized, but his tolerance was wearing thin. After lunch, a strap holding together a bundle of timber snapped, sending five prime trunks down river. Although Henry Olt was able to, one by one, finally retrieve the choice wood, the foreman blamed him for the accident. He docked Olt an hour's pay. After that, Henry was ready to hear whatever it was Scoville had to say.

"I didn't think it would take you long, Mr. Olt," Scoville said, reclining in his office chair that evening. "Are you tired of playing a rigged game?"

Scoville informed Henry that he wasn't the only person to have experienced hardship, rising expenses, and declining profits since the mayor's decree. He explained that while no one went looking for trouble, trying to run afoul of the law, there were honest men who simply refused to bend the knee.

"Good folks are going to do things their own way, and they're increasingly less tolerant of those who arbitrarily change the rules," Scoville said. He dug around in his desk drawer and removed a leather pouch and handed it to Olt. "So, here's what we're gonna do: you're going to take this now but I'm trading it to you on credit. Tomorrow you're going to withdraw the last of your bank notes from your account at the bank and repay me."

Henry Olt emptied the contents of the leather pouch onto the desk between the men with a clatter. Out poured pure copper and fine silver coins of all weights, sizes, and mints.

"It feels like ages since I seen or held these." Olt rubbed a coin between his finger and thumb. "I can't take all this; I ain't got enough to cover it."

"Whatever you can't cover is my gift to you. I saw your poor horse this morning and I talked to Dillon. I hope you'll forgive my intrusion into your business, but he said it could stand a trip to the farrier. Tomorrow, after you've brought me those worthless bank notes, go see Cooper down at the smithy and get that horse shod."

The next day, Henry Olt did as Scoville suggested. Emboldened with a renewed sense of resolve because of the lawyer's directions, he observed the others in the bank. They were conducting business in bank notes, just as they were told, just as George Best planned—to their own peril. Henry saw in them the man he had been only the day before, and he was flooded with pity. He satisfied his debt to Scoville and rode down to the smithy.

Cooper was there early, tending the burning fires and wielding a hammer that sent sparks across the brick floor. Cooper looked reluctantly from his work up at Henry when he requested the horseshoes.

"I know what you're thinkin'," Henry said, "but I ain't here tryin' to pawn off any of them useless bank notes." Cooper only nodded. Henry knew the man well enough to know that if he wasn't talking he wasn't comfortable, so he asked, "What'll you take for 'em?"

"Alright here's the deal, I need ore to cast this iron, I need grain for my belly, hay for my horses, and silver for tradin' the services of others," Cooper said.

A smile spread across Henry's face realizing that Scoville was right, there must be others. This was, for him, an initiation into a secretive loosely organized association of rebels. For the first time, Olt recognized that standing for what is right sometimes meant standing outside the law.

Olt said at last, "Alright, silver it is."

The two men shook hands and Cooper got to work. Before long, Henry Olt had completed his first transaction in a thriving black market that was emerging in Sagebrush. He did not realize how extensive it was, though, until he was party to a conversation between Josiah Rush and his own brother-in-law, Dillon Turk, back at the livery.

"... so then we have 'em pay up in bank notes, just like the law requires," Dillon said, "but then we turn right back around and buy hay, food, textiles, or silver from 'em for the same amount so's we don't get stuck with Best's trash."

"And what you *do* get stuck with gets passed on to me, huh?" Josiah asked. "Pretty clever."

"Yessir, that's why this week's haul is a little lighter, Josiah. I can't believe it's come to this," Dillon said. He handed over a stack of bank notes that Josiah stuffed into a burlap sack.

"Dillon, you're a good man. This won't last forever. I'll see to it that I get a good deal for all this back in the city. Am I good to take my five percent then, to cover expenses?" Josiah said.

"Oh of course, of course."

"Mr. Rush," Henry Olt interrupted. His eyes found a glimmer of steel from the outlawed gun on Josiah's hip. "You mean to say, you're swappin' these bank notes back in the city for the people here in town?"

"Henry," Josiah said, "that's exactly what I'm doin'. George Best never saw Sagebrush as anythin' other than a sandbox to shit in, so a bunch of us are sendin' it all back to stink up his own yard. In the process we're reclaimin', piece by piece, everything he stole from us."

"Dillon, you've got the boys to think about. What if you get caught? Ain't this a pretty big risk?" Olt said.

"It is," Dillon agreed. "If we do this, we risk losin' everything; but if we don't do this, we're guaranteed to lose it. Am I supposed to just sacrifice all I've ever worked for? Supposed to give our time and services away for nothin'? Why? 'Cause someone up and decided that they's gonna try to print our way to riches? Nonsense. The mayor don't know what's best for me and my family!"

Dillon was getting worked up, so Josiah put out his hand and generously took over. "You see, Henry, things in the city are bouncin' back after the last run on the bank," Josiah said.

Dillon took a bucket of rye to the pasture as Josiah continued. "Mr. Olt, it appears as though people there have regained their trust in these bank notes 'cause Best was able to satisfy their frightened withdrawals with the gold an' silver he took from Sagebrush. Next time he may not be so lucky. As far as I'm concerned, there is a very short window where we can get rid of *these* things," he patted the bag full of bank notes, "an' get back all the genuine funds we can recover."

"So you're arrangin' this for everyone? All the business owners in town?" Olt asked.

"Well, obviously not everyone, but there are enough. Still, don't go advertisin' that all around town, Henry. I hope you can appreciate it if I don't name names."

"Well, that's mighty fine of you," a voice bellowed from behind them. They turned to see Nicholas Scoville withdraw a pocket full of bank notes.

"Well look-y here," Josiah said. "What are you doin' carryin' those around, Scoville? Can't say I've ever known you to cave to public pressure."

Scoville balked. "Have you ever known me to blatantly shirk the local polity, either? Josiah, I'm a lawyer for heaven's sake."

"Ah, that just makes you slow to come 'round is all. Still, your part in all this stays under wraps, too."

"That's why I trust you with this." Scoville placed the crinkled bank notes in Josiah's hand. He counted them as Scoville wrote down the amount in a ledger that both men signed. "I will warn you, though, the marshal seems keen to enforce the new mandates. Earlier today I argued against the confiscation of silver that an unaware traveler used to try and pay for a ticket at the Depot. So be careful," Scoville nodded at Josiah's sidearm, "especially with that."

"That's a shame. Thanks for lettin' us know," Olt said.

Josiah spoke again after a brief pause. "Well, gentlemen, it seems that's the last of what I need, so I'll bid you farewell. I'm off to meet our buyer in the city. I'll be back on the eight o'clock train in three days' time. Till then!" Josiah tipped his hat, grabbed the burlap sack, and headed across Main Street to the Depot.

20

Josiah's trip to the city proved to be a profitable one and would have easily seen the vendors in Sagebrush paid handsomely in sound money had it not been for the misfortune that befell the prideful Henry Olt. The day before Josiah was set to return, Henry finished a shift at the mill and marched into the foreman's office. He'd grown bold after successfully bargaining in silver again for a few days and decided he would demand his wages in coin, not by the stroke of a pen in a ledger at a bank he no longer trusted. The foreman kicked up his boots onto the timber framed desk and reclined in his chair. He placed his intertwined fingers behind his head, offered a confused face, and asked for clarification.

Olt, suddenly intimidated, began to lose his nerve and set about shaking and stammering, trying to backtrack his request. After failing to pacify his boss, Henry turned to leave.

"Just wait right there," the foreman said. He had finally grown tired of Henry's demands, tardiness, and mishaps. "I owe you some wages and I want to settle up. It'll be the last you draw from this place of business. Thank you for your service to the company. You say you'll only accept silver?" The foreman took off a ring and tossed it to Henry. "That'll be all."

"Sir, I . . ."

"That'll be all. You dally any longer and you'll be trespassin'."

Henry left dejected. He repeatedly mulled over the conversation in his head, the ring spinning in his fingers. Main Street was different now, without the promise of hope that this town once provided him. He sat for a long time on the bench in front of Scoville's office, feeling sorry for himself and regretting the principled stand he made that cost him his job. Henry was embittered and fearful. He would have given anything to take it back. He felt let down, hoodwinked, by the motivational ploys of Scoville and Josiah. They were quick to welcome him to their clandestine alliance, but where would they be when the bills were due and Henry didn't have the money to pay up?

As he was stewing in front of the law office, waiting for the opportunity to give Scoville a piece of his mind, Marshal Oglesby approached.

"Afternoon, Mr. Olt," he said.

"G'day Marshal."

"What have you got there?" Oglesby asked, pointing to the ring with which Henry was fidgeting.

Suddenly, Henry's heart sank and the color drained from his face. "Uh . . . nothin', sir."

"That's not what I hear." The marshal stepped menacingly into the sunlight and cast a large shadow. "I hear you accepted that as payment from the Lumber Mill after you refused legal tender. That's a crime now, Mr. Olt. I had you pegged as a better man than that."

Scoville, curious upon recognizing the marshal's booming voice outside, drew near to the window and overheard him talking to Henry Olt.

"Unfortunately," the marshal continued, "it's my duty to execute the laws of the land regardless of my personal friendship with the perpetrator. Do you understand, Mr. Olt? I consider you a friend, so perhaps we can talk like men and come to a friendly arrangement that doesn't end with you before a judge. What do you say, Mr. Olt? Let's take a walk, shall we?"

Olt nodded feverishly and followed the marshal down to the courthouse. They passed through the courtroom and a small corridor to an empty jail cell. Oglesby pulled two chairs through the bars and left the door open. Olt hesitated before joining him inside the cell.

When both men were seated, Marshal Oglesby was uncomfortably quiet until Henry finally broke the silence.

"What are we doin' here?" he asked.

"Adjustin' to your new quarters unless you can give me a reason why I shouldn't lock you up for violatin' the law."

"What do you want?"

"Henry, I know you're a good man and still relatively new to town. Since I'm a forgivin' person, I can overlook the misdeeds you've committed durin' your attempts to learn which kind of folk you'd ought to be associatin' with here in town." He cleared his throat. "There are indeed certain kind of folk you'd ought not to be associatin' with, and I think you know just who it is that I'm talkin' about. There's rumors goin' 'round of a scheme, of sorts, to challenge the authority and lawful governance of this territory. You wouldn't happen to know anything about that, now would you?"

"No sir, I . . . well . . ." Olt could only recall the anger he felt over what it cost him when he listened to Scoville and Josiah about the silver. And Oglesby was a lawman, after all. Perhaps he'd do well to tell the marshal what he knew and avoid the cold damp fate that awaited him otherwise. Then again, what kind of man was the marshal? The kind to put down a sick man and act as a hired gun for those who buy political influence?

Henry Olt was at an impasse.

"Yes, Mr. Olt. Go on," the marshal said.

Henry found his nerve again, "What's in it for me?"

"You mean aside from not rottin' in this hell-hole while you await trial?"

"Yes, exactly!" Olt said.

"Well, you know what *I* want. What else do *you* want?"

Since neither the marshal nor Josiah commanded his allegiance, Olt opted for evasion. "I want you to buy my horse."

"Excuse me?"

"That's right, I want you to buy my horse. It's the last thing of any real value I still own. I'll take payment in silver coin, not in bank notes, and I want a train ticket out of town."

Marshal Oglesby smirked and rocked his head side to side as he pondered the proposal. Before he could respond, Henry Olt delivered the clincher. "You promise me that," he said, "and I'll promise you Josiah Rush." The smile drained from the marshal's face, and he leaned in closer.

The offer was one he could not refuse.

According to Henry Olt, Josiah would be arriving armed and with luggage containing contraband destined for the cabal of business owners whom Oglesby viewed as insubordinate. Not only would the marshal have the satisfaction of detaining Josiah Rush, but this would quell the heart of rebellion that was fomenting throughout Sagebrush.

Dusk settled upon the territory the night of Josiah's return. Oglesby could hear the cadence of the eight o'clock train in the distance, so he slinked into the shadows of the alley and waited. Henry Olt was there with all that remained of his earthly belongings crammed into a small duffle sitting beside him in the dirt. Olt removed a coin pouch and counted his silver as he looked sidelong at the livery. He felt a pang of guilt for not saying farewell to the Turk family, but he could not conceive of a convincing story for his abrupt departure. Dillon would have seen through him and would never understand Henry's decision. Olt was suddenly afraid for the boys. He had not considered how his actions could impact them. It was too late though; Henry had made his deal and would be better off leaving town and never coming back.

The train halted with a creak and a hiss. From the shadows the marshal watched a handful of passengers disembark until finally a dark figure stepped onto the platform and donned a crooked hat. As the figure descended the deck and neared the alley, Oglesby hastily emerged with his gun drawn.

"Josiah Rush," he said, "you're under arrest."

"Is that right?" Josiah asked, raising his hands. His eyes followed Henry Olt who passed the two men while on his way to the train. "Have anything to do with the word of this Judas?"

The marshal bound him and ordered an attendant to have Josiah's bags brought out. "This has to do with your violation of the edicts in this land regardin' the carry of firearms." The marshal gave Josiah a pat down, expecting to find his sidearm which seemed to be an extension of the man. Instead, he found an empty holster.

"Nothin' illegal about wearin' one of those, is there?" Josiah chuckled.

Marshal Oglesby's heart dropped. He had a suspicion that although he was the one making the arrest, Josiah was controlling the situation. He shoved Josiah's face into the wall causing the tattered black hat to fall to the ground. Blood poured from his eyebrow and stained the shirt Lorraine had once laundered with such care.

"I hope to fare better than the last prisoner I seen you with," Josiah said.

"We'll just have to see, won't we?"

Oglesby hollered for Henry Olt who had already boarded the train. He considered following Olt to demand an explanation, but in his panicked deliberation he couldn't justify leaving Josiah unattended or run the chance of missing the employee with the bags. The hope of recovering the money was worth more than the pleasure of making Henry Olt answer for his bad intel. So Marshal Oglesby watched through the window of a railcar as Olt took a seat. *Good riddance, you weak, pitiful man*, he thought.

With Josiah handcuffed, Oglesby waited in the dark alley for the luggage. Finally, the attendant rounded the corner with Josiah's belongings as the whistle of the steam engine blew. After struggling under its weight, the attendant dropped the suitcase with a heavy thud that stirred up a dust cloud in the alley. In the distance, the train lurched forward and picked up speed. Henry Olt was already departing Sagebrush when Marshal Oglesby opened the duffle. Instead of a bag of riches, Oglesby learned that Josiah Rush had arrived with a bag of rocks.

At the same time, somewhere in the prairie not five miles east of Sagebrush was a lone rider. He was barreling along the tracks but would soon divert his course and follow the river. It was Cooper Emmons, carrying Josiah's pistol and a bag containing the community's earnings. He had waited under the railroad bridge outside of town just like Scoville told him. When the train passed, the bag had dropped just like Scoville told him. He was now bound for a keen one-armed horse breeder who would know where to stash it safely, just like Scoville told him.

Back in town the door of the jail cell slammed shut.

"You can't hold me like this, Oglesby!" Josiah said. "What are you chargin' me with?!"

"You'll find out tomorrow." The marshal snuffed out the lamp and shut the door as he exited.

21

Josiah awoke the next morning on a cot in the jail cell. He propped himself up on one elbow and yawned. Rubbing the base of his skull, he massaged away the pain of a stiff neck. The voices in the corridor that woke him grew louder.

Josiah recognized his friend Nicholas Scoville by his indignation, "Marshal, you are completely out of line! Holding my client without any charges for another minute will result in serious problems for you! I'll see to it that—"

"That what, Scoville? I swear if it'll get you to shut up, I'll consider it."

The door to the cell block opened and Scoville stepped through in a burst of excitement. He carried a stack of papers and was visibly relieved to see Josiah.

"This power drunk heathen wouldn't let me back here to see you for the longest time," he said, pointing to Oglesby. The marshal rolled his eyes then turned around and left.

"Good to see you, too, friend," Josiah said.

"I'm sorry to have left you in here all night, I just got word this morning . . ."

"It's alright. Did Cooper make it?"

Scoville lowered his voice and reassured Josiah, "Yes, yes, everything went according to plan. I *knew* to trust my suspicions when I saw Henry get the shake down from Oglesby."

"I tell you, when I got the telegram that you wanted me to dump all that money off them tracks I thought you was crazy." Josiah looked around at the inhospitable cage. "Turns out though, I'd be spendin' a whole lot longer than one night behind these here bars if it weren't for you."

"Don't mention it. Look, there's something I want to talk to you about. I had hoped it wouldn't come to this but given that you now most undoubtedly have a target on your back, I think it's time we handled it." Scoville slipped a few papers through the cell bars. "I took the liberty of drawing these up. I hope you don't mind, it's just that I'm sure your concerns are elsewhere. I don't know what trouble awaits once Oglesby has you released, but this is . . . well, just in case."

After stretching, Josiah took the papers. He sat back down on the bunk and read them closely. Scoville understood that by signing at the bottom Josiah would be accepting a grave reality about his situation. Josiah knew there would be a price for making a stand, but the potential cost of his convictions was more than he had wagered. Signing the documents, however, was clearly the most selfless and righteous thing to do—if not also the most difficult. Josiah swallowed hard, attempting to clear the lump forming in his throat.

After a long silence, he reached for Scoville's fountain pen. When the last ink droplet had dried on his signature, Josiah folded the pages and returned them to Scoville.

"Trust that I'll keep these safe, and pray the time never comes when we shall need them," Scoville said. The lawyer turned and left.

As the door was closing, Josiah heard him say to the marshal, "You haven't charged him. Release him, right now." Before long, the clatter of keys and the clank of the cell door were the song of Josiah's liberation. The marshal didn't say a word; he simply walked off and left Josiah to find his own way out.

Stumbling onto the street with squinting eyes adjusting to the daylight, Josiah took in a deep breath of fresh air. Although his incarceration was brief, he moseyed up the road with a newfound appreciation for the cloudless day. Josiah walked to the livery where Dillon had been boarding Nero. It was on this short walk that Josiah resolved to never again be subject to the confines of men. He was not in the business of creating victims so there should be no reason for him to ever submit to the misguided long arm of the law. A very basic and primal notion overwhelmed him. He drew breath, moved about freely, and no one had any natural authority to take that from him. It was more than that, though. Josiah resolved that if anyone ever felt they did, then they were welcome to try.

Josiah retrieved Nero and arrived back at the ranch. He was greeted by Lorraine and Carson with open arms, long hugs, and an abundance of kisses. He beamed as he drew back to take a good look at Lorraine.

"Oh, Josiah!" she said through tears, "I was so worried about you. I can't believe, I . . . when I got word I just—" Lorraine buried her head in his shoulder and squeezed him tight.

"Easy now, shh, shh, it's fine. Look, I'm here, I'm free, all is right with the world."

"Promise me you won't ever put me through something like that again!"

"Now you know I can't do that," he said, caressing her hair. "But I can promise you I won't ever get tired of these arms wrapped around me. Or the taste of your perfect lips."

She pulled away to wipe her eyes and struck a flirtatious pose. It delighted Josiah when Lorraine handed Carson over and set about making breakfast. He lifted the boy into the air causing the little one to burst forth with giggles.

"I invited the Turks for dinner tonight," Josiah said. "I know I just got back, and I want to spend some time with you, but it came up in conversation and you know how it goes."

"Oh of course, darling, it'd be lovely to see Rebecca. Are the boys coming?"

"Didn't think to ask, but I imagine so."

While Josiah and Lorraine discussed dinner plans, back in town Nicholas Scoville had finally returned to his office after running errands. With Josiah's documents in hand, he went to a filing cabinet. He stopped suddenly with the drawer half open and pondered the risks involved with simply filing them away. Instead, he closed the cabinet and turned to the safe in the back corner of his office. He stashed the paperwork and was closing the door when a voice from the doorway startled him.

"Don't bother doing that, Mr. Scoville." Marshal Oglesby had entered silently and was watching the activity. Scoville turned around to see the marshal step aside, allowing the mayor into the office. He took a seat as the marshal paced toward the safe.

"Looks like you haven't upheld your relationships with those in power, Mr. Scoville," Oglesby gloated. "That's too bad. When those associations sour, certain privileges get appointed to other more trusted agents. Such is the case with your role as treasurer."

"What? What is this nonsense?" Scoville said.

"I assure you it is not nonsense. I'm here to relieve you of your duties—effective immediately—and return the territory's funds to its elected officials. There will be a new treasurer assigned in your stead. Someone more aligned with the vision for the future of Sagebrush."

"And who would that be? Who is more capable or careful than me?!" Scoville turned to the mayor, "Who will be controlling these assets now?"

The marshal answered, "He's not made any official appointments yet, but I'm sure he'll pick the *Best* man for the job." Oglesby sneered, then read off Scoville's total. The mayor confirmed that the ledgers matched and the two of them hauled away the funds disregarding all Scoville's further protestations.

Outside, they passed Dillon and Rebecca Turk, each carrying an armful of fresh vegetables. Oglesby leered at Dillon who was alarmed to see him emerge from Scoville's office. Dillon hoped to check in with the lawyer, but Rebecca insisted they had a slew of things to manage before seeing Josiah and Lorraine that evening. The Turks loaded the greens onto a mule cart and set about their business.

When the time for fellowship arrived, Rebecca stood on the doorstep of the ranch and knocked. Dillon joined her, but Cassidy and Jasper had run off to the stables to see the horses. Lorraine greeted the Turks. She ushered them into the dining room where Dillon unloaded an armful of food which was promptly replaced by an armful of baby. Carson cooed. The house was rich with the buttery smell of biscuits. From the kitchen, Josiah whistled a tune while pan frying wild mushrooms. Rebecca, quite at home wherever she went, insisted on taking over and kicked Josiah out of his own kitchen so she and Lorraine could cook and converse. All too happy to oblige, Josiah poured a drink and joined Dillon in the other room. The two men with baby Carson stepped outside to watch for the boys and ended up taking a walk to the stables themselves.

Nero stamped and snorted when Josiah rounded the corner to the barn. Little Jasper Turk spooked and took a careless stride backward. He stumbled into an empty pale Cassidy had just used to give the Percherons water. The elder boy heard the commotion and turned in time to see his little brother falling and extended his hand. Jasper caught it, but Cassidy was unstable so they both fell. Covered in hay and laughing heartily, the boys wrestled as Dillon watched with pride. Josiah smiled and observed their playfulness with fresh eyes. Before him was a poignant example of the joy of freedom he had only recently reclaimed. It cemented Josiah's resoluteness to appreciate and exercise it.

"Alright boys, saddle up," Josiah said.

The boys' excitement was heard from the house. However, once the first horse was brought out, little Jasper changed his mind. He had grown significantly this year but wasn't quite confident enough to handle a horse on his own. He opted for grooming Nero instead. Dillon watched with amusement as Cassidy stayed one step ahead of Josiah's instruction. Slipping on the bridle, positioning the blanket, throwing over the saddle, cinching the straps—all of which he accomplished with the expertise of a veteran horseman. He had watched his father do these tasks a thousand times. Finally, he mounted the horse and trotted for the round pen.

"Where you off to, boy?" Josiah asked.

"Pen, Mr. Josiah."

Josiah checked with Dillon, who gave a nod. He then turned back to Cassidy, "There's enough daylight left, take her to this western meadow where we can still see you, but go ahead and turn her loose!"

The only thing keeping Cassidy's jaw off the ground was the smile drawing up the corners of his mouth. He reined around with a "hyah" and began racing the long shadows cast by the pines stretching out from the edge of the pasture.

After a little while, Josiah remarked to Dillon about the bravery of his boys.

"I know they scared the daylights outta you a while back durin' that robbery. I seen you haul ass to scoop them up across the street."

"Foolishness," Dillon shook his head. "Coulda been killed runnin' out like that against a whole gang of armed robbers."

"I hope you weren't too hard on 'em. World needs men that ain't had the courage whooped completely out of 'em as boys."

"Well the world, and their momma, needs these boys to live to become men."

"Look at 'em, Dillon," Josiah said. Jasper was brushing Nero in the stall and Cassidy was a stark black silhouette against the late burnt orange sunset. "They're well on their way."

"Yeah, I suppose you're right. Strategy can always be learned."

"Yup. They can learn that anywhere, but it's *your* job to impart to them what it means to be a man."

"It's my *honor*, you mean." Dillon witnessed Jasper feed Nero an apple.

Just then, Rebecca popped out of the doorway and rang the dinner bell. Cassidy rode in, quickly unsaddled the horse without instruction and raced Jasper to the house. The two older men sauntered back with the baby and washed up as Lorraine set the table.

When everyone had gathered, Josiah said the blessing. They passed the food and with every plate full, there was still a second helping left for the growing boys. Josiah found more joy in his life as he enjoyed more life with others.

Josiah admired Lorraine as he noticed her exceptional talents as hostess. Her elegance was on full display as she graciously steered warm conversation. He witnessed the Turks respond to her natural comfort as he did, exchanging fears and sadness just as easily as gladness and laughter, of which there was plenty.

When plates were empty, Dillon asked the boys to find something productive to do while the adults shared in grown-up matters. When they had gone, Dillon spoke frankly and directly.

"Josiah, we want to express our regret over Henry's actions. We think it downright cowardly what he done. I wished I'd have know'd what all he was plannin' 'cause I'd have whooped him. Know that."

"My sister didn't have the best taste in men," Rebecca said. "In fact, she was utterly lousy when it come to it."

Lorraine noticed that Rebecca spoke more critically than her good nature usually allowed, but she was sympathetic.

"Well, I appreciate that," Josiah said. "I just want to make it real clear that I don't blame you for his actions or hold any grudge against Henry." He said this in case there was any lingering attachment the Turks may not have liked to admit. Secretly, Josiah entertained the idea that Henry Olt might meet a grisly and untimely end. While Josiah did not truly wish that upon the turncoat, he surely never wanted to see the man around Sagebrush ever again.

Having the most difficult of topics out of the way, the Turks were fortuitously interrupted by a knock on the door. Lorraine began to stand but Josiah stopped her. He grabbed a rifle and peered through the window. The floors creaked as he shifted back on his heels in relief. He set down the repeater and unlocked the door for Levi and Cooper.

"Pardon, are we interruptin'?" Levi asked when he noticed Josiah had company.

"Not at all!" Dillon answered. He stood and met the men in the living room to shake hands as they removed their hats and dusters.

"Ooh wee!" Cooper sniffed and rubbed his belly. "We come by to drop off these hinges, but it was really just to see what you was cookin' up Ms. Lorraine."

"I think the boys are done if you want to help yourself to whatever's left," Lorraine said from the other room.

"Cooper! Yay!" "Hi Uncle Cooper!" the boys shouted as they ran into the room at the sound of his voice. Little Jasper tackled him, and Cooper pretended to buckle over. Cassidy, however, halted, looking hesitantly at Levi.

"Cassidy, quit yer starin'," Rebecca said.

"Ah, it's alright," Levi replied. "The kid's just waitin'..." he pushed an arm through his sleeve "... to see THIS!" He teased the boys with his scarred limb and laughed wildly.

Little Jasper pretended to be afraid, screamed, and ran off. The showmanship was enough to win over the elder brother though, and as soon as Cassidy cracked a smile, he walked over and gave Levi a big hug. When the chaos quieted, Cooper helped himself to a plate of food. Levi casually tossed a copy of the *Sentinel* on the table as he sat down.

"What's this?" Josiah said.

"Breakin' news. Figured you'd want to celebrate the arrest of that dangerous Josiah Rush, like the rest of the town's supposed to be doin'."

"You kiddin' me? It's already hit the papers?"

"What? This can't be right!" Lorraine grabbed the article. "Oglesby must have gone to Porter last night!" She scanned the page. "Josiah, this doesn't mention anything about him releasing you without pressing charges. This isn't journalism! This reporting is an attack on your good name."

"Yeah, but it don't sound like that Porter fella's the one who wrote it neither," Cooper said. "Writin' is all wrong."

"Ah hell, I ain't worried 'bout what folks got to say 'bout me," Josiah said.

"Well, if that's the case, Josiah, this is still reckless," Lorraine said.

"How you figure?"

"If Porter didn't write this, but he was bullied into printing it, then it demeans his work. What's worse, Josiah, is they aren't telling the whole story. Instead this is designed to change the way people feel about you."

"Folks is always gonna have someone tell 'em who the bad guy is, been that way far longer than that paper's been around.

So long as they ain't come up here with torches and pitchforks, to hell with 'em."

"Goodness me!" Lorraine gasped. She had been half listening and half scanning the page. Josiah sat upright.

". . . aaand there it is," Levi said. "Reckon you'd find that one interestin', too."

Levi referenced an opinion piece written by George Best. In it, Best detailed at length the economic woes the town was suffering, the transparency issues concerning the bank and the town's savings, as well as the inflationary pressures the citizens of Sagebrush were experiencing. All these things, according to Best, directly resulted from mismanagement on the part of the branch manager, Peregrine Page. George Best publicly vowed to remedy these ills and restore the economic prosperity he now took credit for bringing to town.

"Goodness me, indeed," Rebecca said.

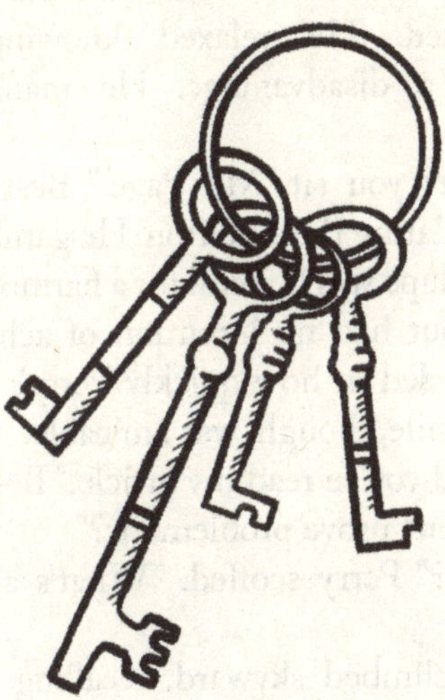

22

The heavy iron doors swung open. Peregrine Page's heels clicked across the marble floor of the city branch of Best's Bank and Trust. The morning after Best's article ran in the *Sentinel*, Perry was on the first train to the city. Exhausted after the late arrival and operating on four hours of sleep, Perry was the first person inside when the bank opened. He brushed past an unfamiliar teller straight down the hallway toward Best's office. The flustered young man initially chased Perry down but retreated in fear at the glare he was shown by the determined trespasser.

George Best sat in his office admiring a new timepiece when Perry burst through the door. Perry held a copy of the *Sentinel* high above his head which he then thrashed down on the desk. Best's chair slammed forward at the intrusion and the two men stood opposite each other, gorilla-fisted, leaning over the mahogany desk.

"Mis-MANAGE-ment!" Perry shouted.

Best squinted. He relaxed knowing that Perry's anger betrayed a disadvantage. He managed a cordial, professional tone.

"Please, won't you sit, Mr. Page." Best sat down first, effectively deescalating the situation. He gambled that despite Perry's rage, the dupe was hopeful for a harmonious resolution. Best was right but had no intention of achieving any such outcome. He reveled in how quickly Perry's anger turned to timidity. Best's smile, though, was amicable.

"I understand you've read my article," Best said. "I should hope that this won't prove problematic?"

"Problematic?" Perry scoffed. "What's a little libel here and there?"

Best's gaze climbed skyward, recalling the events that led to their business agreements. "And what's a little slander here and there?" His eyes slowly moved from the ceiling and cut right through Perry. He saw a fragile plaything. The man across from him was porcelain.

Perry's face fell flat. He swallowed hard and his pulse pounded at his temples.

"Perry, you look as though you've just hung your queen. Please, sir, don't embarrass yourself. Pull it together."

All Perry could hear was the ringing in his ears. He didn't feel the expensive threads in his suit, he could only focus on the heat rising from his neck up and across his face.

"This has been part of your plan the whole time? To disgrace me like this?" Perry said.

Best was savoring the revenge. "You didn't think you could run my name down for years all over that place, try to blackmail me, and then we were really just going to be business partners, did you?" Best paused. "Oh, you did. Pity. That's not how it works. I mean, you embarrassed me. You hurt my pride, and for what? So you could be popular with some backwards sodbusters? That was a mistake, Perry."

"Okay, so now you have settled the score. You've humiliated me in front of my hometown. Are you satisfied?"

"Oh, completely!"

"Good, well I hope you enjoyed that little stunt. I suppose I can handle the indignity so long as I leave here with at least *some* of the reserves. The temporary orders mandating bank notes for trade in the territory are set to expire soon and I have customers who wish to withdraw their deposits."

"Temporary, ha! What's more permanent than temporary government measures? You still don't understand. You're not walking out of here with anything. Not so much as an ounce of copper for those poor people, and definitely not with your title! I'm revoking your privilege to use the name Best's Bank and Trust—effective immediately!"

"You can't do that! *I* bought that bank! I have the rights to it!"

Best savored the knowledge that Perry had not paid attention to the details of the arrangement. "Except, you bought that bank with my money, and you don't read the fine print." Best laughed. "I can call the loan, Perry. At any time! And as a matter of fact," Best leaned forward and put a finger on the desk, "*I am*!"

"What?!" Perry said. Best withdrew a contract from his desk drawer and let Perry examine it.

"That's right, it says 'immediately upon request.' Do you have the means to repay the loan you swore for Best's Bank and Trust?"

Perry gulped. He stuck a finger in his collar to loosen it. "You know I don't." Out of shame he shied away, and his eyes caught a scrap of paper with Best's scribbling.

"Well, that's it then. Thank you for your time, Perry. Please leave your keys on the way out."

Perry began rationalizing the situation. The blow was so crushing and sudden that in its wake he could only cling to whatever hope he had left. He considered that maybe it was for the better that his business with Best was finished. The man was a con artist, after all. *At least*, he thought, *I can go back to running the Parlor.*

Suddenly flushed with concern, Perry jerked his head up to meet Best's gaze. The man had his head down and his eyebrows raised, eyeing Perry with sadistic amusement.

"No, you don't mean to . . . surely you wouldn't . . ."

"I do mean to," Best said. "I'd call the loan on the Parlor immediately, too, if I could. Instead, according to my older contracts, you have, let's see," he scanned another document, "ah, thirty days." Best let out a belly laugh.

In a last-ditch effort to exact revenge for the loss of his livelihood and all he'd ever worked toward, Perry threatened to make good on his promises to expose their joint corruption.

"I'll go to Porter High at the *Sentinel* right now. I'll tell him everything. The bank note scheme, financing the Depot, the fire—EVERYTHING!"

Best yawned. "Peregrine Page," he said, "just who, at this point, will believe you? You're a failure who can't pay his debts." Perry's head dropped. "As far as the people are concerned, you're responsible for the circumstances that saw their savings shipped away to *my* vault." Best kept speaking while Perry ran his fingers through his greasy hair. "They resent you for it. Those people will now see that you're in default on your loans. What a disgraceful situation." Best kept adding salt to the wound, but Perry got a closer view of the scribbling on his scrap of paper. "Anything you say now will seem like the desperate ramblings of a man who has presently lost two businesses." The verbal assault made possible the conditions for the image of the paper to be burned into Perry's subconscious. "Besides," Best continued, "you have no proof but your word, which is no good here any longer. I made sure of that. Your fall from grace is complete."

Suddenly, as if doused by a deluge, Perry's anger washed away from his head to his feet. He had found his breaking point. The man stood, tossed the bank keys to George Best, and left the office. On his way out he began to laugh hysterically. He untied his bowtie and threw it on the ground. His golden cuff links followed. He tore off his suit coat and tossed it to the teller he'd ignored on the way in.

Bursting forth through the bank doors, Perry emerged lighter and happier than he had been in a long while. He patronized a city bar. By the time he left, he was barefoot wearing only his slacks and cummerbund. He then boarded the next train back to Sagebrush.

When he arrived the following day, he teetered, hungover, from the alley down to the Parlor. His entrance drew the attention of everyone, including Josiah and Scoville who were conferring over a pint. Perry approached the two men.

"Easy fella," Josiah said as Perry advanced on their table. Josiah stood with his hand out in a defensive manner. Perry pulled out a chair and bumped the table as he sat, nearly spilling Scoville's drink.

"Can we help you?" Scoville said.

"More disdain, please," Perry replied. Scoville thought he smirked, but Josiah interpreted the smile as one of a man experiencing the relief of penance.

"Just what are you doin' here? Lawrence says he ain't seen you step foot inside this place for months." Josiah was more inquisitive than accusatory. Still, he crossed his arms and his head favored one shoulder.

"Well, good sirs, I've been given the boot. I'm done over at the bank; and this place, well, let's just say I hope you're both here making memories," Perry said. Josiah nodded and leaned back in his chair. Neither he nor Scoville were surprised by the news given Best's comments in the paper. Josiah *was* surprised to feel pity for the man, though.

Perry continued. "Perhaps your treasurer can now be the man to make your change."

"No sir, evidently we've both been dismissed," Scoville said.

"What do you mean?"

"Oh, so you haven't heard either. I was just telling Josiah that I have been relieved of those duties. I no longer manage the town reserves."

Something clicked inside Perry's brain. A connection was made between this new revelation and a bit of trivial information picked up casually in the throes of turmoil. Perry recalled with vivid detail that piece of paper from Best's office. The scribbling he once passively regarded as irrelevant, now suddenly made sense.

In a final, guilt-provoked attempt to undo any further damage set in motion by his involvement with Best, Perry saw an opportunity to foil the banker's schemes. This would, Perry hoped, also serve as an opportunity for recompense.

"They're moving that money," he said.

"Well, we figured that much," Josiah admitted.

"But I know when and where!"

"You do?" Scoville was skeptical.

"I do, I saw the schedule in Best's own handwriting!" Perry's enthusiasm bordered on maniacal.

"Josiah, perhaps we should take a moment to discuss this." Scoville said, noting the intrigue in the man's face. Already his wheels were spinning.

"You don't trust me, I understand," Perry said. "I wouldn't trust me either, I've been lousy. But this is my chance, not to make it right, but to prove to you that I know I was wrong."

"Lousy is an understatement. You've destroyed livelihoods! And the savings of these hard working, honest people! The economy here in Sagebrush! And you did it to ensure that you could afford, on a whim, whatever manner of luxury you so desired." Scoville was drawing attention to himself.

Josiah noticed the staring faces around them and put an arm on Scoville to calm him down. "Okay, okay, let's talk," he said.

They stepped aside where Scoville whispered, "Josiah, the man's so crooked he'd swallow nails and pass corkscrews!"

"Maybe, but somethin' broke him. I know it, I can recognize it when I see it."

"Which is exactly why he can't be trusted—he's desperate."

"Maybe, but I think the only thing he's desperate for is revenge. While that's no virtue, it just so happens to align with our purposes, and an opportunity."

"What do you mean?"

"Scoville, you go right now and round up Levi, Crandall, Cooper, and . . ." he paused, "yeah, and get Will and Jacoby, too."

"Are you sure you know what you're doing? Those two?!"

"They're rough and they're callous, but they're good men. They got no love for high falutin' big-city wolves come into town intent to devour their people." He nodded as if to fortify himself. "Yup, Will and Jacoby, too."

"Alright, what are you going to do?"

"Meet me back at my ranch with the men at two o'clock. I'm gonna find out what Mr. Peregrine Page knows about stealin' money."

A short while later, Lorraine stood on the porch of the guest house with Carson when she heard the distant rumble of hooves. She watched over the horizon as dust rose then drifted away on the wind. As Scoville's wagon team crested the hill, the rest of the men followed on horseback. Lorraine instinctively sensed trouble looming.

"Scoville," she said walking toward the pen where the men tied their horses, "good to see you. Where's Josiah? Is everything alright?"

"Oh quite, quite, dear. Josiah will be along shortly. Don't worry yourself."

"Very well, gentlemen, please come in. I'll get you all something to drink."

They positioned themselves around the large table in the dining room as Lorraine served refreshments. Scoville had not informed anyone why Josiah sought their counsel, so Levi and Cooper were cracking jokes. Even the otherwise earnest Charles Crandall sported a high-spirited grin. That changed, however, when Josiah finally arrived.

He stepped through the front door in a rush without acknowledging anyone, even Lorraine. He hung up his duster and hat on the coat rack by the door and made a beeline down the hall. The men grew silent and exchanged confused glances. Lorraine turned to Scoville and crossed her arms. Everything was definitely *not* quite alright. In turn, Scoville put a hand up and shook his head. Lorraine stormed off to the kitchen. When Josiah finally emerged from down the hall, he did so with two boxes of ammunition and a second holster on his belt containing a gleaming revolver. He grabbed six cartridges and stuffed the rest of the ammunition into the pockets of his duster.

Josiah drew his second gun. He spun the pistol over his index finger, forward then back catching the grip panels firmly each time. He released its cylinder and pushed the ejector rod. A single empty case bounced to the ground with a clink, clink, clink. The room was silent enough to hear the case roll around on the wooden floor. Josiah pushed six shiny brass cartridges into the cylinder and gave it a spin sending the ratcheting system buzzing. He then slammed the cylinder home with a quick flick of the wrist. After inspecting the sights, he took a brief but noticeable pause. Everyone watched as Josiah moved his primary pistol to his left hip and replaced the gun with its lustrous steel framed twin.

Finally, he turned his head to see the men sitting at his table. Will Richardson's knee shook with anxiety while Charles Crandall's skeptical scowl studied the display. Josiah stepped to the oblong table and took a seat in the first open chair. He didn't say a word but, after deliberately looking each man in the eye, he motioned toward Scoville.

"Well, now that we're all here," Scoville cleared his throat, "I think I'll go ahead and start."

Scoville proceeded to inform the men that the treasury had been liquidated and he no longer served the town of Sagebrush in any official capacity. His tale was met with responses of sorrow and outrage. The cold realization that the only wealth in the land rested in the private savings of a few families, those cautious of Best's swindle, left the men little reason for hope. Scoville commented that not only had the gold and silver of a generation of diligent pioneers been mostly pilfered, but now the politicians and lawmen were complicit in the embezzlement of the last of the territory's resources. These precious commodities, he explained, were being exchanged by government fiat for a phony currency controlled by those with the illegitimate authority and power to manipulate it for their own benefit.

"They're takin' your money, and the money to oversee Sagebrush's welfare, to secure our future," Josiah said at last. He leaned forward, "Or at least they're gonna try."

Crandall was the first to determine the purpose of the meeting. "You want our help to stop it."

"That's what I'm askin' of you," Josiah said. There was a sudden commotion in the kitchen and then Lorraine stomped out the door, down the hill to the guest house. Josiah briefly appeared troubled but continued.

"Look, we've been able to recover at least a portion of the business losses. But given that the last attempt ended with a night behind bars for yours truly, and we're on borrowed time with our buyer in the city, this may be our last chance to make a stand and stop this thievery. Now, I'm aware of some information about just where, when, and how the contents of the treasury are bein' moved. I think we have a responsibility to ourselves and our neighbors to act on that information and recover what is rightfully ours."

"Just what are you proposin', exactly?" Levi asked.

There was a pause. The air hung stale and dry. Will Richardson licked his lips and Scoville bit at his thumbnail. Levi never so much as blinked as his eyes stayed locked on Josiah. Cooper grinned at the prospect of ruining the plans of the men that ruined his smithy.

"Gentlemen," Josiah said at last. "I propose we intercept the money as it's transported by rail tomorrow mornin'."

"You want our help *robbin' a train*?!" Cooper bellowed.

Chaos erupted, full of both enthusiasm and dissent. Amid the yelling, there wasn't a single point made by anyone that affected the disposition of any other. Insults flew across the table as questions were posed along with accusations and demands.

"I knew you could think like a criminal, but actin' like one?!" Levi said.

As voices raised, so did eyebrows. Soon Josiah was the only one still seated, refusing to participate in the bickering.

At last, he shouted, "Enough! Pull it together!" When everyone settled and assumed their seats, he spoke again. "Now I know you've got questions, comments, concerns. I know you've got reservations, too, but we've got to talk about this with some sobriety and order. Levi, I need you on board. What d'you say?"

"Sounds foolish and dangerous," Levi said.

"Probably so," Josiah answered.

"I mean, before we even get into the right and the wrong of it, just how exactly did you come by this information?"

"Heard it from the horse's mouth: Peregrine Page."

Cooper slammed his fist on the table and stood up, "You've *got* to be kiddin' me, that lyin' scoundrel. Why I oughta head for the door right now on that bit of news alone! You know he can't be trusted; this already sounds woolly-headed. You walkin' us into some trap, Josiah?"

Scoville interjected, "Cooper, we'll get to you in a moment, please!" It was too late, however, for as soon as Scoville scolded

Cooper, Will started objecting to the disorder and Levi hollered that he had not finished; the whole thing devolved into an unruly shouting match. Before long, Josiah was again the only man seated, cradling his head in his hands. When he had had enough, he slammed the table, calling their meeting to order.

Everyone reluctantly returned to their seats. "If we're gonna do this, I need you to be more disciplined and have a little more trust in me," Josiah said. "Now Levi, it turns out that Scoville ain't the only one been pushed out now that Best has his hands on all that gold. Perry came in earlier—and Scoville can attest to this—lookin' like a whooped pup. He got the ax as well. He didn't just lose the bank, though, he's losin' the Parlor, too."

There was an audible gasp as the men began to understand. "We all know that from the time Perry got involved with that bank he's only been lookin' out for himself. Well now, he wants revenge, and his interests align with ours. So yes, I think we can trust that he's tellin' the truth."

"So now what? We're the errand boys for some washed-up, greedy cheat?" Levi asked.

"Please. You think Perry's gonna see an ounce of whatever we recover? Not a chance. We ain't doin' this for him. We're doin' this for folks like the Turks; shoot, we're doin' this for us."

Levi nodded, still reticent, but conceded the floor to Charles Crandall.

"Josiah, Scoville," Crandall said, "I know y'all mean well, but we got ways to handle these kinds of things; ways that don't include doin' more harm than good by actin' like vigilantes. Ain't we commanded to submit to the authorities or dishonor God?"

"Crandall, my friend, I do appreciate your point of view," Josiah said. "You are perhaps the best of us, but ain't we also commanded to seek justice and love mercy? Commanded to rescue those stumbling to slaughter? We're a people of laws, not rulers, so when the authorities themselves don't submit to the law of the land, then what? We have suffered under a murderous marshal and a corrupt mayor compromised by an outsider who's changed our laws so he could use his bank to steal from us. To what other earthly authority might we appeal our cause? Some judge who sat by and allowed for the mayor's illegal orders? No sir, good men are their own recourse when all else fails."

"Ah, ah, ah," Crandall shook his finger, "Deputy Butch Eaton is still sworn to execute the laws of this territory. We must attempt an appeal to him before even entertainin' this dangerous nonsense."

"Good luck findin' him," Josiah said. "Has anyone seen Butch since the day that robbery resulted in the whole town findin' out the bank vault was empty?"

"Come to think of it," Scoville pondered, "I haven't." Everyone shook their heads.

"Then we must wait until he is reached," Crandall said.

"And by then it will be too late," Josiah replied. "Gentlemen, this has to happen tomorrow or not at all."

"Then I wish you luck. I will pray for your success; but I cannot be a part of this." Crandall said.

"I'm sorry to hear that, but you're free to follow your conscience. I've lost no love or respect for you, Crandall." Josiah moved on. "Cooper? What do you say?"

"I say we shoulda taken care of the marshal earlier this year. Maybe we wouldn't be in this mess. You said back then it wasn't wise, I don't see how this exactly fits that bill either!"

"Back then, Oglesby wasn't jailin' innocent people on the orders of private interests."

"Nope, just killin' 'em. Funny how it ain't 'til you're the one affected that you come out guns blazin'!"

"What do you want me to say? Okay, you're right! We prob'ly shoulda done more about Oglesby back then, but we can do somethin' about Best right now."

Cooper crossed his arms. "This is bad for Best?"

"It is."

"Perry gets nothin'?"

"Not a thing."

"Sagebrush gets the gold back?"

"Yup."

Cooper threw his hands up, "Alright, I'll ride with you."

Josiah motioned toward Will Richardson. Will patted Jacoby's shoulder reassuring his friend, "Josiah, looks like it's just me. Don't seem like Jacoby's got a good feelin' about all this." Josiah expressed his appreciation for Will's help.

"Alright, Levi," Josiah sighed, "back to you."

"How many guards?"

"Don't know."

"They ain't gonna take kindly to us tryin' to waltz in there and take what they're hired to protect."

"Nope."

Levi stood up and walked over to the lone brass casing on the floor. He crouched down and rolled it in his hand before holding it up between his index finger and thumb.

"Josiah Rush, I thought you was done takin' lives for gold."

"And what do you think takin' gold *is*, Levi? That gold represents the lives of your friends and neighbors. It's the countless hours of honest toil from good, peaceful people. That gold is what they have to show for their time, their lives! When it's taken from them by men like Best, what's actually taken is the hours they spent achin' and stressin', laborin' and tradin'. What's taken is their freedom to choose what they value and what they trade their lives for." Josiah snapped his fingers. "Gone with the stroke of a pen for phony paper that don't keep, Levi, 'cause they just print and spend and print and spend until it's all worthless."

"Then we just start over."

"And become a target for men like Oglesby? No, sir. Now look, I ain't sayin' we murder no guards, but I won't be pushed around any longer."

"For a long time after my service," Josiah continued, "I resented violence. But now we have the opportunity—no, the responsibility—to step up and finally be a force for good in this world. I've fought my whole life to survive, but now I've found somethin' that I'd sacrifice my life fightin' for." Josiah glanced around the room, ". . . the freedom and the lives of my neighbors and friends."

At last, Levi said, "Alright. I guess I'm in." All around the table, the men sighed and cheered. "For the record, though," he interjected, "it ain't on account of some pretty speech. I just can't let you go out there with only Cooper and Will at your side. Good way to get yourself killed."

Cooper crumpled up a place mat and threw it at Levi in response to the jest. It only reached half-way before coming undone and falling to the floor.

"Thank you," Josiah said. "Alright gentlemen, we need to go over a plan. Crandall, Jacoby, you're welcome to stay if you'd like."

"Might as well," Crandall said, "but I didn't have any part in this, y'all understand?"

Everyone agreed. Josiah noticed Scoville rub his chin as though having an idea, but he did not share it straightaway.

The men plotted for the next few hours and agreed to meet back at the ranch at dawn.

23

Josiah awoke just before daylight. After dressing and pulling on his boots, he sat down on the edge of the tousled bed. While he would routinely start for the door and begin his day, he instead took a moment to enjoy the splendor of the first few rays of sun peeking over the horizon. It was framed by the window in the room overlooking the subtle hills of the ranch. A breath of wind animated the chimes on the porch, the tall grasses in the meadow, and the row of trees wedded to the river that gave life to this land. Josiah captured that breath of wind inviting in the aroma of pine, cedar, and wheat before letting it out slowly. He felt for a glass of water on the nightstand and pondered the degree to which peace is appreciated by other men during the overtures to conflict.

Josiah stroked the stubble of his beard. He made a deliberate effort to unclench his jaw and relax his brow. Still breathing. He focused on overcoming his body's propensity to betray the conviction of his will during times of great stress.

The door creaked, but Lorraine otherwise entered silently. She crawled onto the bed and settled behind him. Resting a hand on his shoulder and her head on his back, she studied his heartbeat. The tension in his chest fled at the gesture. She said nothing, but Josiah was still disarmed by her commentary; as though he was hearing her pleas, yet again, with every thought.

Would you not endure this suffering for my sake? Must you rush off to danger? And what of your soul?

She knows his response. *Does a man not have the liberty and responsibility to wield the sword in righteousness against iniquity? Does God ask of us to forfeit unto evil men that which He has gifted and entrusted to us to steward?* She does not know his doubts, however. *Whose kingdom am I really serving?*

The silence was broken by the first words spoken between them.

"I love you," she said. She had surrendered to Josiah's determination and wanted him to know that it would not cost her affection.

There was a knock at the front door of the cabin. Lorraine watched Josiah stand then place his hat crooked upon his head. He opened to an unseen man at the threshold and exchanged a few inaudible words. Josiah then closed the door and turned back to Lorraine. She ran through the bedroom to the living area and threw her arms around him out of fear, collapsing into violent wails. Josiah held her up and held his grief. Lifting Lorraine in his arms, he kissed her then set her down on a kitchen chair. She watched Josiah retrieve his bandana but was too distraught to say goodbye.

He took one last look at her. "I love you, too." Josiah then stepped outside to join his bandits.

Nero flared his nostrils as Josiah mounted up, sliding his rifle into the leather sheath attached to his saddle. Josiah, Levi,

Cooper, and Will stampeded off as the morning sun crested the pines.

They avoided town and took a route north of the river. The plan was to meet the tracks where they crossed over the water and follow them toward the mountains. While plotting, Crandall had shared his knowledge of a railroad bridge that he suggested as an ideal location to await the train. Beyond that bridge, the landscape shifted to a significant graduation that would slow the progress of the massive locomotive enough for Nero and the other horses to keep pace. The gang would need them fresh, though, so the morning was slow-going to conserve the animals' energy.

The easy ride gave Josiah the opportunity to allow his thoughts to wander. The longer he rode, the more attuned he became to his surroundings. The last time he departed with a group of men into the wilderness he had been on the other side of the law. He found relief discovering that nature's pronouncements did not discriminate between sinner and saint. She still took the measure of a man. Depending on his marrow, her ancient voice existed as that of a maiden or banshee. Her wind nevertheless carried wisdom, that liberating and terrifying truth too sacred to compete with vanity for an individual's attention; a reminder that "you *are from* this dust and to this dust *you will* return." The invitation to contemplate the inevitability of one's own demise accompanied the warning that it will be met sooner rather than later if he disrespects her dangers.

As the horses proceeded across the dry, open land toward the inclining hills, Josiah wondered how such revelations never led him to a temper of despair. He found them alluring, as though a challenge were issued. Daring him to rise. Live. Embrace this dominion. It was an offer to take sustenance from and care for her resources, for the sacrifice would be returned when the body rests in the soil and the soul rests in the spirit. That offer was her gift, a chance to become someone without the fear of death but with a vigorous will to truly live life and live it rightly. Josiah figured none of it could ever happen from the safety of civilization, something which ironically proved more dangerous to a man's soul.

Josiah identified with the heart of the natural world as he listened to the horses' rhythmic canter pulsate across the landscape. He was a student of her lessons; a student of himself. He had known what it was once like to fear both men and death. He had tasted the bitter fruit of those motivations and understood the roots of that fear to be shallow, but hardy and plentiful. He had spent a long time tending to the fields of his own nature. And yet . . .

Josiah fought to refuse his body any pleasure it still tried to take in the excitement he was feeling now that the party approached their destination. There was a shift in Josiah's disposition akin to slipping into a comfortable old pair of well-worn boots. This time, however, there was no internal conflict or restlessness. He was settled. His divided nature, which once screamed for him to step aside and ponder his path, had been resolved. The reality of his situation forced Josiah onward toward certain means to uncertain ends.

His holsters, heavy under the weight of the revolvers, struck his hips like the ticking of a clock. Josiah had learned that before a fight, a man may be persuaded by patriotism, roused by religion, incensed by ideology, or coerced by his own sense of duty, honor, justice, or adventure. He had seen even the most undisciplined and apathetic men provoked to violence when pushed to the brink of desperation, having nothing more to lose. Josiah had also experienced, however, complex and lofty ideals become reduced among blood and bullets to nothing more than a visceral battle to satisfy one's innate compulsion to survive or, more powerful still, to avoid failing the men fighting at one's shoulders.

Josiah was no longer subject to an artificial, willful, and unwavering pride in the illusory bonds that laid a powerless claim on his allegiance to the present ordering of men. Nor did he find religion to be a personal motivation for adopting the use of force, but instead one of the greatest deterrents to it in general. He granted it was the prerogative of a person to individually discern, and the curse of mankind to collectively debate, which values may govern their circumstances, but he did not doubt the reality of virtues, by which all men do abide at least some—in their own fashion. He felt no sense of official duty, but instead a moral obligation out of the love he held for his neighbors, including the three brave men beside him. He reasoned it would be dishonorable to deny them a chance for justice, though he questioned the righteousness of man's communal sense and application of it, and more importantly his own worthiness to impart it. Nevertheless, that is what he sought to do. He was not apathetic nor was he a desperate man. He cared little for that legacy which once brought him notoriety, fame, infamy, among men. He thought it may be even poetic and fitting, if it came to it, to encounter finality the way he once introduced it to both soldiers and fugitives alike. Forgiven as he was for the guilt he bore from a past most men would laud, Josiah marveled that it was yet ultimately the powerful strength of the ties to his kindred that held him on his course.

There was no doubt that the actions of Best were reprehensible. Josiah did not hesitate to denounce them. But he had seen justice dispensed at the hands of men who considered themselves impervious to having their methods scrutinized. His fear was to become like them. If men are beholden to reason and not exempt from eternal consequences, then they ought to be wary of the haughtiness of fancying themselves above reproach for questionable ethics influenced by otherwise unimpeachable moral convictions. Josiah was familiar with the taste of that particular recipe for atrocity.

But then, how would he fare if he ignored his conscience, forsaken the aspiration to see the town's sustenance reimbursed, and instead left well enough alone? Would the marshal and Best continually perpetrate their crimes against life and property? Would Josiah continually turn a blind eye to suffering? Would he pretend such acts of the devil himself were of no account even though they found themselves on his own threshold? These, too, would not abide.

As the railroad bridge came into view, Josiah made peace with the fact that he could be held accountable should he fail to provide persuasive justifications for his actions. He knew there would be confusion and misunderstanding. People would question and doubt the righteousness of his path. He assumed he would face condemnation from a great number of people, but he resolved to face their convictions with sympathy. He remained convinced, however, that his calculated actions were simply the least ruinous. Even if Josiah would not become accountable to others, then he was still undeniably accountable to himself, and eventually to God. A warrior, Josiah figured, needed a lawyer, counselor, *and* a savior.

Roughly four hours after they began their journey, the horsemen arrived at a dry riverbed beneath the railroad bridge. Here they would stage their ambush. The men had little time to lounge before the earth started to rumble and their hearts began to pound. The four of them looked at each other and saddled up again. The increasing noise of the approaching train progressively drowned out Levi's prayer.

The rhythmic pulse of the clanging metal gave beat to the steam whistle as it resounded through the fields. The conductor rounded an easy bend and, with the incline now in view, throttled up the pistons that propelled the powerful machinery across the prairie. Black coal smoke poured from the chimney as it belched heat and soot, which rose and dissipated before it could offend the senses of the patrons in the caboose: an attractive bank teller and her two guards. They traveled in George Best's personal rail car. Unaware of their impending appointment with the moral marauders, the trio was unsure whether their dizziness was due to the back-and-forth rocking of the speeding train or the bubbles in their glasses of French champagne.

When the weight of the train first hit the bridge above Josiah, he fought the urge to flee from his position under the flexing timber and steel. He wasn't the only one concerned with the untrustworthy appearance of the arches either. Will Richardson ducked and still held the back of his head. Levi covered an ear with his good hand to protect it from the painful, deafening noise of the speeding rail cars. A gust from the passing train swirled in the ravine and nearly stole Cooper's hat. Josiah took heart from the childlike enthusiasm for adventure written all over Cooper's face as he held onto the brim. When the train had passed, the men looked to Josiah who, upon drawing a devious half smile, cracked the reins. Leading the men, Josiah drove Nero up the gully in pursuit of the locomotive.

On either side of the tracks, they rode in pairs. Nero broke ahead and was the first to gain on the train as it struggled against the rising elevation. The late autumn prairie grasses were dry and low, whipping against the hooves that sent clods of packed earth soaring in the wake of the team.

They closed the gap quickly. Josiah and his men remained unnoticed by the two guards, distracted by the playful bank teller. When the riders reached the rod iron railing enclosing the small porch of the caboose, Josiah tossed his reins to Levi and stood up in the saddle. On the other side of the rail car, Cooper gave control of his horse to Will and did the same. The two men leapt forth onto the back of the train. Cooper's boot slipped from the deck and dragged over multiple railroad ties. He nearly fell completely but was able to pull himself back up and climb over the railing. The railcar shifted under the weight of the hijacking men, alerting the guards.

Once steady on their feet, both Josiah and Cooper turned around to catch a payload of handmade explosives, courtesy of

Martin Kelly's delayed network of suppliers back east. Josiah had intended to use the powder for experiments in reloading cartridge ammunition for the rifle that currently occupied the sling adorning Nero's shoulder. That would have to wait, however, as he now had more pressing needs for the propellant.

The rear door of the luxury car swung open with a violent clang as the metal handle dented the caboose's side wall.

"Hey, what's this all about!?" howled one of the guards. Josiah ducked as a fist sailed his way. He dropped the explosives on the deck and buried his shoulder into the stomach of the guard, tackling him into Cooper. Cooper had been securing his share of the safe-busting munitions so when the struggling men hit him from behind, he lost control and dropped the bundle overboard. He watched in horror as it fell against the tracks, cracked open, and spilled pounds and pounds of unburnt black powder across the steel rails and tar-covered wooden ties.

Cooper turned around and, out of his frustration, put the guard in a choke hold as the other emerged from the caboose. The second guard held up his unbuttoned trousers with one hand and gripped an unshouldered lever-action in the other. When Josiah rolled over to see the barrel of a gun pointed in his direction, he mule-kicked the Casanova in his coin purse. The rifle fell from the guard's hands and slid off the back of the train. After a second kick to the face, the guard stepped back, tripped on the powder, and flipped over the rail. He landed across the sprinting horses, face up in Levi's lap.

"You don't even get the good one," Levi said as he bloodied the young man's nose with his stump and pushed him off the horse. Levi didn't bother turning to see the guard stop rolling, stand up, and raise his fists defiantly in the air.

With the first guard now unconscious, Cooper and Josiah stepped into Best's rail car. Beyond the regal green curtains, behind a red-buttoned leather settee was a trembling woman in a chemise holding an unsteady revolver in the general direction of the two men.

"Easy now, we ain't here to hurt you," Josiah said, stepping toward her. Cooper began to flank her position around the other side of the couch. Just when it appeared as though she was going to drop the gun, Cooper tripped on an end table and knocked over a metal pitcher. The noise startled the already frightened teller. She turned toward it and jerked the trigger.

The sound of gunfire was followed by a cry of pain and Cooper clutched his side. The horrified woman dropped the pistol and retreated beyond the mirror emblazoned with the initials GB.

"Cooper!" Josiah shouted.

Removing his bloody hands to inspect the gunshot, Cooper said "It's low and left." He winced. "Just finish this and let's get the hell outta here." Cooper ripped off a sleeve and packed the wound.

"Looks like it went clean through but we're goin' straight for Lorraine when we get back," Josiah ordered. He retrieved what was left of the explosives and stepped over the unconscious guard on his way back inside. Josiah kicked down the door to the car's sleeping quarters. Against the back wall was the large safe that allegedly housed the entirety of Sagebrush's remaining resources.

"It's bigger than you said," Cooper complained.

"Yeah, it's bigger than Perry said."

Josiah glanced at Cooper who raised his hands as if to say, "I told you so."

"Alright, well it's twice the size and we've got half the boom, but we've got to at least try," Josiah said. The two men crouched down—with Cooper hissing and clenching his jaw in pain—and began staging the explosives with their backs turned to the doorway when they heard scuffling and shouts.

Startled, they turned around to find none other than Charles Crandall planting his boot firmly on the neck of a struggling, but conscious, guard. Beside him was the runaway teller. He bent down and retrieved the guard's pistol.

"You two fools about had it. Glad I know'd better than to let you try and pull this off yourselves."

As Josiah helped bind the guard, he looked to Crandall for an explanation.

"I done some thinkin' after I left your place last night," Crandall said. "Way I figure it, we're still deputized agents of the law. I was never decommissioned after the Waddell manhunt, were you?"

Josiah laughed, "You saved our lives, Crandall!"

Crandall continued, "Savin' lives and recoverin' stolen property, it's all in a day's work. I bought a ticket this mornin', didn't wanna interfere with the plan, but reckoned I'd be here just in case y'all needed any help. Good thing, too. I heard the shot and when I seen this young lady runnin' through the passenger car I had a feelin' things was headed sideways."

"Let's catch up later, shall we gentlemen?" Cooper asked as he glanced down at his red-stained shirt.

They finished securing the guard and Crandall ushered the teller to the safe. He inspected the explosives rigging on the hinges. "Hmm," he said at last, "That prob'ly woulda done it."

Crandall wasted no time, and instead of setting the charges, he nodded to the young woman who unquestioningly addressed the large silver dial on the iron door. A moment later, the door swung wide open and inside, from the floor to the ceiling, was more gold and silver than Josiah had ever seen in one place.

Crandall shoved a duffle in each of their hands and pushed them aside to begin filling his own. When he had finished he addressed the teller.

"Listen closely," he told her. "When you see George Best, you make sure to tell him to keep his litter to his own yard." With that he pulled out two stacks of large denomination bank notes and placed them gently in her hands. "Now, go see to your friend."

When the safe was empty, the three men rushed to transfer the bags to Levi and Will and make their get-away.

"Hurry!" Will said, patting the neck of the aging black stallion he rode, "This hoss can't take much more!"

Cooper tossed the bag, then made the jump back to his horse safely, landing with a distinct thud and gasp of pain. Josiah offloaded his and Crandall's bags to Levi.

"Crandall," Josiah said, "Jump!"

Charles Crandall, ever the gentleman, first took the time to apologize for frightening the young teller and encouraged both her and the guard to seek honest employment elsewhere. Once he and Josiah made the leap from the train, the five men stopped the horses for a rest.

There, amid the sprawling sage, the horses caught their breath as the men lost theirs from celebrating with hoots and hollers. Even Cooper managed a small exclamation then doubled over in pain as the adrenaline wore off. Having accomplished their mission and refreshed their steeds, the gang headed west, back to their homes, returning with the treasure of their people.

Shortly after the crew started back, Perry paced throughout his office above the Parlor. Somewhere in the relentless cycle of anxiety and guilt, he lost his perspective for the boundaries of proper ways to cope with his grief. George Best, Perry had determined, was a wicked man. The Parlor, a place to which he had once given all his efforts, was to be foreclosed on by a banker that needed to be stopped. Perry felt powerless to do much else beyond his confession to Josiah the day before. Riddled with shame and hurt by the betrayal he felt, a sinister calm settled on Peregrine Page. He would come clean.

Perry marched over to the marshal's office where he found Oglesby immersed in a book.

"What is it you want, Perry?" the marshal barked.

Perry began to lose his nerve, "Oh, I, well . . ."

"Are you here to waste my time?"

Images of shackles and jail cells flooded Perry's mind so, rather than boldly presenting the whole truth about their corruption and the ensuing arson that paved the way for his and Best's influence in Sagebrush, Perry cowered. "No sir. I'm here to tell you that George Best is behind some of the crimes that have beset Sagebrush in recent years."

In a pitiful plea, Perry further attempted to implicate Best in the arson without implicating himself. The marshal could not have been any less interested in the yarn he spun. With a slamming door he dismissed Perry, just like Best said he would.

Blinded by hatred, rather than attempt to persuade public opinion with an answer to Best's hit piece in the *Sentinel*, Peregrine Page snapped. He stormed across the street as the sun sank low on the late afternoon horizon.

Perry forcefully cut through the crowded saloon, bumping shoulders and spilling drinks of men much larger than himself. He paid no attention to their threats, however, as he stomped upstairs to his office. He paced and paced. Back and forth in a rage, he watched the afternoon drag on into the evening.

The inconsequential effect his story had on the man sworn to uphold the law had Peregrine Page feeling disillusioned. Hurt like a beat pup, alone, scared, angry, and ashamed, Perry lost all sense of purpose. Vengeance being his only consolation, he resolved to mete out as much destruction as he could to make up for the loss of everything he'd ever known.

Perry opened a desk drawer and grabbed a snub nose revolver. He then went to a glass display case housing two vintage flint locks to retrieve a pouch full of gunpowder. He stepped into the hallway on the second floor of the Sagebrush Grand Hotel and fired off three shots into the ceiling. Hotel room doors flung wide open as people fled the area. Convinced there was no one left, Perry poured out a thin line of gunpowder all the way down the hall that descended the stairs and stretched into the lobby where he fired off another shot. As people ran out into the streets, Perry set his eyes on the Parlor. Through the glass, he saw a bug-eyed Philippe La Brune and mouthed the word "run!" When the music stopped, Perry fired again, advancing on the saloon. Lawrence Hoak ushered people out of the swinging doors as Perry entered from the lobby, firing into the air again. He still trailed a steady line of gunpowder behind him. As the bar emptied he upended tables, breaking bottles of high proof alcohol across the floors. He gawked at the large red velvet curtains hanging down across the stage and started to laugh madly. Perry shuffled his feet, dancing out onto the wooden boardwalk then down the stairs. A crowd formed around him, screaming for him to stop, but it was too late.

Peregrine Page struck a match and ignited the line of gunpowder. It raced up the stairs catching the boardwalk on fire. Advancing into the saloon, a wave of blue flames overtook the floor as it encountered the spilled alcohol. The fire burned the wooden card tables and climbed the curtains. It proceeded through the lobby of the hotel where the carpet caught fire and scaled the stairs. By the time the second-floor hallway was overcome with flames, large plumes of black smoke rolled out of the downstairs windows. The Sagebrush Grand Hotel and Peregrine's Parlor were both engulfed in a fiery blaze. Perry continued to dance and kick up dust in the middle of the road.

As the flames grew, Josiah and the returning men approached Sagebrush and initially mistook them for the last gasps of the setting sun beyond the western horizon.

While Perry danced and the crowd gawked, Deputy Butch Eaton pushed his way through the chaos with a stranger at his side. From the other direction, Marshal Oglesby also fought the horde of onlookers. At once, the three men broke through the madness into the circle that had formed around the arabesque arsonist.

"There you are, Butch!" the marshal said, "Just where in the *hell* have you been? After you arrest this fool, you've got plenty of explainin' to do." Marshal Oglesby pointed his finger at Butch which presented an opportunity.

"Oh, I'm here to make an arrest alright, but he's gonna have to wait." With that, Deputy Butch Eaton grabbed the marshal's arm and wrenched it behind his back. Oglesby protested as Butch slapped on handcuffs.

"Butch! Have you lost your mind?!" Oglesby said.

Just then, the stranger with Butch Eaton spoke up, "I'm Edgar Carmichael, Capital Prosecutor. Felix Oglesby, you are hereby under arrest for racketeering; for engaging in untoward business activities resulting in a conflict of interest, and abuse of your power—"

"That's preposterous!" the marshal cried. "Butch, if you go through with this, I'll see you gutted for it!"

"I'm not finished, Mr. Oglesby," the prosecutor said. "You are also hereby charged with treason for the enforcement of unlawful edicts, and now threatening the life of an officer of the law, and—" there was a loud crash from somewhere inside the burning building. Glass shattered and the glow of the flames danced in the glare of Oglesby's spiteful eyes.

Carmichael, the capital prosecutor, continued, ". . . and finally, the murder of Colton Waddell." There was a sobering realization that Oglesby had misjudged Butch Eaton's response to the events of the manhunt earlier in the year. "Mr. Oglesby," Carmichael continued, "you have been stripped of your title and all authority."

Butch Eaton ripped the star from Oglesby's lapel. "You've disgraced this."

The raging fire illuminated the night as a shadowy Felix Oglesby was led through the streets to a jail cell.

The next morning, hundreds of miles away in the city, George Best sat on a station bench awaiting the train carrying his gold reserves. He was greeted, instead, by an empty safe and the resignation of his most trusted employee. Already angry, he arrived back at the bank to a telegram informing him that his Sagebrush Grand Hotel had burned to the ground during the night.

That evening a furious George Best came home to find a letter waiting. The letter came by way of the capital and originated from a handful of his fiercest competitors. Some of them, it seems, caught wind of Best's exploits out west and were rather impressed by his subsequent net worth. Included in the letter was an invitation to an exclusive and secret business meeting where a group of bankers would set aside their competitive interests and instead join forces to lay the groundwork for a consolidated Capital Reserve Bank. The problem they saw with Best's business model, as they called his connivance, was that it was limited in scope to the territories where he could afford to establish bank branches. They encouraged him to unite with their efforts to centralize. They planned to focus on the capital city, as they could therefore "serve all of the united territories," and everyone in it from coast to coast.

With an insidious and revitalized hope for untold wealth and power, George Best did not bother to even try reclaiming the gold lost in the train robbery. It was but a pittance compared to the opportunity that now lay before him. In the middle of the night, George Best abandoned his interests in Sagebrush entirely and departed for the capital to take part in a banking cartel that was pitched to the legislators with bribes and thrust upon the porcelain citizenry as a bulwark of financial stability.

24

Nearly a month later, demolition crews worked on the burned-out carcass of what was once the Sagebrush Grand Hotel when Josiah Rush came riding into town. Saddled atop Nero, he wore his crooked hat and duster; underneath, a revolver on each hip. He did not worry about the legality of carrying his sidearms, as the mayor's edicts no longer oppressed the townsfolk.

After the mayor's involvement in Best's deception and his efforts to implement the wildly unpopular gun control mandates, Nicholas Scoville successfully passed a referendum repealing the offensive statutes. With the help of a petition containing the signatures of hundreds of people from all over the territory, Scoville effectively recalled the mayor and escorted him from his seat of power.

Josiah tied Nero to the hitching post in the center of town then took a gander across the street at the courthouse.

Recalling that, in the mayor's absence, there had been a special election held, he chuckled to himself about the events that had followed. The candidates included the sitting vice mayor, some clown who wore a cowboy boot on his head, and Mr. Charles Crandall who ran for office only at Scoville's exhortation.

In a hotly contested election, Crandall's rumored involvement in the train robbery became the center of a scandalous smear campaign. During the debates, the vice mayor criticized Crandall as an ignoble thief. He accused Crandall of sitting idly by as private citizens' savings were moved back east, but then acting only once the town's treasury was jeopardized. He claimed that Crandall sought to control the coffers and distribute the contents among his friends through civic contracts. At the charge, Crandall merely drew a wry look. He categorically denied any involvement in the robbery that "rightfully returned the wealth of Sagebrush to its people." The cheers resounded as the townsfolk read between the lines.

The arguments at the debate boiled down to whether the people needed a leader with experience to make decisions on their behalf, as the vice mayor claimed, or a public servant who would restore their freedom and one day return to public life to live as an equal among them, as Crandall claimed.

Upon casting their vote, every citizen wrote down their place of residence and signed the paper ballots in front of a small panel of witnesses, each representing a different candidate. When the votes were counted it proved a close race, but it was Charles Crandall who ultimately won the electorate. On a cold day in early winter, Crandall humbly took his oath as the new mayor of Sagebrush.

Josiah turned his attention back to Nero and dug through his saddlebag. He petted the horse with some soothing reassurance while withdrawing a small leather pouch. From over Nero's shoulder he saw Butch Eaton passing by on his way up the road. Butch sported some fancy new hardware on his lapel thanks to Charles Crandall's first act as mayor.

After suffering the abuse of the marshal, Crandall had made a wildly popular proclamation rejecting the jurisdiction of the capital over the territory. He sought to bring complete political control back to the people, and one of the measures included a law enforcement department accountable to the locals, not some far-off unelected bureaucrats. Carmichael, the capital prosecutor, was at the time the only Capital representative in the territory. He made known his objections, but he alone was powerless to prevent the implementation of the new declaration. In order to maintain a peaceful transition, however, Crandall nominated former capital deputy, Butch Eaton, for the newly reestablished position of sheriff.

"Butch, huh?" Josiah had ridiculed the decision.

"Look, he's kind of an idiot, but he's proven himself to have a moral compass. Besides, it makes political sense right now," Mayor Crandall said.

"You already sound like a politician."

With unanimous support Butch was duly elected and sworn in. He and Crandall reversed the enforcement of unlawful dictates regulating the use of specified currency and the carry of personal firearms within the town limits. When Porter High asked Sheriff Butch Eaton to comment for the *Sentinel*, he promptly followed the answer with an inquiry into whether Butch planned to pursue the mystery bandits who robbed the train a month prior.

"Do you believe there is any connection between them and the gang that robbed the bank, too?" Porter had asked.

Butch had held out his hands saying the railroad was a capital matter and deferred to Carmichael for comment. Carmichael leered at Mayor Charles Crandall before going on record in the *Sentinel* as saying he believed the train robbers were long gone and posed no further threat to the people or institutions of Sagebrush.

He concluded by saying, "Seems they're your problem now, Butch."

Josiah smiled at the recollection then latched his saddlebag. Tossing the pouch in his hand, he gazed up at the facade of the brick building that used to be home to the Sagebrush branch of Best's Bank and Trust. The old marquee had been taken down and destroyed when the town's reserves were returned. Porter High braved the mob and stepped in to save some of the signage for "historical reasons." What was left of it now hung in the printing room of the *Sentinel* as though in a museum; a constant reminder of his investigative duties and responsibility to objectively deliver these stories to the people.

While there was still some cosmetic work to be done on the outside of the building, inside the bank was fully operational again. Levi Holdegel had taken the early admonitions of Nicholas Scoville to heart. After three profitable auctions throughout the year and a healthy distrust of bank notes as a reliable store of value, Levi had enough real capital to make an offer on the business when the town auctioned off the seized asset. Holdegel's Depository, as it turned out, was not in fact vulnerable to security breaches as George Best and Perry had claimed. That was an excuse to pacify any dissent to their plans to consolidate the wealth. The vault, in fact, was as solid and uncompromised as ever. After setting a new combination for the lock, Levi was in business.

With Crandall in the mayoral seat, and Levi operating the bank, the town's funds were discreetly moved to the Depository vault for safekeeping without so much as a whisper of it getting to Porter High at the *Sentinel*. With the prosperity of Sagebrush securely in the hands of good men, Josiah felt comfortable enough to entrust a share of his own savings to a friend.

"Good afternoon, Levi," Josiah said entering the bank.

"Never thought I'd see the day . . ." Levi said.

"Well, if I don't get this back I can always take it outta your hide."

Levi laughed and the two shook hands. Josiah opened an account with the Depository and, for a reasonable fee, confidently delegated the protection of his valuables to his friend. Josiah hadn't been Levi's first client, however. That esteemed privilege belonged to Lawrence Hoak. Lawrence had proven his abilities to operate a lucrative saloon, and Levi was hopeful for the future, once again. Interested in further investing his equine profits, he procured from the Lumber Mill the materials needed for the construction of the Grande Hoak Opry. Lawrence's vision for a saloon, gaming hall, and entertainment venue featured the talented Philippe La Brune hosting a variety of traveling performers and attractions.

Involved in the construction of the saloon were two men destined to become regulars. Josiah had been on site the day that Lawrence approached Will Richardson, the project foreman, and his assistant, Jacoby Sutton, inquiring after potential future employees.

"You loved the Parlor," Lawrence said to Jacoby, "and I need some help around here. Don't suppose I could convince you to come work for me?"

Lawrence was merely being polite and had turned to walk away when a voice behind him said, "I'm interested in drinkin' whiskey, not servin' it."

Both Lawrence's and Josiah's eyes bulged when they realized that the voice they heard belonged to Jacoby Sutton. Will let out a deep belly laugh that sent the rest of the men into a fit.

"Lawd-a-mighty! Jacoby, I thought you's a mute," Lawrence said.

That was all they could get out of the man, though, as Jacoby simply shrugged and continued about his business.

Will Richardson told Lawrence he knew of a man in the dying town of Buffalo Junction that was hard as nails and loyal as a rescued mutt, just the kind of guy he'd need. After some up-front silver and a long weekend on the trail, Will and Jacoby had returned to Sagebrush with the sombrero-laden, mule-riding bartender from Buffalo Junction. Josiah recognized him from the pursuit of Waddell.

The trio happened into town just as the former marshal, Felix Oglesby, was being extradited to the capital to stand trial for his crimes. He and the bartender recognized each other from afar as Oglesby was led in shackles from the jail to an ironclad wagon. Lawrence's new hire returned Oglesby's ominous and familiar gesture, pointing at the disgraced lawman then tapping his temple a couple of times as if to say, "I'll remember this." Oglesby lashed out against his chains, powerless over his circumstances. Porter High had been there covering Oglesby's extradition so when he saw the exchange, he walked over to meet the new arrival. Upon referencing his sombrero, the newsman greeted him with a "Bonjour, mon frère!" in a butchered accent.

"What is it with the people from this town?" the bartender was overheard saying.

Back at the bank, Josiah finished his business with Levi and the two of them stood at the counter talking when Cooper poked his head through the door.

"It's time, gentlemen!" he smiled.

"Good to see you up and about," Josiah said.

Levi locked up and closed the Depository early. The three men started across the street toward the Auction House where Dillon and Rebecca Turk were wrapping up a deal with Nicholas Scoville. Scoville sold the property and business, along with the Commercial Docks, to the Turks. It was a difficult decision, but now that things had settled down in Sagebrush, Scoville felt called back east. The Turks recognized that the future of transportation did not lie with horses and wagons, but with cargo on the rails. They were eager to take on a venture that would support them into their twilight years.

Scoville planned to slip away quietly once his affairs were in order, but Lorraine would have none of it. She organized a surprise going-away party. She and Carson met Josiah, Levi, and Cooper just outside of the Auction House.

"Where's Crandall?" She asked.

"Right here," he said, coming up the road from behind. Accompanying him were Lawrence, Will, and Jacoby.

With gifts and food in hand, they all poured in with a "Surprise!" when Dillon Turk opened the door. Scoville, delighted by the show of affection, began to tear up. After receiving the well-wishes and parting gifts from his friends, he collected himself and addressed them all.

"I am so very appreciative of each and every one of you. My life is better with you in it."

"It was weariness," he continued, "of political infighting that led me to embark upon a journey out west in search of something real, something pure, something to remind me of the reason I pursued a study of the law in the first place. That pursuit has led me to you good people, who I am blessed and privileged to call my friends. The events of this year have taught me that one cannot outrun evil. It is, however, because of your inspiration that I have recovered my drive to fight for our rights, to determine our own destinies, and to possess the tools, whatever they may be, required to achieve them. I vow to continue that fight against any power that would take advantage of good and honest people like yourselves. That vow is what ultimately leads me to make this sacrifice, for it is within the borders of the capital that I will be most effective in that crusade, not hundreds of miles removed in a secessionist territory. Sagebrush will always hold a special place in my heart, though. So, my dear friends, will you."

Scoville removed a handkerchief and dried his eyes while receiving hugs and warm farewells.

"Scoville, I'm gonna miss you lookin' out for us," Josiah said, placing an arm around Lorraine.

"Oh, I'll still be looking out for you," Scoville smiled. He turned to his case and withdrew an envelope for Lorraine. She took it and opened finalized adoption papers. Carson was fully and legally her own. Lorraine wept. She hugged Scoville and Josiah, then set off to celebrate with Rebecca.

"Treasure of a woman," Scoville said.

"That she is," Josiah replied. "You know, everything seems to be workin' out, but I gotta say I just hate it that Best weaseled away."

"Perhaps for now," Scoville said. "A man like Best, I'm sure he'll show up again. And the next time he comes peddling his cons, we'll be wise to him."

Scoville committed to keeping in touch. He promised to write so long as Crandall was able to keep the mail going, given his newly acquired duties as mayor.

"Say Crandall, what will become of the Post now?" Scoville asked.

Crandall was happy to share that he had a specific young rider in mind to take over those responsibilities. "Same rider, as a matter of fact, who delivered the warrant for Waddell if you recall. A good boy, honest, though a bit ornery." This seemed fitting and pleased the lawyer.

When his luggage was all loaded, Josiah walked with Scoville to the Depot and saw his friend off safely, waving from the platform as the train departed.

At the same time Josiah was bidding farewell to Scoville, Martin Kelly was next door at Dodge's Emporium and Dry Goods. He was deep into a bottle of whiskey. As he looked around at his empire of dusty unsold merchandise and listened to the deafening silence, he was faced with the ugly reality of his own loneliness. For the first time since losing Pearl, he felt remorse. Finally accepting the reality that baby Carson was, in fact, his son troubled Martin now that he had lost his opportunity to raise the boy. Ashamed of having laid his hands on Pearl and Lorraine, he was also crippled by overwhelming disgust upon examining the Emporium's fancy renovations. These projects he would be paying off for years to come. Martin wallowed in his comparisons to George Best and hated himself for the efforts he wasted trying to impress the mogul. He failed to attain his delusions of acquiring the wealth and favor of a man like Best. Those delusions that once offered hope, now mocked him as the overdue bills bearing Best's name continued to roll in. He opened one such bill for the renovations and, without having the money to make the payment, let it fall to the floor. He then stumbled to a shelf, grabbed a rope, and threw it over the very same beam he repaired with the first of the money borrowed from George Best. Martin Kelly downed the last of his whiskey and hung himself.

25

Josiah cinched the straps of his saddlebags after double checking his provisions. He'd be traveling light; hunting and foraging along the way. It would be a long journey and he didn't want to burden Nero any more than necessary. Josiah led him out of the stables where he flicked his tail and snorted at the shock of the falling temperature.

Lorraine walked over to Josiah from the guest house. In one arm she cradled Carson, and in the other was a napkin of fresh, hot biscuits. She handed them to Josiah with a kiss, then cheated shyly away.

"I got Cassidy and Jasper comin' 'round to look after things," Josiah said. "They're gonna tend the herd, take care of the horses and whatnot. I've left details about the harvest and spring plantin' schedules, and some contingencies just in case."

Lorraine shook her head as if to say she could not handle the small talk.

"You'll likely be up and runnin' soon," he continued anyway. "You sure you can handle a shop and the boy, both?" he asked.

"Are you leaving me a choice?"

"All I mean to say is you know there's plenty of folks 'round here to help, if you need it."

"I know." Lorraine looked away again. She did not see Josiah's intense admiration.

"I'm proud of you. I think this apothecary idea of yours is gonna be a blessin' to a whole lotta folks in need."

"Well, I couldn't have done it without Scoville's generosity," she said, "without him advancing that store front." Her tears flowed, but not because of Scoville. "Said it was his gift to me, so I had some time to turn a profit." She wiped a tear from her face and tightened her squeeze on Carson, using the child as a distraction from the pain of saying goodbye.

"Speakin' of Scoville," Josiah said. He reached into his back pocket and removed a thick folded-over packet. "When I got arrested after tradin' in the city, it was Scoville who was responsible for makin' sure I only spent one night in that cell. Without him, things would have turned out a lot different I'm sure." Josiah handed the packet to Lorraine.

"When he sprung me from jail the next mornin' he had these papers drawn up. They're just in case somethin' bad was to happen; to protect this place."

Lorraine opened the packet to find the deed to Josiah's ranch transferred into her name. It bore Josiah's signature on the bottom.

"We done it so's to make sure that if I got into any more trouble, they couldn't touch the ranch. This place wasn't gonna be looted by the marshal or the mayor. They'd just as soon turn around and auction it off cheap to someone like Best."

"Josiah I can't . . ."

"Just take it now." He closed her hand around the papers. "I mean to return, but it's a wild world. If I don't chance to make it back, this ensures that you and the boy have a place on this land; a place in this town—in this world."

Lorraine pleaded, "Oh Josiah, why do you have to go?"

"Lorraine, right now there's a man out there who's likely lost everything he's ever had. Lost the money from his herd to a thief, gold that's stashed away somewhere in Buffalo Junction. Lost his wife and boy to that same thief. Lost his chance at justice thanks to a rattler and a trigger-happy lawman. Lost everything; just like I could have lost everything. It's been eatin' at me for a long while now and I feel compelled to track down Reuben Ward. I *have* to make sure he knows there is a place where he's welcome should he choose to join us back here in Sagebrush."

Josiah spoke slowly and deliberately, "I want you to know somethin' though Lorraine. I am in love with you, and when I return the first thing I aim to do is change your last name. What do you say Carson grows up with a mother and a father, in a family where he's loved?"

"Alright then, cowboy," she said, nodding through a tearful smile. "You hurry home."

At that, Josiah Rush reined Nero around, put the east behind him, and rode off into the sunset.

CPSIA information can be obtained
at www.ICGtesting.com
Printed in the USA
JSHW031006240323
39392JS00003B/8

9 798985 062809